THE ACCESSORY

THE
ACCESSORY

Mary Lockwood

Random House　　New York

That which is not felt by the criminal is his crime.
That which is not felt by the innocent victim is his
own innocence.

—Simone Weil

It is natural for the mind to believe, and for the
will to love; so that, for want of true objects, they
must attach themselves to false.

—Pascal

I. THE FACT

In the Park

the great soprano sang (recorded) of springtime and yearning, and the lunch-hour throng assembled: office girls unwrapping sandwiches from paper bags, salesmen smoking behind their newspapers, students with briefcases, taut-girdled ladies resting on their way to Lord & Taylor. The old men had come to the park at midmorning, taking their customary seats, and now appeared as fixed and worn as the benches on which they sat, flannel shirts buttoned to their wrinkled throats in the dappled shade of the June day. The stone bulk of the public library blotted out the brilliant metallic swarm of Fifth Avenue to the east; somewhere in its depths a turntable revolved, shooting the long arrows of music into the afternoon. A sheet of paper tacked to the announcement board near the Fortieth Street entrance gave the day's program in neat typescript beneath the heading of the date and the year, in the late 1950's: Mozart's Concert Rondos in D, K. 382, and A, K. 386; Beethoven's Seventh Symphony; "Four Last Songs" of Richard Strauss; Bartok's Concerto for Strings, Percussion, and Celeste. It was almost one o'clock. The pneumatic drill which had yammered ceaselessly throughout the Beethoven from the direction of Sixth Avenue was silent at last; only the distant rumble of trucks and the fitful hooting of the cabs on Forty-second Street now beat against the green shores of the park. "*In dämmrigen Grüften,*" sang the soprano ecstatically, "*träumte ich lang von deinen Bäumen und blauen Lüften . . .*"

On a bench facing the broad steps that led to the lower level of the park sat a young man on his way to an appointment. Patches of sunlight shifted with the breeze across his narrow strong-boned face and cropped blond hair, but he did not blink or lean away; his eyes under triangular lids regarded the strolling crowd with a steady speculative gaze that expressed neither distaste nor approval. His neighbors on the bench held themselves a little away from him, as if acknowledging instinctively some quality in him of self-containment or aloofness. The young man did not look at them, only dropping his gaze from time to time to glance at his wristwatch. It was clear that he considered the segment of time separating him from his appointment to be of small interest; equally clear that he would not or could not retreat from his surroundings into any private reverie of memory or expectation. His eyes observed and recorded tirelessly, incurious but obedient to some habitual discipline.

The young man, who was a doctor, had studied German at one time. Although he did not care for music, his ears had begun to register automatically the words of the song—such of them at least as he could make out, for the music kept floating away from him, entangling itself in the fluttering leaves of the trees like some ethereal balloon whose string hovered always just out of reach. Still he caught the words "light" and "wonder," and thought briefly that there was indeed a sort of radiance, a restless shimmer, in the music that almost justified its intrusion on the spring air. Romantically it denied the artifice of machine and amplifier, it denied the city itself echoing so thunderously about it, as though it sprang from some forgotten stubborn source within the rock.

The seconds ticked on, mechanically recording themselves in some independent recess of the young man's brain, while he studied a pair of girls who had arrived at the top of the steps opposite him and stood talking in the full sunlight, looking about idly and swinging their large patent-leather bags against their slender thighs. One was a Negro girl in a linen dress, sleek and self-possessed; she was smiling in a remote, tolerant way at the chatter of the other girl, whose pretty face was animated and gay between soft wings of brown hair, and whose expressive gestures drew the eye to her rounded figure in its light summer suit. The young man observed that both girls wore earrings and bracelets of heavy gold costume jewelry, buttery in the sunlight. A wide flat necklace gleamed against the dusky throat of the Negro girl; and as the other girl turned slightly in his direction, he was almost blinded by the glitter of an enormous spiky pin at her shoulder, as exaggerated in size and shape as a low-comedy badge or medal. His mouth twitched ironically, but he looked away as the girl's glance swept toward him and paused for a fraction of a second on his face.

The music changed, became tremulous and melancholy, lost itself once more amid the light clashing of the leaves. *"Der Garten trauert,"* sang the soprano, and something about rain, the end of summer . . . Along the benches, conversations lapsed, faces turned inward for an instant, becoming closed and private, as the melody rose and fell in elegiac rhapsody. A student hooked his scrawny wrists around his knees and gazed up into the tattered sky of leaves with a beatific frown. The swarthy man who had been pacing angrily and aimlessly along the center of the promenade plunged his fists into the pockets of his windbreaker and halted, scowling at the pavement.

The young man felt an unfamiliar apprehension, an almost physical discomfort. He looked unnecessarily at his watch and thought: The most important thing is to be on time. In fact, it's probably the only important thing—the old bastard's way of testing me, deliberately waiting until the last possible moment to see me (not that he needs to see me, anyway), picking the most inconvenient and inappropriate place he could think of. If he has so little time to spare, why doesn't he fly? Why should he insist on taking a boat . . . ? Tired, the young man thought after a moment. Yes, Beddoes is tired, feeling his age; he needs the rest and doesn't want anyone to know it. He had a quick positive image of the great man lying slack in a deck chair, his eyes closed against the slow pulsing of the sun, with no one but a passing steward to observe how the flesh sagged away from the square grim face, flattening its heavy lines, or how the long liver-spotted hands lay passive along the wooden arms of the chair.

He stared thoughtfully at the pretty brown-haired girl, who,

aware of his gaze, lifted her chin and glanced away.
ter should leave enough time. It was quarter-after now.
... thought: I'm damned if I'll hang around in some mob at the
bottom of a gangplank, waiting to be summoned into the Presence. Three minutes late, possibly five; yes, I can afford that. The
soprano sang now of her mortal weariness, pleading for release
in exquisite tones which the breeze dispersed, until the thin
voice of a violin, almost inaudible at first, ventured a fresh rhythm,
a rising melody; and the full orchestra, drawn by this thread,
surged forward with a kind of mournful joy, washing stone and
leaves and flesh in its own grave light. *"Und die Seele unbe-
wacht . . ."*

Naturally, the young man thought: the soul, what else? But his
body relaxed for a moment on the hard seat, his gaze lengthened
over the sunny brick walks and flowers below the steps. He wondered idly what the music was, who had written it. It was the
lightest, most random thought, a mere habitual tug of curiosity;
but it had the effect of shifting his glance once more, this time
toward the announcement board, half hidden now in a cluster of
people. There's a program or something there, he thought, maybe
I'll take a look at it before I leave. His gaze roved on over the
heads of the crowd in the direction of the Fortieth Street entrance
—and so he was looking squarely at the man in the brown suit
from the moment he staggered into the park, clutching at his
chest and struggling for speech.

A drunk: the old men on the benches regarded him apatheti-
cally from the depths of their private stupors; the shoppers
dodged him mechanically, without a backward glance. Only a
pony-tailed girl started back in alarm and revulsion as the man
lurched past her and crashed heavily up against one of the posts
supporting the announcement board. Convulsively he flung an
arm about the post and clung to it. In the long moment before he
slid to the pavement, the doctor had an unobstructed view of the
pale, sweating face, whose lips, faintly frothed, still worked in a
last mute effort of explanation and entreaty.

The delicate leaf-shadows played across the brown shoulders
of the fallen man; the music soared. There was a general murmur
of dismay. The swarthy man in the windbreaker dropped to his
knees beside the man, but rose almost immediately and cried

loudly, with an air of gloomy triumph, "He ain't drunk. No smell of liquor or anything. Guy must have had a heart attack. Somebody find a doctor." Already a small crowd was gathering, pressing forward to see; heads turned and stared along the promenade, while the forgotten orchestra played the introduction to the last of the four songs, intimating a strange new landscape, zones of emptiness and peace.

"A doctor! Is there a doctor here?"

The cry was taken up and repeated obediently. Those nearest the fallen man looked over their shoulders sternly, searchingly, at the people gathering behind them.

"Oh, God," exclaimed the pretty brown-haired girl, backing away. "Can't somebody do something?"

The people on the outskirts, unable to see over the shoulders of the others, gazed about vaguely, shaking their heads at the questions of newcomers. A few were already leaving. "Guy's had it," said one with a shrug. But now there was a stir at the center of the group where the man lay. "Artificial respiration," a woman said knowledgeably to her companion. "You got to keep the lungs working. That's what Frank did when my uncle had his attack up at the lake last summer, remember? He saved his life, the doctor said." "And oxygen," her friend said, nodding. "That's the big thing these days. Don't forget oxygen."

On his bench the young man sat motionless, his hands clasped in front of him. The sunlight flickered on the blond hairs of his wrists and on the metal band of his watch, which said that it was now time for him to leave the park. No, he told himself again. There isn't time. If I had to try massage, tourniquets . . . Even if I didn't, even if there was nothing I could do for him, it would still be ten minutes at least before I could get away, probably more . . . Ah, what are they doing now, the idiots? For through a gap in the crowd he could see someone bending over the victim, tugging at the brown shoulders. An argument had begun: the swarthy man stood glaring, his hands on his hips. He yelled furiously, "You want to walk him around, it's your responsibility, buddy. I say leave him be!"

Ten minutes. I can't. It's twenty-after now. Beddoes said one-thirty, no later; they clear everybody off at two. If I don't show up—

The doctor rose. "Tell them to keep him quiet until the ambulance comes," he said in a harsh voice to the woman next to him, who stared and clutched at her fur stole defensively. He turned away, almost colliding with the girls in the gold jewelry, who were making their way toward a bench vacated in the commotion. "Wouldn't you think there'd be a doctor?" the brown-haired girl was saying. "I mean, look at all these people—oh, excuse me," she said, raising her eyes to his face as he brushed by her; he caught the unconscious flicker of approval and invitation in her glance. Muttering an apology, he strode away toward the Forty-second Street exit, away from the murmuring crowd under the trees and from the fading strains of the music, drawing now to its close on the last faint cry of the famous voice. "*Ist das etwader Tod?*" Is this perhaps death?

In the cab, speeding westward, the young man said to himself: The guy was probably gone anyway. Sure, somebody must have called an ambulance, it'll be there in a few minutes. Or another doctor . . . in all that miscellaneous collection of people there must have been another doctor, he told himself angrily, someone who had time to play the Good Samaritan and no appointment to keep. He stared ahead at a patch of sky now visible above the river, ignoring the dark-skinned children with their sticks and balls who sprang out of the path of the cab between the gleaming bumpers of parked cars. For a speculative moment he saw the letter he might have written to the professor, explaining the circumstances. A medical emergency . . . no choice except to remain at the scene . . . But the letter—the cable?—arriving too late, the chance of a lifetime (yes, of his lifetime) given to another.

The cab plunged between the dark pillars supporting the West Side Drive and skidded up against the curb at the entrance to the United States Lines, almost pinning a chauffeur to the glossy trunk of his limousine. Paying the driver, the young man inhaled the damp gray smell of the river and saw in his mind the cold immensity of the ocean beyond, where no man ventured at random. He thought fiercely: I am at no one's mercy; no freak of circumstance can deflect the course I have set for myself at such expense, over so many years. Once admit the claim of an anonymous man in a crowd and you might as well sink back into the

crowd yourself, relinquishing will and pride and purpose as
the luxuries they are, property of the lucky few.

If anyone knew—

But no one did or could, except himself.

With that thought, the deliberate tide flowed in upon the marsh
of memory, flooding the green island and the brown-sleeved arm
that clutched its spar of painted wood . . . The young man
made his way through the excited chattering throng to the first-
class gangplank and strode up into the carpeted belly of the
ship. The door of the great man's cabin stood open; he raised a
square expressionless face from the folder on the desk as the
young man knocked against the sill. With difficulty, he smiled.

Someone had left an evening newspaper on the arm of a chair
in the waiting room outside the clinic. Sheldon picked it up on
his way to the elevators, as much from an instinct for tidiness as
from any curiosity about its headlines. An apartment-house fire
in Queens, he saw, the front page given over to a murcky photograph of a fireman aiming a hose at a fourth-floor window; right
out of the files, Sheldon thought, probably the standard plate
they haul out whenever there's an apartment-house fire. But
the pictures inside were specific enough—children clinging to
the skirts of draggle-haired women, a blanketed body being
trundled into an ambulance, a man slumped on a curbing against
a lurid background of smoke and shattered glass.

Sheldon folded the newspaper in distaste and jammed it under one white-coated arm as he entered the cafeteria. It was still
crowded at this hour, but he couldn't wait to eat if he was going
to have time to check his cultures before evening rounds. "What's
your service right now?" Beddoes had said, frowning at the folder
before him. "Bacteriology? Well, that ought to leave you some
spare time . . . Of course, you're not officially responsible to me
until July, but I have several private patients who might interest
you if you have nothing better to do. Dr. Ramsay's covering for
me, I doubt if he'd have any objection to your taking a little night
duty now and then. Who knows"—smiling ironically—"you might
find something interesting." Well, I'll find more than that ass
Ramsay ever would, Sheldon thought; as Beddoes knows damned
well.

He took a tray and moved impatiently through the cafeteria line, nodding to acquaintances but choosing the vacant end of a long table where he would not have to speak to anyone. While he ate his soup he scanned the pages of the newspaper from back to front: baseball scores, a Hollywood interview ("basically I'm a very insecure person"), a recipe for poached salmon, a syndicated psychologist's bland advice to the mother of an evidently paranoid child; editorials; an espionage scandal in London; Congressional comments on the Administration's latest tax bill; finally, the double-page spread on the fire. He was about to push the paper aside when his eye caught a small headline in the lower right-hand corner of page three.

MAN COLLAPSES IN PARK,
DIES ON WAY TO HOSPITAL

Milton S. Kalb, 56, a salesman, was pronounced dead on arrival at Roosevelt Hospital after he collapsed in Bryant Park early this afternoon. Medical authorities attributed his death to coronary thrombosis. In commenting on the efforts of several onlookers to revive Kalb by walking him around, they emphasized that exertion in such cases may be injurious and even fatal.

Witnesses among the lunch-hour throng, gathered to listen to the public library's daily concert of recorded music, said they believed the man was drunk and at first paid little attention to the tragedy.

Kalb is survived by a wife, Mrs. Anna Kalb of the Bronx, and two children, David Kalb, 30, of Queens, and Mrs. Sylvia Pretzel, 27, of Manhattan.

Pretzel, thought the doctor; that must be a misprint. No one is named Pretzel, for God's sake! He stared at the smudged print, waiting to feel some connection between himself and the death of Milton Kalb. Bryant Park—he had not even known its name, and the words evoked no picture in his mind. With a slight effort, as though he were raising a photographic slide to the light, he found that he could see the scene once more in all its detail, but from a distance: the toy trees, the moving people, himself a tiny anonymous figure seated motionless on a bench.

Refusal to give aid, denial of duty, he thought, looking at the tiny figure. Could I have saved him, anyway? He frowned, cut-

ting the fat from his pork chop, thinking now not of Milton Kalb
but of the impossibility of measuring alternatives in such a matter. How could you speak of making a choice between two
courses of action, medical or otherwise, when you knew before-
hand that you would have only one set of consequences to eval-
uate? True choice is a matter of logic, it deals with known factors.
It's raining, and if I carry an umbrella I won't get wet, though I
dislike being encumbered; if I leave the umbrella behind, on the
other hand, I will be unencumbered but wet. Choose. But such
choices are rare; scientifically speaking they occur only in the
laboratory, and then only after the alternatives have been artifi-
cially established in advance: subject identical specimens to different stimuli and eventually you'll have sufficient data on which
to base a choice. But when you deal with the living tissue, the
human being himself, where are your identical specimens, and
what confirmation can you hope to have of the correctness of
your choice—to operate, to prescribe a certain course of treatment, to do nothing? Sheldon told himself that the concept of
successful choice was meaningless in such circumstances, and any
assignment of personal credit or blame a crude presumption.

Milton Kalb was dead, who might have been saved. But there
was no way now, and never would be, of retrieving the crucial
moments in the park—of pushing the doctor forward from his
bench to do whatever needed to be done; of letting the clock in
the first-class stateroom tick on into the afternoon, over the long
sea miles; no way either of measuring an old man's spite. In a
few days it would be announced that Dr. Nicholas Sheldon had
been awarded the Thomas A. Ettinger Fellowship for Research
in Neurology; and Milton Kalb was dead. Just "and"—no need to
presume "therefore" or "because." If you did, you must also presume the number of lives to be saved or at least prolonged by
the efforts of Dr. Nicholas Sheldon in the course of a long and
brilliant career . . . Sheldon struck the thought away impatiently;
it was the sort of rationalizing he despised. Yes, cut your morality
to fit your behavior, he thought, it's easy enough if you have the
leisure and the inclination. The truth is we act to save ourselves:
ourselves only and always.

He folded the newspaper and raised his coffee cup, and in that moment his glance fell, impossibly, upon the smiling face of the girl in the park.

She stood just inside the cafeteria door with an intern named Paul Griffith, murmuring over her shoulder to him while her wide-eyed gaze floated over the crowded room to rest briefly—for a fraction of a second, for eternity—on the rigid white-suited figure of Sheldon sitting at his table twenty feet away, the coffee cup held motionless at his lips. Griffith said something in her ear, leaning close to her; she laughed, shrugging her shoulders, and took the tray he handed her. They joined the line at the counter.

Sheldon looked around and reached quickly for the coattails of a passing intern. "Hey, Ernie!"

The intern looked down, surprised, over his loaded tray. "Hi, Nick. How've you been?"

He started to move on, but Sheldon said, "What's your hurry? Join me."

"Well—sure, thanks, I will." He took the chair Sheldon pulled out for him. "I hear you're in line for resident fellow under Beddoes," he said, unloading his tray.

"It isn't confirmed yet, but I ought to hear soon."

"Great. I never understood why they even considered Fraser. I mean, he was a nice guy and all that—"

"Beddoes liked him," Sheldon said briefly.

Griffith and the girl were collecting napkins and silverware, their backs half turned to him; and he had his camouflage, was no longer a young man sitting alone as she had seen him in the park. But too late, too late! he told himself angrily and incredulously, as though the quickness of his own reaction should have canceled out the moment of her recognition. She saw me; she knows. Has she seen the paper? But no, the question of whether the guy lived or died doesn't concern her. All she has to know is that I'm a doctor who ignored a summons. One word from her—

Ernie said, grimacing over his soup, "I didn't think old Beddoes liked anybody. You ever hear the story about him and the nurse? This is supposed to be years ago, when Beddoes was a fairly young guy. This gorgeous babe is assisting him in a neurological exam, and she keeps twitching her ass and rubbing up against him, you know, but he doesn't bat an eye. Finally, when they're all through, he turns to her and says, 'My dear girl, as raw material you are undoubtedly well endowed, but I'll have you understand that in this hospital we do not tolerate crude technique in any form. Refine, refine!'" Ernie laughed, sputtering a little.

"I've heard it told about him, and about Granger and Schmidt and Tillinghurst," Sheldon said with indifference. He swallowed the last of his coffee. The thing to do now is get out, get away, he thought. Maybe I'm wrong, she isn't the same girl at all; or if she is, she didn't recognize me, it was just my imagination, or the way I was staring at her.

Ernie had been looking around the room, his prominent blue eyes restless and avid. Now he gave Sheldon an adolescent nudge and said, "Speaking of dolls, Griffith's got himself a cute piece, all right. See her, up there at the counter? She used to date Al Piper before he went off to join the Foreign Legion or whatever. Griffith just moved in where he left off. Bobbie Willis, her name is; I got it written down in my little black book. Griffith never lays the same girl more than a couple of months. I give him another few weeks at most. Then presto, the guard changes. I got him to promise to give me the good word."

Sheldon forced himself to keep his eyes on Ernie, whom he now remembered he disliked; but Griffith and the girl had reached the end of the counter, in a moment they would be turning, coming in his direction. He rose abruptly, giving Ernie a careless slap on the shoulder with the folded newspaper. "Well, I've got to run, Ernie, see you around."

"So what's your hurry?" Ernie was buttering a piece of bread, gouging the frozen yellow square into the soft dough; now he stared at Sheldon, the butter knife poised in midair, and said, "What's the matter—you regretting your sociable instincts already?"

Sheldon shrugged, managing a smile. "Sorry, I've got things to do, and I didn't realize it was so late."

"Look," Ernie said, with a belligerence that made Sheldon wonder if he could have been drinking—but no, the guy was hypersensitive, always taking offense over nothing, he ought to have remembered that. "You were the one who asked me to sit down, remember? I mean, I didn't invite myself."

Oh, Christ, Sheldon thought, as heads turned in their direction. But Griffith and the girl weren't paying any attention, just scanning the room for an empty table. Someone waved at them from a corner and they moved forward with their trays. Sheldon had an unobstructed view of the girl's profile as they passed. Yes —the same girl, the same curving mouth, the glossy wings of brown hair.

And at this split second of his certainty, as though she had been waiting for it, deliberately offering herself to his scrutiny, the girl turned her head to look directly at him, smiling the faintest of mocking smiles, and winked. Behind her Griffith steadied his tray and gazed over her shoulder, intent on reaching the table; in another moment they had moved on.

He said quickly, "Look, Ernie—I really am sorry to run out on you like this, but I just didn't realize what time it was. We'll get together soon, okay?" Ernie nodded sulkily, only partly mollified, and did not return his smile. Sheldon strode swiftly toward the door, his tall shoulders hunched, the newspaper pressed tight under his arm.

The single window of the room stood open on a square of darkness, admitting the beat of a radio from an adjacent window, the swish of late traffic on Riverside Drive several blocks away, the importunate yowling of a tomcat in the chill spring evening. Sheldon sat at his desk staring down at the tiny crowded print of the Manhattan telephone directory, which lay sprawled open on the green blotter at a page in the W's.

Bobbie could be Barbara or Roberta. There were two listings for Willis, Barbara: a Mrs. Willis on West Ninety-second Street, and a plain Barbara Willis on Christopher Street. No listings for Roberta. Christopher Street, in the Village. It figures, he thought.

Well, then. He would telephone her, make an appointment to see her; try to explain. And of course she would—what?

She had not said anything to Griffith tonight, he was sure of that. He had stayed at the hospital until Griffith was due back on duty in pediatrics—where, as he stepped from the elevator, he found the intern backed up against the main desk by the formidable head nurse, who was lecturing him in a fierce whisper. Sheldon had nodded as he approached, watching the muscles of Griffith's face at the instant when their glances met; Griffith grinned at him, and while the nurse stopped for breath, produced a comic grimace for his benefit, rolling his eyes at the ceiling and clutching his midriff. Sheldon had laughed and walked on, feeling the sweat break out. Nothing, then—nothing that was not in keeping with their casual acquaintance, with Griffith's own gregarious and clownish nature.

But why? he thought now. Why hadn't she said something right away? A limited capacity for moral indignation? A shrewd sense that Paul Griffith was not the most suitable recipient for such a tidy little piece of information? Or maybe it was only that she wasn't very bright and had yet to grasp the significance of what she'd seen. (Sure, and just happened to wink at him because she thought he looked vaguely familiar. Try again, Doctor.) Hell, she was Griffith's girl, and several others', if Ernie could be believed; she would be around (had been, might have noticed him before, for all he knew—she was not his type), a frequent and casual visitor at the hospital, and sooner or later—

Leave well enough alone, he told himself angrily, half fearfully. For Christ's sake, leave it alone! She may already have decided it's none of her business, she . . . Once more he examined her face in his mind, enduring again the light, lazy mockery of her glance, her flickering half-smile. Yes, he thought, as soon trust a cat to stay out of the cream. "Oh, by the way, what's the name of that tall blond doctor—a resident, I guess he is? You know, the good-looking one with the bony face who always seems to be in such a hurry? Because honestly, it's the funniest thing, but I could swear I saw him down in Bryant Park the other day, when this poor man keeled over with a heart attack or something, and they were calling and calling for a doctor . . . I mean, he didn't have a bag or anything, so no one *knew* he was a doctor; but aren't you supposed to—I mean, aren't doctors expected to . . . ?"

Money. But he didn't have that kind of money—and even if he did, would she take it?

To go on through the weeks and months, even the years, knowing that a casual word from her at any time could destroy him: the single blot on the record which he, of all people, so surely and swiftly headed for the top, could not afford. Not that anything would happen to him publicly; the medical profession could close ranks as discreetly as any other when questions of incompetence or negligence among the brethren were concerned—only privately, where it counted. With Beddoes and the others, with all those within the hierarchy who could give or withhold preferment and recognition, especially those to whom intellectual brilliance in a younger colleague was always a little suspect anyway, implying, as it sometimes (reassuringly) did, a compensating deficiency in other areas. Lack of humility, for instance, or of patience, or of suitable deference to established opinion; sometimes even, though most regrettably, of moral character, personal integrity . . .

Sheldon sat back, tilting the chair, and closed his eyes, fingertips pressed hard against the scarred edge of the desk. He noted with detachment the pathology of fear: the heavy pounding of his heart, and its pulsing echo in his ears; the dryness of his mouth, the dampness of his hands; the involuntary contraction of his muscles against a fluttering interior tremor. Deliberately he gathered himself, deliberately relaxed. Take it easy, he told himself, what the hell's the matter with you? You've got to do better than this, it's not as if she's even put the knife in you yet—and stopped, letting the chair tilt slowly forward until he was staring again at the tiny words "Willis, Barbara, 24 Christopher," lying innocent and passive under the white glare of the desk lamp. I never even had to ask her name, he thought; and knew then what the fear was for.

A true choice, the alternatives known.

He had not had to ask her name. He had found her address simply by turning a page. In this city of millions no one knew, no one need ever know, of the connection between them; and from that fact alone, it might be possible to fling a bridge across the abyss that had opened so unexpectedly beneath his feet. And to cross it swiftly, without looking back . . . Fantastic, unimaginable —possible. Yes, he thought, possible. Don't I see already exactly how it could be done? And know myself capable of it—as of anything, everything, in my own defense?

The horror of the thing, he found—lying awake through the slow black hours of that night—was curiously abstract. Once you contemplated it in specific terms, as a particular course of action undertaken for particular reasons, the horror faded, leaving little emotional residue—except, perhaps, for the stirrings of an ancient, morbid excitement.

Bobbie Willis stepped out into the cool morning sunlight, letting the green-painted door of 24 Christopher Street swing shut
behind her. On high-heeled patent-leather pumps she tapped
away toward Sixth Avenue beneath the translucent young leaves
of the trees planted along the curbing, the full pink skirt of her
dress twitching over its petticoat as she walked. A white sweater
ornamented with carved wooden buttons hung loosely from her
shoulders; she carried a large patent-leather bag in one white-
gloved hand. She paused for a moment outside a florist's on Sixth
Avenue to ask the price of the white-collared clumps of iris set
blazing upon the sooty pavement, but hurried across the street
as the light changed, her pink skirt swaying from side to side. In
the gray half-light of the subway entrance she waited in line to
buy tokens, studying the shiny toes of her shoes and humming
softly to herself. Then, with a swirl of her hip, she slipped through
the heavy turnstile and descended the two flights of stairs that
led through the rumbling darkness to the Sixth Avenue subway,
followed by at least a dozen tall young men wearing light raincoats and carrying newspapers under their arms, who stared ap-
preciatively at the neat shapes of the girls in their summer
dresses.

The D train rushed in, exhaling noisily as its doors gaped wide
on half-filled cars, gathered itself, and shot off once more into the
darkness. From his seat at the end of the next car, Sheldon saw
that the girl neither read nor looked at her fellow passengers, but
merely sat with her arms folded, smiling a little—that damnable
smile, he thought—as if in pleasurable anticipation of whatever
the day might bring. At Fourteenth Street the train filled up; he
moved onto the platform between the cars, leaning against the
clanking metal wall behind his raised newspaper as the doors
closed in a whirl of soot and litter. The train shrieked on through
the blackness. Twenty-third Street; Thirty-fourth next. The girl
was smoothing the skirt of her dress now, inspecting her gloves:
Thirty-fourth must be her stop. Sheldon flattened himself against
the surge of incoming passengers and stepped onto the platform
just in time to see her walking briskly toward a northeast exit.
She was glancing at her watch now, hurrying up the stairs in a
flashing of slender legs and white petticoat. Only quarter to nine
—was her office some distance away, or did she stop somewhere

for coffee? He must be careful; there was little enough chance that she would notice him in the hurrying morning crowd behind her, but if she stopped, had to stand in a line, began to look about her with that careless, smiling, all-encompassing gaze—

The sunlight glittered on the confused rush and surge of Thirty-fourth Street. Sheldon had never been to war, but he thought of the outskirts of some great battlefield, groaning with heavy transport and shrill with the furious cries, human and mechanical, of frustrated progress. Glass walls echoed light and sound, guarding the fragile artifacts of civilization, diverting the eye from the huge steel thrust of the buildings into the mild spring sky.

The girl crossed Fifth Avenue and turned north. Sheldon kept pace with her on the opposite side of the street, and was glad of his caution when he saw, between the crawling buses and cabs, the attentive sideways turn of her head toward the windows of Altman's massive façade. She waited for a light at Thirty-fifth Street, and then—he almost lost her—darted across the sidewalk toward the glass doors of a Chock Full O' Nuts. Sheldon returned to the corner, fixing his eyes on the jaunty tiled sign above the doors, until she emerged and hurried on northward, almost running now. Nine o'clock. The pink skirt whipped across Thirty-sixth Street and turned sharply into a small office building between a cafeteria and—he moved to the curb for a better look —a luggage store plastered with "Sale" signs. He waited a few minutes, watching the dark rectangle of the lobby under its shell-shaped bronze lintel; then, satisfied, he moved on. An ordinary nine-to-five job, apparently. So far so good. He would return at lunchtime to make sure she went back to the office afterward and so would be leaving for the day at five o'clock, like all the others: in the crowds, at rush hour.

Waiting for an uptown bus, Sheldon stood gazing up at the smoky blue shaft of the Empire State Building while the impatient people of the city jostled him unseeingly in the familiar abrasion of contact, flesh against flesh. Two hours back at the hospital, he thought. It should be enough, with the work he had done earlier in the morning. And he would work late that evening —though not too late, he must not risk calling attention to the rather peculiar schedule, even for a slack time in the lab, which he had set for himself on this particular day . . .

At noon Sheldon was opposite the office building once more, moving carelessly in and out of the shops, always staying close enough to the windows to have a glimpse of the doorway across the street. There was a good chance that he would miss her this way, especially when the intervening traffic loomed high with buses and trucks—but he could not risk even a passing glance of interrogation or curiosity, he must keep moving. At one-thirty, when he had decided he must have missed her, or that she had stayed in the building for lunch, he caught the pink flicker of her dress through the shuffle of pedestrians past the doorway, and saw her smooth brown head inclined in conversation with a short man in a bright blue suit—the boss?—for the few moments it took them to reach the door of the neighboring cafeteria. He left the bookstore whose display of garish Impressionist prints he had been pretending to study, and crossed the street to stand at the southeast corner of Thirty-sixth Street, shifting his weight impatiently from one foot to another and glancing frequently at his watch, as though waiting for a tardy luncheon companion.

After fifteen minutes the man and the girl emerged and stood for a moment talking; then, with a wave, the man hurried back into the office building and the girl walked on up the avenue, swinging her shiny bag. Sheldon followed her across Thirty-seventh Street into the fragrant hubbub of Lord & Taylor, where she vanished into an elevator, and stood inspecting ties and socks in the men's department until she reappeared carrying a flat dark green bag slashed across with the slanting white letters of the store's signature. A blouse, he thought idly, or a nightgown. Watching her rapid examination and rejection of a display of evening bags on one of the gleaming counters, he decided that she was probably a wary shopper, less impulsive than she looked, with the inherited shrewdness of her middle-class—Midwestern? —background. She stood aside at the revolving doors to let a pair of tanned suburban women enter; one of them brushed against her and turned, exclaiming in apology, but the girl only smiled vaguely and went on out the doors. That much of a New Yorker, he thought, and wondered for an instant where she had come from, and how long ago—

But these were expensive thoughts, he reminded himself

coldly: things he could not afford to wonder about, much less know. He left the store, only to dodge quickly back into the shadows of the entrance when he saw that she was standing irresolutely at the curb as though considering another errand, looking north along the gleaming tunnel of the avenue, whose great walls rippled now in the full sunshine while flags and pennants whipped color into the blue air. After a moment the girl looked at her watch and turned reluctantly south toward her office, settling the white sweater more securely around her shoulders. From his careful distance a half-block behind, Sheldon saw how the empty sleeves danced and gestured in the breeze of her passage through the crowds.

When he had seen her enter the building again, he walked unhurriedly over to Madison Avenue and had a drink and a sandwich in the nautical gloom of the Whaler Bar, where only the largest of the bartenders and possibly the hat-check girl—a hearty blonde with small cruel features—looked as if they could ever have had anything to do with the sea. Then he made his leisurely way back up Fifth Avenue to Forty-second Street, turning west past small shops selling stockings and cheap negligees and rhinestone jewelry, until he came to the large Woolworth's next to Stern's. The kitchen-goods department was down a flight of stairs, which he descended with sudden diffidence, a newcomer to the city furnishing his bachelor apartment as hastily and cheaply as possible, collecting a small frying pan and saucepan, dishtowels, assorted utensils, including an eggbeater with a glossy red handle, and three kitchen knives—a paring knife, a bread knife, and a third whose domestic function he wondered about briefly as he slid the blade from its cardboard sheath and felt its point with his thumb. Was it meant for slicing? The blade was narrow and firm, a little too long to be handled efficiently, but very sharp at the point.

He replaced the sheath and watched the saleswoman drop the knife into a big flimsy paper bag with the other things, slapping with practiced violence at the cash register to add up the sale. She hardly glanced at him, and at his purchases only to take their prices. One curious or appraising look and he would have to stow this particular lot in a locker, to be picked up later and produced at his apartment in slightly used condition in the very unlikely event that they were ever traced to him; in the meantime he would try another store. But now this alternative could be discarded, forgotten; and emerging into the sunshine once more, Sheldon felt physically lighter, as though each section of his plan were a weight to be detached in its turn, until finally he could return to himself, to his real life, stripped clean and unfettered for good.

Next door, in Stern's lobby, he shut himself into a phone booth, dialed his own empty apartment, keeping his back to the door while the receiver buzzed dutifully in his ear, and reached down into the bag with his free hand for the knife. It fitted neatly into the deep side pocket of his raincoat, with his old pigskin gloves. He left the lobby and jaywalked across the busy expanse of Forty-second Street with the bag under his arm. He felt tall and conspicuous as he reached the curb, and his mouth had gone a little dry: this was the most, indeed the only, exposed moment of his plan. But casually, unhurriedly, he jammed the bag with its tinny contents into a trashcan near the entrance to Bryant Park, where the luncheon concert had long since ended and only the old men in their flannel shirts dozed in peace beneath the shimmering leaves.

At three minutes past five o'clock Bobbie Willis left her office building on Fifth Avenue and joined the southbound crowd surging down toward Thirty-fourth Street, accompanied by the handsome Negro girl who worked in her office. Turning westward, they narrowed their eyes against the slanting rays of the sun, which flared behind the heads and shoulders of the people coming toward them, giving them a ghostly and insubstantial look. Bobbie had a headache, and wished she had remembered her sunglasses. When she got home she would take a couple of aspirin and have a light supper—a salad, or maybe just some cold soup —and see if she could talk Ann into going to a movie. Or Chuck might call, if he wasn't still mad at her . . . At Sixth Avenue she parted from Stephanie, who was going on to the IRT, and descended the subway stairs a slow step at a time, hemmed in by the sluggish crowd, automatically stiffening her nostrils against the basement odor of the subterranean air that rose to envelop her.

The D train was crowded. Bobbie stood near the center door of the car, grasping the slippery white pole with one hand and trying to read a paperback best seller she carried in her bag; but the binding was cheap and stiff, and she had trouble keeping the pages open far enough to see the words at the inner margin. She gave up at Fourteenth Street, when the gust of the opening doors ballooned her skirt around her knees and she had to use the hand that held the book to flatten it. A woman belatedly fighting her way out onto the platform poked the sharp corner of a handbag into Bobbie's ribs; she looked around in annoyance and put the book back in her bag. From a seat near the doors a man in a dirty plaid cap stared fixedly at Bobbie's legs, gnawing his chapped lips, and was stared at in turn by the grim and faded old woman next to him. Bobbie gazed unseeingly over their heads as the train slowed. The rushing blackness of the windows stuttered on the numeral 4 . . . 4 . . . 4 painted on gray girders, and submitted at last to the yellow glare of the station.

She braced herself automatically against the final forward lurch of the train, and then slipped sideways into the stream of departing passengers, thinking as she tapped across the platform toward the nearest flight of stairs: Damn, I left that bag in the office, my new blouse that I wanted to wear tomorrow. Did I put it away in the drawer when I came back from lunch? In her mind she began to search the desk she had just left for the flat green bag with its familiar slanting letters; she hardly felt the entering sting of the knife behind her heart, and had taken another step upward before the sting became an enormous pressure that forced her mouth open soundlessly as she fell. The square green shape blocked the light hugely, a dull green wall the color of shadowed leaves and grasses: Forest green, she thought, forest green . . . With a rush the paper tore and shredded, and blew away like powder before the winds of darkness.

There was a roommate, the newspapers said—Ann Claremont, twenty-three, daughter of Guy Reid Claremont, well-known author of travel books and articles. A graduate of Wellesley College, Miss Claremont was employed in the public-relations department of one of the city's larger art museums. She had no idea who might have wanted to harm her roommate, whose

body she had been called upon to identify. She was being kept
under sedation at her father's apartment and was not available
for comment.

Well, it was a chance he'd taken, had felt he must take—waiting that morning a safe half-block from the green door, deciding
not to risk a look at the mailboxes behind it. Because, he told
himself, even given the very slight possibility that the roommate had been told the story, what could she really know that
was worth knowing? Not his face, not his name. And even if by
some accident she should come to learn those, she would not
know him—what he cared for, what he was capable of.

The days passed. Nothing happened, nothing was going to happen. Miss Claremont, being persistently unavailable for comment,
vanished quickly from the news; Miss Willis herself was not far
behind.

He had bad dreams, of course, in the first weeks of that hot
summer, when sleeping was difficult, anyway, and the whir of
the fan on the window sill kept opening and shutting the subway doors throughout the hours of the early morning. And in the
hospital sometimes, stooping to hear a patient's whispered question, studying the delicate shadows of an x-ray screen, he found
himself clenching his teeth against the sudden derisive voice of
his secret knowledge, which wanted to cry out at the absurd ease
with which it was possible to take a human life, in the face of so
much consecrated labor, such an elaborate armory of steel and
machinery and trained intelligence dedicated to preserving it!
The voice angered and pained him; it was as though he had encountered in a respected colleague an unpardonable betrayal
of professional trust.

But inasmuch as he had little fear of discovery and no com-
pulsion to relive the event, the sense of his crime as a personal,
physical act soon faded. He had not even seen the girl fall, had
heard only the sudden murmur of the crowd behind him as he
went on up the stairs. He was left chiefly with a kind of grim
wonder at the conjunction of circumstance and accident which
had forced him, as he saw it, to such grotesque and melodramatic
lengths. He perceived now that he had made insufficient allow-
ance in the ordering of his life for the intrusions of sheer chance—
chance considered as a propulsive force, not merely as a random

illumination of possibility or desire. It had never occurred to him that its lightning could strike so directly, leaving behind this insistent odor of sulphur, this grittiness of char and ash which the swift stream of time could still not quite expunge.

No. There was a reason for this lingering unease, he discovered. It was the sense of unfinished business that bothered him—the damned roommate, of course. By temperament he disliked having to take things for granted: the stronger the probability, the more strongly it invited proof. Well, then—what? If he could just meet the girl somehow, he thought, could set himself to watch her face at the moment when she first saw him and heard his name . . . Yes, what he wanted from her, he realized, was nothing more or less than a certain look, the kind of glance Paul Griffith had given him that night at the hospital—casual, pleasant, unsurprised; or if the glance was also appraising (he knew his attractiveness to women), charged with only an ordinary degree of interest and sexual wariness.

"Poor Ann," someone, a friend of Griffith's, had said in the course of the subdued talk that followed the news of the murder —he had been careful to hear what he could, while keeping his normal distance—"she must be taking this thing pretty hard. Having to make the identification— God, the poor kid." And the others had shaken their heads.

They knew her. One or two of them might even have taken her out, double-dating with Griffith. An introduction, a handshake— and with it the final confirmation of his own security. It wasn't impossible. He could make no overtures, of course. But he could go to the parties; Griffith and his friends were always giving parties, preferring beer to sleep. If that failed, he might risk the Village itself, her own neighborhood, see where she went for a bite to eat, and then some evening—but careful, careful, at all costs, whatever happened, he must not seem to have sought her out—

But this extension of his plan was unnecessary, as it turned out. One night in July he arrived at a hot and noisy open house in someone's basement apartment to see, standing in a doorway, a tall blond girl whose composed and smiling face stamped itself in that instant upon his mind and senses with a stunning finality, as if it had been the print of a negative he had been carrying around with him all his life. "Let's see, Nick," his host was muttering in his ear, "you know Freddy here, and Al Marks, and this is Julie Turner, Gardner Blake, Ann Claremont . . ." But he was not listening, he had already started toward her, it seemed to him that he had known in that first instant—but in his anger and incredulity he told himself that it didn't matter, it couldn't matter, not now—exactly who she must be, and where she lived, though none of the newspapers had succeeded in getting a photograph of the dead girl's roommate.

II. AFTER THE FACT

ONE

The apartment was on the second floor, overlooking the street. The door from the hall opened directly into the narrow kitchen, on whose end wall— the partition dividing it from the identical cubicle of the bed- room—hung a tall Dufy poster, streaks of pastel over a drawing of the Tuileries. It was a naïve and homemade kitchen, without right angles: the miniature tiles of the drainboard had been stuck together with a haphazard thumb, the soap dish sat askew above the tiny sink, the cupboards sloped. To the right a low arched doorway led into a square little living room furnished by the landlord with three undersized Early American chairs, a stubby coffee table and a desk. On the rough white plaster wall above the fireplace Ann had hung a framed print of "The Peaceable Kingdom," whose stuffed animals gazed benignly into the middle distance. There were also a Morris Graves bird over the desk, a pair of Rembrandt drawings between the two windows, and a print of Gris' "Coffee Mill" above the drop-leaf table near the door. A studio couch covered in gray-green monk's cloth and dotted with yellow cushions like lemon drops extended along the inner wall beneath a long double bookshelf. Loose-woven orange curtains hung at the windows and across the entrance to the bed- room, which held a double-decker bed, a mirror and a scarred chest of drawers.

On this July evening the little apartment was dustless, the cushions exactly aligned, the three ashtrays set out. Ann Claremont, wearing a plain green linen dress and low-heeled shoes, stood at the window looking westward along Christopher Street toward Sheridan Square. Rain had fallen lightly during the afternoon, but now the sky was luminous with late sunshine, which dazzled in the high windows of the apartment house across the street and richly flooded the topmost leaves of the maple saplings planted along the near curb.

As Ann leaned forward against the sill, it gleamed in her thick fair hair and sprang flashing from the small gold pin at her shoulder, the narrow watchband encircling one strong flexed wrist. She was a tall girl with a sturdy firm-muscled body, a little heavy in the hips and thighs. Her face was level-browed, gray-eyed, with a short straight nose and rounded, naturally ruddy cheeks that gave her a smiling look even when her mouth was sober in repose. Her neck was solid and graceful, exactly proportioned to her height and to the weight of the shining hair twisted at its nape. "A striking girl," people said, but with a certain unease; her forthright manner, her general air of assurance and energy, above all the untroubled clarity of her gaze, were somehow disconcerting. Yet in this often formidable composure of hers there was appeal as well as challenge, the odd pathos of the handsome animal whose race is yet to be run.

She waited in the mellow light, looking in the direction from which he would come. It's not that he is late, she reminded herself; only that I am early. As usual. Born with ten minutes to spare, Carlo had once said. But I can't help it if I hate rush and confusion, she thought, and if nobody were ever ready ahead of time—

But now she saw him: a very tall young man in a light summer suit, striding with bent head across the intersection with Waverly Place, his footsteps sounding loud and decisive in the lull of the evening traffic. Ann's fingers tightened on the window sill as she saw how he made directly for the door of her building, glancing neither to right nor left. He didn't even have to look for the number, she thought with a shock; as though he already knew his way to me—just as he came across the room to me the other night at the party, without hesitation, paying no attention

to anyone else, so that I thought at first he must be bringing me
a message of some sort, a summons.

"Nick," she called. "Up here!" She smiled as he looked up and
saw her. "Just walk in, the lock doesn't work; to say nothing of
the buzzer."

With a wave of his hand he ducked into the entrance. She
heard his quick footsteps on the stairs as she went into the kitchen
to open the door, swinging it wide as he came up the last few
steps from the landing. "Welcome!" she said, and held out her
hand. "I see you found your way."

"Oh, no trouble," he said easily, and followed her into the living room, looking around, appraising it. "Nice little place. Does
the fireplace work?"

"Well, that's a matter of opinion. The only time we—I tried
to use it, the tenants upstairs started choking to death and somebody called the fire department. I gather you could smell the
smoke blocks away."

"Chimney probably needs cleaning," Nick said, and turned to
the window. Ann came to stand beside him. In silence they
looked down on the heads of people strolling through the gathering shadows, alone or in couples who murmured quietly together as they passed the window of the small gift shop below.
She saw his frown, the tension of his jaw, and thought: He is
nervous too, and finds the feeling as strange as I do. She observed
lightly, "At least there's always something to watch here. Especially in the summer."

Beneath them a man stopped to turn an astonished stare at
the shop window. "Jesus!" he said to himself, and went on.

Ann laughed. "The copper phoenix. Did you notice it when
you came in?"

"No. Just a lot of beads and some weird-looking ashtrays."

"It's in the back, on the wall—the *pièce de résistance*. I'll show
it to you when we go out." She turned away. "Well, shall we
have a drink here first? Let's see—I've got Scotch, and gin and
tonic, and vermouth, and exactly twelve ice cubes."

"Gin and tonic sounds fine— No, let me," he said, crossing the
room in three strides. "I'll find my way around. Same for you?"

"Yes, thanks."

Ann sat down on the couch, listening to his hands swiftly finding the bottle opener and glasses, snapping open the lever of the ice tray. After a moment she called out, "What's your schedule like these days, Nick? Do you have a fair amount of time off?"

"Oh, compared to interning I keep bankers' hours. It's not bad."

She leaned forward, clasping her hands tightly around her knees. "I don't understand why the internship has to be so terribly strenuous. You must get so tired after a while that you stop being able to learn much of anything, let alone do your job very efficiently. Of course, if it's a matter of staff . . . but is it really necessary to work such long hours, do you think?"

"Yes," he said, coming back and handing her her drink. "It's one very simple way of separating the sheep from the goats. Here, six ice cubes, I counted."

There was a burst of laughter from the street below. Nick glanced at the window with distaste, and said, "Don't you find it pretty noisy here, with all these people underfoot?"

"Oh, not really. It quiets down later on. Anyway, it's kind of fun, when you have nothing better to do, listening to fragments of conversation and trying to reconstruct them. My favorite so far is the man who said to his wife, 'But listen, honey, if we can't use the charcoal, what's the point of buying the parakeet?' We never did figure that one out." Damn, she thought, taking a swallow of her drink.

"We? Do you have a roommate?"

"I did."

"Impossible. There isn't room. Oh," he said, glancing into the tiny bedroom, "a double-decker. That's the secret." He eased himself into the small armchair by the window and saluted her with his glass before he drank, his eyes on her face.

"The landlord's idea," Ann said. "Actually, when I first saw the place the bed was in here—an enormous double bed. It took up the whole room. And black curtains. I never met the former tenants, but they certainly had the gloomiest-looking love nest I ever saw."

"And you've seen a great many, of course."

"Of course."

She noticed that he was looking at the photograph of Bobbie on the radiator cover, the one she'd had taken to send to the boy in Japan. Richard Gowan, his name was; Bobbie always spoke of him as Richard, not Dick. I never wrote to Richard, Ann thought. I wonder if anyone else did.

"That the roommate?" Nick said.

"Yes."

"Good-looking girl."

"That's what they all say."

Then he really doesn't know, she thought. Oh, God, to spend one evening with someone who doesn't know—surely I am allowed that? She said into the silence, aware of his curious glance, "Have you decided where we're going to dinner?"

"Hungry already?"

"Oh, I'm always hungry, I warn you. Despite my sedentary life. It's the subway stairs, or something."

"Or your athletic temperament," he said, and held up a hand when she looked at him blankly. "Oh, I don't mean just the way you look or move, though that's part of it. It's also the way your mind works: always having to know what comes next, what to prepare for."

"And that makes me an athlete? Such an unattractive word."

"Oh, I don't know . . ." He leaned back comfortably, crossing his long legs. "I bet you skied a lot at—Putney, was it? And played hockey at college—"

"Lacrosse, as a matter of fact."

"Good Lord. And crew—don't they have a ladies' crew at Wellesley?"

"Well, yes, but—"

"In fact," he went on thoughtfully, "you're really much simpler than your environment, your probably rather bookish friends, your museum job; hardly touched by them, except in superficial ways. You're happiest when you're working, and your instinctive preference is for physical work, not brainwork. Especially anything competitive."

After a moment Ann said, "I'm afraid I dislike being typed. Particularly by people I've just met."

"Sorry." When she was silent, he added amiably, "I have a bad habit of thinking out loud. And an orderly mind, like you."

"A fellow athlete."

"I never had time for sports," he said, and smiled at her, holding her eyes with his own; and suddenly she felt again as she had at the party, when her heart had begun to pound so violently beneath the thin fabric of her dress that she was sure he must see it —standing so close to her, listening so gravely, with such polite irony, to the laughing chatter with which she sought to fend off her helpless sense of having been singled out and claimed irrevocably by a stranger.

She said with a little shrug, "Well, you did make me sound like a terrible—fraud, or hypocrite, or something."

He shook his head. "That's not what I meant at all." He sat forward, holding his glass between his knees, staring down at it with a frown of concentration. "Don't you ever have this sense of seeing through the complex surface of a person to the natural *working* human being underneath? Through the engineer to the mechanic, for instance; through the architect to the carpenter, the bricklayer . . . Do you know what I mean?"

"Yes, I suppose so. And through the doctor . . . ?"

"Through the doctor to the glorified nurse most doctors used to be. At least that's true of some of us," he said in a tone that excluded himself. "It's as though our psychology hasn't had a chance to catch up with our technology."

"Yes," Ann said. "I do know what you mean. It's something I've felt too, especially here in the city. So much sophistication imposed on people so fast—"

"Exactly. The artisan turns technician, the typist turns secretary, the businessman turns executive. And the upper-class college girl, who even ten years ago wouldn't have been worrying about anything much more burdensome than the Junior League or her boy friend's future at the bank, becomes a conscious member of the intellectual elite—for a few years, anyway."

"Meaning me?" Ann set her glass on the coffee table and looked at him with a smile. "I'm no intellectual, Nick, if that's what you're trying to find out. Despite a few—bookish friends, as you put it. The Village is really pretty middle-class these days, you know; don't let the tourists fool you. Lots of us go to Howard Johnson's for hot-fudge sundaes. Sometimes we even eat ice-cream cones on the street. Furtively, under our raincoats."

"Of course," he said, grinning. "I can see you're the furtive type."

She laughed. "All right. You know, it really is terrible to be so

—straightforward-looking. You can't ever hide anything; at least I can't." When he didn't answer, she said, "Don't you know what I mean? You have the same kind of face I have—firm and definite, without shadows. The despair of the amateur painter."

"Do you paint?"

"I used to. When I was in college I did some portraits of faculty children, just for fun mostly, and I was surprised at how much harder it was to get a likeness of what I'd always thought of as an easy face than of a difficult, changeable, irregular face . . . to say nothing of getting an interesting portrait, one that expresses some depth of personality."

"Instead of concealing it, you mean?" His voice was amused and a little impatient. "I'm afraid I disagree. You and I have the dangerous faces; with practice they can conceal almost anything."

"But do people with straightforward faces have anything to conceal?" she said, and refused to be put off by his smile. "No, really—I think most faces convey personality quite accurately, if you study them closely enough. Or maybe it's partly the other way around: our appearance conditions our character."

Nick looked down at his hands. "What about the wolf in sheep's clothing? The gangster with the choirboy face?"

"Oh—" Ann shrugged. "The people who manage to look simpler than they are. Yes, I know, but the exceptions only prove the rule. I really do think you can judge a book by its cover most of the time."

"Most of the time," Nick repeated with an odd ironic emphasis, and got to his feet. "Drink up, girl, we have a reservation at Le Bijou as of now."

Ann rose, smoothing down her skirt, and met his eyes, dark blue and speculative under slightly hooded lids, before he bent his head to pick up her glass and take it to the kitchen.

"A reservation yet," she said, looking around for her purse and deciding not to bother with it. "I'm impressed."

"I thought you might be."

As they went down the stairs Ann said, "This business of faces reminds me of Thomas Mann—the distinction he makes between fair blue-eyed people and dark-eyed ones, the moral difference he feels between them. It's a northern-southern thing, partly;

you get it in D. H. Lawrence too. Do you remember in *Women in Love*—or is it in *The Rainbow* . . . ?"

"Read much?" Nick said.

Ann looked straight ahead, feeling the color burn in her cheeks. "Sorry," she said briskly. "It must be my bookish friends. It's too bad they aren't interested in jet planes or horticulture or stamp-collecting, I suppose I could be quite chatty on those subjects, too—"

He held the door for her, smiling to himself. "Are you such a chameleon as all that? I doubt it. You strike me as someone who makes a plan and sticks to it, regardless of what anyone else says or does. Isn't that true?"

"A plan?" she said, disconcerted in spite of herself. "Well, I don't make very many plans these days. But yes, I do believe in finishing what I start, if that's what you mean."

They made their way along Christopher Street to Sixth Avenue, where the rushing metal flanks of two-toned cabs gleamed under the evening neon, and urgent *Don't Walk* signs halted the casual throng in its nightly promenade toward Eighth Street and MacDougal and the Square. Nick walked at a rapid, even pace, one hand in his pocket, the other holding Ann's elbow lightly. She saw how the eyes of passing girls, boy-girls included, flicked at him and lingered appraisingly. Lord, she thought, he is good-looking, isn't he? But doesn't seem aware of it; or if he is, probably regards it as irrelevant.

He said, as though pursuing an uninterrupted train of thought, "Generally speaking, though, you are not a compulsive person. Or at least only about small things."

"Oh," Ann said lightly, "I suppose we all have our compulsions." When he turned his head to look at her squarely for the first time, she added with a little laugh, "I mean, we'd have to be supermen not to, wouldn't we?"

He said, still watching her, "Anything in particular you're compulsive about?"

Ann shrugged. Not now, she told herself, not tonight.

"What does that mean?" he said, imitating her shrug. "Are you always so noncommittal about yourself?"

"Are you always so inquisitive?"

"Oh, I just like to get the facts. It saves time in making a diagnosis."

"I'm quite healthy, thank you."

He guided her around a drunk who was shakily trying to light
a cigarette stub from a box of kitchen matches. "Oh, yes, I can
see that. In fact, it's the first word that would occur to anyone
seeing you—health. Health rampant, health triumphant. Do you
have any idea how appealing that is to a careworn medical man?"

His smile at her was open and direct, but she thought: I was
wrong about the shadows, they have been there all along; and
there is something subtle and even strange about him that he has
learned to control, if not quite (whatever he may think) to conceal.

They came out of the restaurant into the warm, dense atmosphere of the city evening, shapes of color and light, darkness
falling like ashes from a cindery sky.

Ann took a deep breath and blew it out again, making a face.
"I've lived here most of my life, and I ought to be used to it, but
in the summertime I still feel as if I'm about to suffocate."

"You probably are. Medically speaking, I mean. Fantastic to
think of all the people who actually choose to live here, inhaling
this poison for a lifetime."

"Including you."

He said drily, "Oh, like everybody else I'm sure my lungs are
immune, pure as the driven snow . . . No, it's the self-destructive
atmosphere of this place that really gets me. You keep hearing
all this crisis talk about traffic and housing and air pollution and
crime, the whole mess, how the place isn't fit to live in—yet at the
same time you can see people getting a kind of morbid pleasure
out of it all. The sheer size of the mess is impressive, I suppose.
And, of course, the more monumental it gets the less personal
responsibility anyone has to feel."

A short stocky man in a pale topcoat and hat pushed past them
rudely, his bitter pugface clenched in a scowl, eyes squinting
ahead into some private tunnel of necessity or despair. Behind
him drifted a girl in a black leotard and corduroy skirt whose
dark hair hung in heavy folds about her drugged sleepwalker's

face. Ann said slowly, "There's a certain pride in just being able to survive at all, you know."

Nick laughed harshly. "So you let things go to pot as completely as possible in order to congratulate yourself on your own powers of survival. That's a pretty negative form of satisfaction, even in this neurotic old world."

"I suppose it is," Ann said. "But then, I'm a city girl."

She stooped to peer into a basement shop displaying straw and leather handbags against an elaborate landscape of silk scarfs and jewelry. "Oh, look! Nick, do you mind if we go in here for a minute? I see exactly the bag I've been looking for all summer."

The shop was empty except for a boy reading a paperback edition of William James, his sneakers propped up on a scarred desk. He finished his paragraph before he stood up, yawning, and said, "Help you?"

"Yes. That bag in the window—the big one."

"Twenty-nine ninety-five," the boy said, unfurling one of the silk scarfs and handing the bag to her. "Italian. Nice job."

Ann inspected the bag, which was large and rectangular, with briefcase-type leather straps and buckles.

Nick said, "That's practically a suitcase! What on earth do you want with something that size?"

"Oh, I carry lots of stuff around," Ann said vaguely, giving one of the straps a strong tug. "My book and my lunch—" Finding him smiling at her, she added, "I used to be the shoulder-strap type, until my friends convinced me I wasn't stylish enough for midtown. I still think it's the only sensible kind of bag. But this—" She thought for a moment, then turned to speak to the clerk. But the boy, bored, had gone back to his book.

Nick said, "Would you mind helping the lady here?"

The boy raised his eyebrows and stared at him.

Ann said quickly, "Could you put this aside for me until the morning? I'd like to buy it, but I don't have any money with me now. I can stop in before work tomorrow."

"I've got some money, Ann. Let me pay for it, and you can give me a check later."

"We don't open till noon," the boy told her, ignoring Nick. "But you can pick it up tomorrow night, I'll put it aside till then. Actually, I'm not supposed to do it, but what the hell, you have an honest face." He found a pencil stub in the pocket of his shirt. "I better get your name, though."

Nick took three ten-dollar bills from his wallet and laid them on the desk. "You don't need her name," he said coldly. "We'll take the bag now."

"Oh, look, really—" Ann began.

"There's a tax on that, mister," the boy said.

"Well, suppose you tell me what it is, and we'll let you go back to your book, all right?"

As they climbed the steps back to the sidewalk, Nick said between his teeth, "Of all the stupid, sloppy, half-baked ways to run a business—"

"You're in the Village," Ann said. "You have to leave your uptown expectations behind."

"I can't stand seeing a job done that sloppily, that's all. If it's worth doing at all—"

"It's worth doing well," Ann finished for him. "I know; it's our upbringing. But as a friend of mine once said: If a job's not worth doing well, it's not worth doing at all. That's the prevailing attitude around here, and you have to admit it has a point."

"Any work that has to be done is worth doing, and worth doing well," Nick said. They walked on in silence toward Washington Square.

How refreshing to meet an inflexible man, Ann thought. Inflexible Man—it sounds like the title of a book. But I am so tired of everybody's being so tolerant and open-minded all the time, of having to look at every side of every question so interminably. I'm even tired of Carlo these days, with his everlasting air of amused objectivity. Maybe it's just the amusement I'm tired of . . . Without looking at him, she had a sudden vivid sense of Nick's presence beside her that was more than the sense of his body, his masculine breadth and height: as of some brilliant metal deliberately forged and shaped in defiance of the common mold. She felt her own body gather itself against his force, whether to meet it or resist it she did not know.

She said, "I'm embarrassed, because I should have asked you before—but what field of medicine are you specializing in, Nick? I mean, what is your fellowship for?"

"Neurology."

"Oh. Well, do you do research, mostly, or—I guess I'm not sure just what the practical side of neurology involves—surgery, or . . . ?"

He said impatiently, "There are a great many diseases of the nervous system and a great many ways of treating them, of which surgery is only one. To answer your question, a fellowship is usually given for research, and if you're lucky you may actually see the inside of a lab once in a while. In my case, the great Dr. Terence Beddoes, whose humble protégé I currently am, has more important things for me to do."

"Such as . . . ?"

"Such as writing up his reports and nursemaiding his interns and answering the telephone when his secretary isn't around, and—oh, the hell with talking about it, if you don't mind."

Ann stared at him. His face had gone tight and rigid; he looked ahead unseeing as they entered the park between the tables of chess players, hunched in frowning absorption over their games. She started to speak, but thought better of it. In silence they walked on toward the bright inner circle of the fountain, where the ice-cream vendor presided busily over his cart and the young men lounged to watch the girls go by. Dogs quivered on their leashes along the walks, or prowled in illegal freedom under the trees, whose leaves, unnaturally green in the lamplight, made intricate patterns on the heads and shoulders of the lazy sauntering couples. Beyond the screen of leaves the walls of the city receded sullenly into the sky, impotent against this vestigial frivolity of living flesh and vegetation, this murmurous shadowy grove in which the lightest, most delicate shiver of air produced a thousand motions, various and surprising.

Ann said, "Well . . . ?" and looked at him. "Do you want to sit down for a while? There's an old man who always brings his radio and listens to chamber music. We could see if there's a free bench near him." When Nick shrugged indifferently, she came to a stop, swinging the straw bag against her thigh, and said with an annoyed laugh, "We don't have to stay here at all, for that matter, if the idea bores you so much."

He looked down at her; his face cleared. "Ann—" he said, and put his hands on her shoulders. She returned his gaze steadily. He let his hands fall away, and gave her a wry smile. "I don't mind. You sit and listen to your music. I'll watch the human comedy. There seems to be plenty of it around."

They found an unoccupied bench under a lamp. Nick sat with his hands clasped loosely between his knees, his head raised to watch the passing crowd: recording it all, Ann thought, studying his taut profile, not for any purpose, but automatically, because his mind always has to be working. Two benches away the radio played a Mozart quartet, the violins skittering gaily through the soft darkness.

"I take it you don't like music," she said at last.

"No."

"Well, but—some music? You can't just say you don't like it categorically, can you?"

"Why not?"

"I don't know. I guess I just assumed everybody liked music. One song, at least—'White Christmas' or 'Stardust,' or something."

"I don't know much about it," Nick said. "Do you?"

"Well—not formally. I mean, I'm no musician. I guess I just grew up hearing a lot of it, that's all."

"Of course, there was a grand piano in the Gramercy Park apartment."

"Yes, there was."

"And the house in the country—Cornwall, Connecticut, isn't it?"

"Yes. A concert grand, as a matter of fact. Do I apologize now or later?" she said, looking at him. "A lot of our friends just happened to be musical. I gather my mother was."

"Was?"

"She died when I was two."

"I'm sorry," he said, frowning.

"A ruptured appendix. Not very glamorous of her, was it? She and Dad were cruising on someone's boat up in Maine. By the time she said something about it and they got her to a hospital, it was too late. An athlete to the end."

"Ann—"

"So my father quit his brokerage job and hired a housekeeper and started going off on long trips by himself, and after a while he wrote a couple of travel articles about out-of-the-way places he'd been and managed to sell them, and he's been in the business ever since, as I guess I told you. When I got old enough, he taught me how to use a camera and took me with him. So I've traveled a good deal and really had quite a pleasant life, and now have a stepmother I'm very fond of."

He said, "I didn't ask for your autobiography."

She stood up. "Well, you said you were interested in facts, and since the evening seemed to be more or less dying on the vine—"

"Ann." He caught her hand and pulled her down beside him. "Look, I know I'm not a very sociable type, but I thought you wanted to listen to the music. If you want to talk—"

She looked down at their joined hands, feeling her own begin to tremble, and drew it away before he felt it too. Oh, God, she thought helplessly—what is it, what's the matter with me, why can't I just walk away and leave him? Now, before it's too late.

He said, smiling, "I haven't told you much about myself, have I?"

"No. But please don't feel obligated—"

"I'm from Hartford," he said. "Or at least I was born there, and my father lives there now. We moved around a lot when I was little, but never very far—just up and down the river towns." He was silent for a moment, staring off into the shadows. "My mother was Polish, but my father is old Yankee farming stock. Some of his cousins still own a little land in the valley, but most of his generation just get along these days doing odd jobs—a little carpentry, a little plumbing, a little tool-repairing. If they're fortunate enough to live near a fancy suburb, they also mow lawns and do a little weeding. Oh, yes, and snowplowing in the winter."

He turned his head to look at her, and went on in a neutral, pleasant voice. "My father was more ambitious, unluckily. He aspired to merchant's status. Small grocery stores, mostly, and once or twice a lunch counter in one of the larger towns. There never was any money, because my father drank. Drinks, I should say. We lived by barter—a pair of shoes in exchange for a sack of flour, more or less. When all the sacks of flour were gone, he would sell the store—custom was always good, people liked him, and I suppose felt sorry for me; I forgot to say that my mother left us when I was four or five. No one ever found out where she went. So we'd move on, usually to a smaller town and a smaller

store. Once," Nick said reflectively, "he was hired to manage a
Rexall drugstore, but of course that didn't last long."

Ann said, "What does he do now—your father?"

"Lives with a more successful nephew, my cousin Harry, who
has a paint store in Hartford. Harry gives him room and board,
partly for waiting on customers in his sober moments but mostly
out of the goodness of his heart. I send him beer money once a
week. As a doctor, I'd give him ten years to live; as his son, I
don't doubt that he'll survive to be a hundred and five and be given
a birthday party by all his relatives and neighbors, with his picture in the Sunday paper over a caption reading, 'Attributes his
longevity to hard work, sobriety and the fear of God.'"

Two girls strolled by, talking dreamily, their soft cotton skirts
floating, sandals slapping delicately against the pavement. Nick
glanced at them and then back at Ann, who said, "It doesn't sound
like a very pleasant childhood. How did you—I mean . . . ?"

"How did I escape to achieve my present eminence?" He gave
a short laugh. "I just quit when I was fourteen. We were living
in one of the Haddams at the time, I forget which one. I wrote a
letter to my cousin—the same good cousin Harry, who's about
ten years older than I am and who had just bought into the paint
store then—telling him I wanted to go to high school in Hartford
and would work for him afternoons and Sundays to earn my keep.
Harry wasn't married then, he was living with cousins of *his*"—he
smiled faintly—"and they had an extra room, a storeroom, that
they said I could have. So I lived in the storeroom for four years
with a lot of old newspapers and broken lamps and bicycle
frames, going to school and selling paint, and in the summers doing highway maintenance work during the day and then cleaning
up for my evening's stint at a diner . . . I was an old hand as a
short-order cook at sixteen."

He leaned back, folding his arms. The light glinted on the fair
hair at his temples and on the long bony line of his brows. "In
my senior year the local Yale club waved its magic wand: full
scholarship to New Haven, which unfortunately didn't include
the price of books or clothes, so I also learned to drive a cab
and to wait on tables at one of the better Italian restaurants. I
even learned a few phrases in Italian; I used to tell the Smith
girls I came from the north of Italy, where blond children are not

uncommon . . ." He paused, his eyes still fixed on Ann's face. "Then, after four more years, presto! Another full scholarship, this time to the medical school. More cabs, more lasagna. Virtue triumphant. Horatio Alger rides again."

"I think it's rather admirable," Ann said.

"Anyway, it's a good story for your liberal friends, who will no doubt consider it deplorably old-fashioned, straight out of the benighted nineteenth century."

"They'll say it shouldn't have been that hard," Ann said slowly. "And they'll be right."

He shook his head, grinning. "You're very sweet. And so wrong. Don't you see the tremendous advantage I have in this fat and happy age—over all the fat boys, over everybody who hasn't done what I've done? I'm tough, I know what I want and how to get it. No sympathy, please." He said this self-mockingly, but Ann caught the sudden sharp light of exultation in his eyes and thought: Ah, he means that, that really is what he thinks, and he will do anything to get where he wants to be.

This thought seemed to her so melodramatic that she said lightly, "And just think of all the other professions you can fall back on if medicine palls."

"Sure. I'm a good Italian waiter. I could even be an Italian waiter in Italy. Venice, say. Or better yet, a gondolier. After all, I was brought up on the river."

"But you can't sing."

"Can't sing! What a thing to say!" Without warning he stood up, threw his arms wide, and bawled out the first two lines of "Drink to Me Only with Thine Eyes" in a harsh clownish baritone. Heads turned all over the park, and the chamber-music audience near them hissed in indignation.

"Nick, stop it!" Ann said, laughing, as he pulled her to her feet and led her off at a half-run along the path toward MacDougal Street, swinging the big straw bag in his free hand.

"Quickly—there are talent scouts all over the place, and I'm not ready to be discovered yet."

"Well, slow down then, it's less conspicuous."

"All right. We'll travel incognito. Pretend we're just out for a picnic." He staggered under the imaginary weight of the bag.

"Oh, look—let me take that, I don't want you to have to lug it

around," Ann said, trying by her tone to break into his clownish-
ness, which now seemed forced.

"Shh! They're after us. Look, they've even called out the dogs."

They had come to the corner; in spite of herself Ann glanced
over her shoulder. A woman was emerging from the park behind
them with a Weimeraner at the end of a short leash. The dog's
coat gleamed silver in the light of the street lamp; as his mistress
pulled him to a halt, he gazed up at Ann with strange pale eyes.

"It was only a matter of minutes," Nick said, rushing her across
the street as the light changed. "Of course, they're really not
talent scouts at all; that's just an ingenious disguise. On the other
hand"—he lowered his voice, breaking into a run—"they have no
idea what's really in the picnic basket."

"You mean all those ham sandwiches?" Ann said, laughing, as
they raced past the Christian Science Reading Room and a store
selling expensive sandals.

"Ah, it only *looks* like ham; nothing, my dear, is what it seems."
He dodged into a shadowy doorway so quickly that Ann had to
retrace her steps to find him. "Just testing your reflexes," he said,
and kissed her. They were both breathing hard with laughter
and exertion; when Ann drew back in sudden agitation, staring
up at his face, Nick said, "That was just for camouflage, of course."

"Of course."

"I mean, it would never have occurred to me otherwise."

"Naturally not."

"And anyway—there's something you should know about me."
His arms were still around her. "What?" she whispered against
his chest.

"I'm a counterspy," he whispered back. Ann laughed, pushing
him away, and they walked on. "Actually, I'm a quadruple spy.
That's a double counterspy. I used to be a triple spy, but it got
too confusing, so I sold out again."

"I'm a homicidal nurse," Ann said as they turned the corner
into the hot glare of Eighth Street. "I work the old people's
homes. Forged wills and overdoses."

"So!" Nick stared down at her, his eyes gleaming as if with
some private amusement. "It occurs to me you know too much."

"So do you," Ann retorted.

"Then we are bound together," he said. He took her hand and

gripped it hard. "Repeat after me: we are bound together until death us do part."

"Ouch! Take it easy!" Ann pulled her hand away.

But he stood waiting, looking down at her with a fixed smile, his body suddenly held in a high tension and poise against the relaxed shuffle of the crowd around him, the tinny throb of the traffic at his back.

"No oaths without a Bible," she said, forcing her gaze away from his.

"Quick, then—to the bookstore."

"No, no!" she protested, laughing. "Really, I ought to get home. Tomorrow's a working day, and all that."

"Then we'll get the Bible at your place. All nurses own Bibles, don't they? Part of their professional equipment, I imagine, especially for the homicidal ones."

But the hilarity had gone, and on the way back to Christopher Street they said little, walking along steadily without touching. At the door Ann said, "Heavens—I haven't been that silly since I was in school."

"Years and years ago," Nick said, nodding, and handing her the straw bag. "Take good care of the sandwiches. Well, I've enjoyed the evening, Ann. I hope we can have another one soon."

"Do you want to come in for a drink? I'm not sure if I've got a Bible, but—"

"No, thanks," he said quickly, as though he had decided this earlier. "I've got to get back."

They looked at each other. Ann tried to keep her face friendly and noncommittal, but his eyes were so somber that suddenly she smiled in spite of herself, and his arms went around her, his mouth came down on hers swiftly, firm and hard like the rest of his body against her. When he let her go and turned away—too soon, why so soon?—she felt a moment's piercing sensation of physical loss, so intense that she almost cried out like a child to bring him back. But he was already striding away from her toward Sheridan Square, his light coat a blur in the darkness. He did not look back.

TWO

Careless and violent,

the city shimmered in the heat of midsummer. There were gang fights in Harlem, bombs exploded in public lavatories, several drownings in the East River. (Ann remembered a Circle Line trip taken with her father years ago—her childish shock at the naked swimmers, some of them boys her own age; how their bodies gleamed out sallow and startling from the dark shapes of piers and bridges, how one perfect dive had left a ring of scum upon the thick green surface of the water.) On the tropical subways girls carried sweaters over their arms against the chill of office air conditioning, and the ink of newspapers came off on their fingers like volcanic ash. At five o'clock the buildings seemed to rock against the sky with the impact of the day's accumulated glare. People coming out of darkened lobbies complained of dizziness and wondered if they were coming down with something. Voices at night sounded low-pitched and hesitant, and sometimes whole neighborhoods seemed muffled by the heat, as though snow had fallen, deadening sound.

On Christopher Street, dropping his daughter off after dinner at a nearby restaurant, Guy Claremont said uneasily, "You're okay these days, aren't you, kiddo? No nightmares, no nerves?"

"No."

"Good. It was one hell of an experience, I know. But the police

did all they could, you believe that, don't you? The best thing
for you to do is just try and forget the whole thing. Unless—" He
shrugged, looking up at the windows of Ann's apartment. "Marge
and I were wondering if you might like to get out of this place,
find another apartment."

"Oh, no. I don't think so. It's all right, Dad, really."

His heavy face with its square-cut mustache, unnaturally
pale because of his city summer, wore an unfamiliar and ponder-
ous look of concern. "You sure? You'd have to break the lease, I
know, but we'd be glad to stake you to whatever you'd forfeit,
and also to a month's rent on a new place."

"Thanks, Dad, but I'd really just as soon stay here. And the
money's no problem—I've got plenty."

"Well," Guy said reluctantly, "suit yourself. But remember,
you've got a standing invitation to come cook for me any time
you feel like it. With Marge up in the country I'm getting tired of
cornflakes and TV dinners. Or you might just drop in sometimes
and say hello. My own daughter living in the same city, and I
never see her."

"But you're never home," Ann objected, smiling. "You're such
a man about town no one can keep track of you. If I were Marge,
I wouldn't stand for it."

"Oh, friends—" Guy gestured vaguely. "I don't know, people
keep blowing into this town from the four corners of the earth,
and who is the one guy they insist on looking up? The other day
I had a call from a guy I had a drink with once in Bombay in
1936—1936, I'm not kidding—wanting me to show him the town
and incidentally straighten out some hassle he was having about
his hotel accommodations. I didn't even recognize him when I
saw him."

Ann laughed. "Well, you were always telling people to look
you up if they ever got to New York," she said, hearing again in
memory all the café conversations of her childhood, the hotel-
lobby farewells, the voluble partings in airports and railroad
terminals.

Guy said, "Well, what the hell, when somebody says, 'Let's get
together sometime,' you don't think they *mean* it as a definite
date. It's a gesture, that's all. You certainly don't fly halfway
around the world to take them up on it." He sighed. "Anyway,"

he added with his broad wry smile, "I do sleep at home, kiddo."

"I know you do."

"Well, I just didn't want you to get any funny ideas about my summer bachelor kick. If I could work in the country, I would. Christ, it's late," he said, looking at his watch. "I better go grab a cab. Take it easy, sweetie, and give me a call sometime, won't you?"

Ann kissed him on the cheek. "Thanks for dinner, Dad."

She watched him plunge off toward Sixth Avenue, the wide skirts of his unnecessary raincoat flapping about his knees. Dad and his props, she thought, letting herself into the dim hallway: the poor man's Hemingway, only without the guns and the women, which leaves the fishing and the wine, and even there he's never gone exactly overboard. Underneath the phony glamour—and he knows it's phony, that must be what's so endearing about him —he's really a very moderate man. With only a moderate capacity for love. No, I don't know that, she told herself, thinking of her dead mother. But I always enjoy him more than he does me. I'm not casual enough, not restless enough; I make him nervous just by sitting still. Whereas someone like Marge, or Bobbie—

At the door of her apartment she paused, her key in the lock, fighting off the nightmare illusion that still assailed her whenever she came home too casually, absorbed in her own thoughts, unprepared—for surely she smelled the light fragrance of Bobbie's perfume, heard a soft drift of dance music from the phonograph, and in a moment would find Bobbie herself curled in the chair by the window with her shoes off, waiting to talk in her sweet breathy voice about the latest date, the latest man, the new romance . . .

Ann shut the door firmly behind her and went through the dark kitchen into the little living room, which held only shadows, only the last street noises and the fitful drip of the bathtub faucet which she kept forgetting to have fixed, since she herself took showers and no one used the tub any more.

Forgetting? But I don't forget things like that, Ann told herself, turning on a light and pulling down the shades. I just haven't wanted to do anything about it. It's part of the same obsession— wouldn't most people call it that?—which has also kept me from getting rid of her things, as I told her parents I would. Her poor, dazed parents ("grief-stricken," as the papers had said): if they knew, they would think me ghoulish beyond belief . . . She slid her dress onto a hanger and took her nightgown and robe from the closet, where Bobbie's clothes still hung voluminously, filling what was supposed to have been half but was more like two thirds of the cramped space, next to Ann's own neat summer wardrobe from which no button or snap was ever missing, no hem or seam left unrepaired.

And in the bathroom—Bobbie's jars and bottles and eyebrow tweezers, even her box of talcum powder, half full, on a corner ledge of the tub. Her flowered silk robe still hung on the hook behind the door. I ought to put that away, at least, Ann thought, brushing her teeth vigorously: I don't want to advertise my obsession, after all, and it really doesn't look like something I'd wear. Turning out lights, she went into the bedroom and stood at the mirror to smooth her hair back into a loose ponytail for the night. The high spike heels of Bobbie's shoes protruded from the shoebag they had nailed to the strip of wall beside the bed; two of the four splintery drawers of the bureau still held her handkerchiefs and slips and sweaters.

Ann got into the bottom bunk of the double-decker and lay staring up through the semi-darkness at the patterned whorls of rusty springs, thinking of the evening she and Bobbie had spent with her father and stepmother last winter. "That's a very pretty and accommodating little roommate of yours," Guy had said afterward; and although Ann had known he meant too accommodating—were there men in the apartment at all hours of the day and night?—she had also seen how effortlessly Bobbie had charmed him with her amusing chatter, her artless curiosity about Guy's own cosmopolitan (she'd actually used the word) career. Guy had been laying it on thick that evening for her benefit—at Charles, wasn't it, where they'd all gone for dinner? Yes, and Marge had even been a little jealous, her expression tolerant and amused but her eyes sharp on Guy's face as he leaned to light Bobbie's cigarettes.

But it was only one evening. Why should she have expected him to turn detective for Bobbie's sake, a girl he hardly knew— and after the police had, as he said, done everything they could? It was his daughter, the living girl, who concerned him now.

Marge might understand, but Marge was in Connecticut and would be most of the summer. You could hardly discuss something like murder through the mail, on monogrammed stationery, Ann thought, with a bleak smile in the darkness. And in any case, the chances were that Marge, understanding, would nonetheless tell Ann to stop beating her head against a wall and get on with her own life. Marge was nothing if not practical.

Nick—but she had not heard from Nick. Nothing at all in two weeks. Of course he was busy, and perhaps there had been a lot of night duty; if residents had night duty, she didn't know . . . Or working late at the lab. Oh, come on, she told herself angrily, stirring beneath the clammy sheet, you might as well face it: he isn't going to call. He got his facts and made his diagnosis and found you didn't interest him after all. His privilege. Healthy, he had said; meaning too healthy? For a despairing moment Ann saw the image she must present to the world: robust and self-sufficient, her surface as whole and taut as the skin of an apple, with a predictable core—yes, and virginal, not yet cloven by the blow of love, indeed hardly bruised so far. I suppose he saw that too, she thought.

And yet—the sense of fatefulness, almost of complicity? "We are bound together," he had said with that brilliant, arresting gaze. Maybe nothing more than a habitual intensity of manner; or maybe even a deliberate technique—how many girls at how many other parties might he have approached with that same effect of urgency and command? How many were fools enough to fall for it? But no, Ann thought stubbornly, my instinct can't have been that wrong, at least not about the physical attraction. An electric charge that you feel to your fingertips, the roots of your hair, can't be all self-generated, it has to be something that runs back and forth between two poles. I couldn't have felt it so strongly if he hadn't felt it too.

If I had told him about Bobbie, she thought . . . Oh, God, surely I wouldn't use her in that way, would I? After all the running I've had to do from people who only wanted to know, to hear all about it—and now to use it as some kind of grisly bait, how can I even think of it? And for someone so difficult and arrogant and probably impenetrable, a man most people must dislike, who practically invited me to dislike him, and then just walked away. Yes, but next time—if he should come again, if I should let him come—he will recognize the photograph he has already half recognized, and ask me why she looks so familiar, and I will have to tell him.

I would put the picture away, she thought, if I had any sense; except that it is the only thing—it and the leaky faucet, perhaps, and the Dufy poster, Bobbie's one contribution to the décor— that I have kept out of sentiment, no matter what anyone might think about the clothes, the face creams, the shoes and handbags. Because as long as there is the slightest chance that they can tell me something, something I have missed—if only by releasing some trivial memory in which there might be a key at last, a clue—

A late bus wheezed in the street outside. Ann turned over and shut her eyes tightly; at once, like one of those black balls given to children whose rotation brings a tiny message floating to the surface, her mind tipped over and released the words of the vow she had made to herself on that first terrible evening. Immaculately the letters spelled themselves out against the darkness of sleep, white on black:

Someone murdered Bobbie. There was a reason. I will find it.

She worked long hours at the museum, accepting stray invitations to lunch but giving none herself, content to spend her free time on a bench in the museum's famous courtyard among the sun-struck gesturing sculptures, or on the terrace of the roof-top cafeteria, where a sooty breeze dulled the hot incessant rumble of the traffic below. She had used up her vacation time in March on a ski trip to the Laurentians, and now could not summon up the energy for the bus or train ride which separated her from a country weekend with Marge or with married friends in the suburbs. In the evenings she often walked alone through the convivial streets of the Village, lingering on Bleecker Street to watch the hectic games of Italian children at play and to listen, translating earnestly, to the shrill bursts of domestic conversation that rattled like gunfire between the stoops. She wore sleeveless blouses and khaki shorts and a battered pair of loafers, and easily turned aside the speculative glances of strolling men by her air of purpose, her firm athletic stride.

Her old friend Carlo took her to a play, and said during the intermission, as they stood outside the theater in the warm dazzle of the night, "Who is he, anyway, the guy you keep looking for every place? Anyone I know?"

Ann looked at Carlo, whose dark eyes had ceased their habitual darting scrutiny and were regarding her intently.

He said, "Am I psychic, or am I not?"

"You are, I guess. No, it's no one you know. A doctor."

"Well, I know *some* doctors. We professional men sometimes meet in passing," said Carlo, who was a lawyer. "What's his name?"

"I said you wouldn't know him." Ann looked down, smoothing a glove.

"Now come on, Annie—what's the big mystery?" Carlo sounded amused and brotherly.

"No mystery."

"Sounds serious," Carlo said, puffing on his cigarette.

"Oh, Carlo, for heaven's sake! I've only gone out with him once, and I may never see him again."

"Aha—that's the trouble, is it?" People were starting to move back into the theater. Carlo took her arm, grinding out the half-smoked stub of his cigarette with a polished shoe tip. "How long since you saw him?"

"About two and a half weeks, I guess."

"You guess. Ha!" They made their way through the lobby and began the smoky, perfumed climb to the balcony. "If he's a doctor he probably doesn't have too much time. Is he interning, or what?"

"He's a resident—or he has a fellowship or something." She added defensively, "I'm not so sure I want to see him again, anyway."

"No? You've got it bad, kid." Carlo examined his program as they sat down. "Not even a lousy change of scene. If you're going to write a dull play, the least you can do is change the sets once in a while. Especially a dull play at Broadway prices."

Ann said, "I don't think you'd like him."

"Probably not."

"I mean—I'm not even sure *I* do."

"Worse and worse."

"Oh, Carlo—" She glanced at him. He was slumped in his seat, gnawing on his thumb with an air of gloomy irritability. The lights were going down. "Do you want to leave? I don't think the play's all that bad, but I wouldn't mind skipping the rest of it if you want to go."

"Go? Me? I never walked out on a play in my life. Or a movie. You never know what might happen. An actor might knock over a vase or go through the springs of the couch or have an epileptic fit or something—"

"That's not funny, Carlo," Ann whispered. "Anyway, you have so walked out on a movie. Remember *Rashomon?*"

Carlo groaned. "It was the second time I'd seen it, thanks to you. Just seeing it once, you get the story told four times, for Christ's sake. I couldn't take it *eight* times. If I'd had to sit and watch those guys with the swords trip over their own feet once more—"

Ann swallowed a laugh as the people around them glared for silence. "It has something to do with Japanese etiquette. They were being polite, or something."

"The inscrutable East," Carlo agreed, and they subsided to watch the third act.

Later, taxiing back down to the Village with the windows open to the neon-streaked darkness, Carlo said, "Tell me more about this guy, Ann. The doctor. I might as well know what he's got that I haven't."

"There isn't anything to tell. I told you, I've only been out with him once."

Carlo said thoughtfully, "Well, I'll tell *you*, then. He's good-looking, of course, in an ascetic sort of way. Intelligent. Serious about his work. Plenty of charm when he feels like using it. And —let's see, probably not to the manner born." When Ann was silent, Carlo sighed and took her hand. "The fascinating thing about you is that you're so damned predictable."

"Thanks."

"Oh, Annie . . ." Carlo kissed her lightly with his mouth, which she always felt guiltily—but why guiltily, she couldn't help it?— was too fleshy and warm, and a little damp. He drew his head away and looked at her with a wry smile. "You know why you're scared of this guy, or uneasy, or whatever you want to call it? Because you're still a virgin, damn it."

"Carlo!" Ann said, mortified, looking at the back of the cab-driver's stolid neck; but Carlo ignored her.

"It's certainly no thanks to me," he said, sitting back and light-ing a cigarette. "Here I've even offered you marriage, and you still won't let me make love to you. It seems to me that's the least a girl can do in exchange for a proposal. Especially if she doesn't intend to accept it."

Carlo had been proposing to her ever since she was thirteen, never seriously.

"I've had a strict upbringing," Ann said lightly.

"The hell you have. It's just you."

The cab was nosing its way down Christopher Street. Carlo fished in his pockets for change. "Am I invited in?" he said. "Not to try and seduce you—I'm too tired tonight. Let's just put on one of your MJQ records and drink ice water and let the crystal sounds wash over our sooty little souls."

The cabdriver grunted, accepting his tip, and gave Carlo a suspicious look before he drove away. "He was about to get fa-therly, I think," Carlo said, gazing after the cab. "Did you know you can get drunk on water—just plain H_2O? They've been hav-ing regular orgies in London; I read all about them in my evening *Post*. The cabdriver must read the *Post* too."

Ann said, "Some other time, Carlo, okay? I'm dead, and I have to be at the museum at the crack of dawn tomorrow while they photograph the new exhibit."

Carlo looked at her. "I don't even make it up the stairs any more, do I? Is it just me, or have you got a dead body stashed away in the closet or something?" At the sight of her face he said quickly, "Sorry, Ann, that was a hell of a dumb thing to say." He tossed away his cigarette and did a soft-shoe dance into the dim hallway, bowing with a flourish at the foot of the stairs. "Sweet dreams."

Ann smiled and kissed him on the cheek.

"I wish—" Carlo hesitated, and went on matter-of-factly, "I wish you'd let me make love to you."

"I know," Ann said, starting upstairs. "You've mentioned it before."

"No, listen." Carlo's upturned ugly face was suddenly serious. "I mean because of this guy. I know, I know, you may never see him again—only you will, sure as God made little green apples. And I have a feeling that it's just going to be too much, your being a virgin—that it's going to be such a big deal with you, and if it should be wrong, if he should be wrong . . . Ann, why are you living this way?"

"What way? What do you mean?"

"I mean staying on in this place, for one thing. I don't care how sensible and level-headed you are, how much you like the apartment itself, you can't just turn off what happened, nobody could; and it's bound to give you the creeps at times, living here."

"It didn't happen here."

"You know what I mean. But all right, forget that. It's also your being alone so much, not seeing your old friends, not bothering to make new ones—"

"Just because I got tired of Village parties—"

"I know, you don't like beer, you don't like being mauled, the intellectuals are pretentious, the artists are bores. Well, okay, so you're a snob—nothing wrong with that, your standards are good ones, and anyway you can't help it. But then, what are you doing here? What do you expect to find?"

"All right," Ann said angrily, coming down a step. "You tell me how I should live, please. Back in Gramercy Park, addressing envelopes for benefits and going to fashion shows? On Seventy-third Street with Sue Potter and Marcia Haig, getting all dressed up for Wellesley Club cocktail parties, or joining the Young Republicans to find a husband?"

"I said you were a snob."

"Carlo, please! I'm just trying to get along, like everybody else. Believe me, I'm not trying to prove anything, I only want to live my own life in my own way. Right now that means being alone, among other things."

"Sure." He shrugged, shoving his hands in his pockets. "Hell, I guess it's just that I've always thought of you as being—I don't know, full steam ahead about life. Not gung-ho, exactly, but . . . well, always ready to manage and organize things, always knowing just where you wanted to go. And caring about things more than other people. Like the time at Putney you made us turn ourselves in for drinking that bottle of Chianti or whatever it was that Mike Barrett smuggled in, and we didn't get to go on the Mt.

Washington trip. I was sore as hell at you for that, as a matter of fact I still am, but I admired you—no, it was sharper than that, I envied you—for feeling so strongly about it that you were willing to risk your own standing, your friendships, for a principle." He scuffed at a worn seam in the brown carpet and smiled to himself. "It wasn't even a rule you believed in. Remember the Senior Beer and Wine Association, and that incredibly pompous petition we drew up? I still have a copy of it somewhere."

"Yes," Ann said. "And now there aren't any rules, are there? No more cozy little world of schools and vacations and parties and tennis tournaments to organize and manage. Just a job and an apartment—no fancy scaffolding. Poor little me. Honestly, Carlo, wasn't it high time I grew up?"

"Okay. Speech about grim reality, modern life, city lights. Consider it duly heard and attended to." Carlo grinned, but added, "The trouble is, Ann, you haven't changed, and I don't think you ever will. It's the thought of all that pent-up energy and moral fervor that really bothers me—it has to go some place, or you're bound to run amok one of these days . . . Hey, listen—speaking of running amok reminds me of elephants, and elephants remind me of the zoo. Would you care to do anything so juvenile and fraught with past associations as going up to the Bronx this weekend, see how the platypuses are making out? Or do I mean platypi."

"I'd love to," Ann said, smiling. "Goodnight, Carlo, and thanks."

"Thanks but no thanks, you mean. 'Night, Annie. Take care."

Ann lingered on the landing, listening to Carlo's retreating whistle and looking down into the building's small courtyard, a triangle of sparse grass streakily lighted by the windows around it. She thought: I wonder what Carlo would say if I told him that I was once in love with him, Carlo, for the whole of one blissful, hallucinatory week—five, no, six years ago, my sophomore year in college, his senior year. Exactly a week, from the Sunday night of the Hoffmans' Christmas party to the Monday morning I woke up to find it all gone: an ordinary Monday morning, grimy around the edges, and I had presents to exchange at Saks and Altman's, and a dentist's appointment in the afternoon; and when Carlo came to pick me up that evening for a concert, I looked incredulously into his familiar narrow clever face and thought: Why, it was only Carlo all along! Dear Carlo, who isn't tall enough for me, and whose mouth will never kiss me the way I want to be kissed—

In a tall window across the courtyard a man was standing with his back to her beneath a tasseled Victorian chandelier; his shoulders were jerking oddly, convulsively. He was throwing something, Ann realized—they must be darts—at a target on the wall. An older man sat at a table nearby, turning over the pages of a huge volume that looked like an Oxford dictionary. Suddenly the younger man turned from his game and addressed the other in apparent fury, planting his fists on his hips and thrusting his head forward. The older man held up a hand for silence, and without altering his pose of concentration, drew a handkerchief from the pocket of his dressing gown and blew his nose with such violence that Ann jumped, and was surprised not to hear the sound of it come snorting across the intervening space.

So much for high drama, she thought, smiling; but as she turned away she was remembering how once she had lived in a world containing few ambiguous gestures, few impinging fragments of the miscellaneous lives of strangers—a whole city of known addresses and familiar rooms, in which every object implied a complex but orderly system of reference and association. Yet she had chosen to live outside its walls, seeing it as hardly more than a village within a greater city that was at once truer, more terrible and more beautiful. A vast hunting ground of the spirit, over which she at least would venture, strong and unafraid—was that how she had seen herself? A Diana, heroic and pure, striding forth not to do battle but to search: for the enchanted clearing, the silver tree, a glimpse of the glittering bird upon its bough. "Miracle, bird or golden handiwork,/ More miracle than bird or handiwork . . ." Well, we've all read too much Yeats, that's for sure, she thought; floundering around in our dolphin-torn and—what is it?—gong-tormented sea.

Oh, but whatever I'm looking for, whatever I hope to find—besides a murderer, small practical item; or is that part of it, the brute that lurks among the shadows?—surely it is a true journey, more than the dead-end sum of rejected alternatives: the boys I might have married (but instead stood dry-eyed under the

June elms, attending the others at their sentimental rites among the rich Episcopal voices, the consecrated lilies); the classmates with whom I might have shared a Bing & Bing apartment with a view, during these negligible but rather nerve-racking few years between the campus and the suburbs; my dotted-swiss room in Gramercy Park, strawberries and cream for breakfast—

The little apartment was hot and still in the faint illumination from the street. Ann stood with her fingertip upon the light switch, nerving herself to exert the tiny pressure that would reaffirm her tenancy, flinging forth her solitary shadow upon the wall.

THREE

Nick was waiting
for her outside the museum on Friday afternoon. At least Ann
assumed that he had been waiting for her; certainly when she
caught his eye he straightened at once and came toward her with
a quick smile of greeting. Then why should she have had the
feeling that he had already seen her—leaning there so motionless
against the pale smooth stone of the building, locked in some
private conflict of indecision or calculation—and that if she had
come out a few minutes later he would not have been there at
all?

He said, "I was afraid you might be working late."

"No. Just cleaning up for the weekend."

They walked toward Fifth Avenue. The day had been overcast
and humid, and now a hot wind thrummed against the flanks of
the buildings, raising small eddies of grit around their ankles.

Nick said, "How have you been?"

"Oh, fine. A little limp, like everyone else in this heat."

"You don't look limp. I don't think you could if you tried." But
he barely glanced at her. "I've wanted to call you, but I've been
pretty busy at the hospital, and—oh, I don't know, I just didn't.
More fool I. I see you've put the new suitcase to work."

Ann looked down at her straw handbag, and stopped short.
"Oh, heavens!" she exclaimed. "I never paid you for it, did I?"

"No, you didn't." He smiled briefly, formally.

"But—oh, Lord, why didn't you call me or something? I'm so sorry! Really, I don't know what's wrong with me. I never once thought of it, and here I've been carrying the thing all over town for weeks!" He wouldn't look at her; impossible to tell whether he was really angry or just waiting for her own embarrassment to pass. She fumbled in the bag for her checkbook. "I'll write you a check for it right now. Do you remember what the tax was?"

"No hurry," he said, taking her arm. "And I'll treat you to the tax."

"I just can't understand it—I never forget things like that. Really, Nick, I'm so sorry!" she repeated.

They turned the corner onto Fifth Avenue, where people stood waiting for buses and looking up at the sky to see how soon it was going to rain.

"It's the heat," Nick said. "Also, I don't imagine you're used to owing people things."

"No," she agreed, and looked at him. "I've never been much of a borrower."

"Anyway, I was the one who insisted on paying for it then and there. I understand how it could easily have slipped your mind."

But he spoke a little stiffly. The poor boy and the rich girl, Ann thought. Oh, if it only weren't so hot! The collar of her blue shirtdress was already damp with sweat; her slip stuck to her. How ludicrous to have spent so much time thinking about him these last three weeks—yes, all right, you might as well admit it—and not to have remembered I owed him thirty dollars! Maybe he even thinks I forgot to pay him on purpose that evening, so that he would have to come back again . . . except that it was he who refused to come up to the apartment when I asked him. Was he forgetting about the money then, too, or was he being delicate—or did he just want an excuse to see me again? But why should he have needed an excuse? He's certainly taken his time about using it.

They came to Rockefeller Plaza. Above the gross golden image of Prometheus the flags were flapping wildly in the gusty wind, and the spires of blue salvia planted between the benches glowed purple in the stormy light. Ann slipped quickly onto a vacant bench and drew out her pen and checkbook. Nick sat down beside her, looking up at the livid sky. "It's going to rain like hell any minute," he observed.

"Here," Ann said, handing him the check. "And please accept my apologies, Nick."

He slid it carefully into his wallet. "No hard feelings," he said.

Well, Ann thought. Not "That's all right" or "Don't worry about it" or any of the things people said, however insincerely, to ease an awkward moment. That's something you'll have to learn, Dr. Sheldon; all the tennis and squash and the good restaurants and foreign films and vacations in the right places, all the hours of concealed irritation spent at Dr. What's-his-name's elbow, even all your natural casual grace won't be worth much to you with the people who count if you don't learn how to talk about money—

"Now I can take you out to dinner, if you're not busy this evening," Nick said.

"Oh! Well, if you're sure—I mean—"

"I didn't look you up just to collect, if that's what you're thinking."

She looked away from his smile as a gust of wind flattened the light skirt of her dress against her knees. A man standing by one of the travel-agency windows lost half his newspaper without turning to glance after it, so that the two little girls in smocked dresses and white gloves who scrambled to retrieve it had to tug at his arm twice before he would take the soiled, crumpled pages and give them a stiff self-conscious nod of thanks.

Ann said, "Dinner sounds fine, only I probably ought to go home and change, and do something about my hair. This wind—"

He touched the smooth coil at the back of her neck, tucking in a loose strand with light fingers. "You look fine. The only thing we may need is an umbrella."

Ann produced one from her bag. "It has a retractable handle, or whatever you call them."

"So I see. What else have you got in that thing? A grand piano?" He peered into the bag and took out a small vanity case and a bottle of mouthwash.

"Now wait a minute—" Ann snatched the things from him and dropped them back into the bag. "That's private property."

"It's just my damnable curiosity again," Nick said, grinning. "And after all, I can't help feeling I have certain rights where that bag is concerned."

"All right!" Ann said, letting herself sound as irritated as she felt. "I'll give you an inventory. One wallet, one comb, lipstick, et cetera; a library book, a package of Kleenex; a plastic raincoat, the kind that folds into a little case," she said, glaring at him, "and a pair of shoes—"

"Shoes!"

"Well, slippers, the kind that—"

"The kind that fold into a little case. I know. What else?"

"A toothbrush. And—and one of those little net hats in case I ever want to go to church . . . Oh, dear!" she said, beginning to shake with laughter at the expression on his face. "It does sound absolutely bats, I know. I guess it comes from traveling around so much with my father and always having to be prepared for anything he might take it into his head to do."

Nick said, "I bet you even have one of those collapsible drinking cups—"

"I used to—"

"And those things you hang stockings on to dry—"

"Oh, dear!"

People stared at them, the good-looking blond couple doubled over in a fit of adolescent laughter against the salvia as the first big drops of rain fell. The two little girls were dragged off toward Fifth Avenue by their mother, looking back over their shoulders at Nick and Ann.

"Are you sure you're not a lady correspondent or something?" Nick said at last. "You're certainly all set for a fast getaway."

"I'm a homicidal nurse, remember?"

"Yes," Nick said thoughtfully, "I'd forgotten." He rose, examining the umbrella. "You'd better open this thing for me—it's going to pour any minute."

They fled into a doorway as the rain sluiced down. Three fat women in black dresses and flowered hats teetered wildly on their spike heels in the middle of the promenade, gesturing in opposite directions like characters in a slapstick movie, a burlesque of indecision. Finally they staggered off against the wind toward Fifth Avenue, clutching their hats and shopping bags and shrieking for a taxi.

Nick looked at his watch. "It's early yet. What do you say we have a drink somewhere around here, and then go down to the Village for dinner when the rain lets up? Unless you'd rather eat uptown."

"No, that's fine with me."

They stood looking out at the deserted promenade, breathing in the acid odor of drenched earth and flowers. A pale spasm of lightning flared through the rain, which was thinner now and blowing in the wind. Ann listened for thunder but could not hear it above the steady mechanical rumble of the city, impervious as always to minor cataclysms of the sky. Nick pressed her arm tightly against his side; they smiled at each other without speaking.

They walked a few blocks east in the rain and had a drink, two drinks, in a dark cocktail lounge without geography or weather, a sealed playroom gleaming fashionably with leather and tinted glass. Nick talked about the museum; he had spent an hour or so looking at the exhibits. He was interested in the sculptures and the mobiles and the surrealist paintings—par for the course, Ann thought, half listening, studying his face, so expressive, yet so controlled; a classic American face in its mingling of strains, Slavic bone structure sharpened and elongated to a Celtic clarity, firm-textured northern skin, eyes like a winter sea, or like the blue of deep snow-shadows . . . a severe masculine beauty, made arresting by its look of tension and intelligence, but in essence (she told herself) nothing more than a fortuitous relationship of skin and bone and pigmentation—

"What are things like at the hospital these days?" she asked. "With all your fellow interns scattered across the country it must be a bit lonely. I mean, of course it's a big hospital—"

"It is a big hospital," Nick said in a flat voice. "What's that got to do with Chagall?"

"Chagall?"

"Sorry. It must be boring to have to listen to a lot of uninformed remarks on a subject you know something about." He signaled to the waiter for the check. "I suppose I'd feel the same way if

you started talking about all the people you've heard of who
have multiple sclerosis or cerebral palsy."

"Please, Nick. I didn't mean to interrupt." She added in spite
of herself, "Is that the kind of thing you're working on—multiple
sclerosis?"

"That and other diseases of demyelination, etiology unknown.
It's not a very cheerful list." She saw that he was angry. He got
to his feet. "Shall we go?"

Outside she waited under the dripping canopy while Nick
went off to find a cab, ignoring her offer of the umbrella. The
storm had blown on over the city into the suburbs, but the rain
still fell, glittering through the headlights of passing cars, explod-
ing sharply in pools of reflected color upon the pavements. Nick's
tall hatless figure sprang like a dancer's from one corner of the
intersection to another; when he came back to her, running along
beside the captured cab, she saw that his manner had lightened,
was even gay, as though the brief physical exertion had released
some pressure within him.

In the cab he said, "I'd like to put my arm around you, but I'd
just get you wet."

"Well, you wouldn't take the umbrella."

"Too undignified—a lady's umbrella. We uncultured physicians
are sensitive about our dignity."

"Oh, please, Nick. I *was* interested in what you were saying
about the paintings, but I guess at the moment I was more interested in you—I mean, in looking at you and thinking, wondering—" She stopped, overcome by her own admission, feeling that
she was on the verge of saying something enormous and irrevo-
cable; but Nick said nothing. His face had become thoughtful,
almost somber. They leaned back against the damp leather seat,
looking out their separate windows at the great city gleaming
darkly in the summer rain. After a moment he took her hand and
held it.

When Ann came out of the bathroom, Nick was sitting in the
chair by the window, holding a small snifter of the brandy he had
bought on their way from the restaurant to the apartment. He
had taken off his jacket, and his white shirt revealed the long

powerful curve of his back as he leaned forward, studying something. Ann saw that he was looking at Bobbie's picture.

She went over to the phonograph and took a record from the small rack beneath it. The Gershwin piano concerto: surely he won't object to Gershwin, she thought—if he even hears it.

He said, "You know, your ex-roommate looks so familiar. I have a feeling I've seen her somewhere. Maybe even met her."

"You might have. She used to date some of your fellow interns, among others." The record flapped down onto the turntable. Ann waited until the slim arm had swung over and down to meet it, and carefully closed the lid of the phonograph.

Nick said, "No, it's more than that. Or maybe it's just the photograph itself. Did she . . . ?"

"You probably remember it from the newspapers," she said. All right, she thought wearily; here it is, here we go. "The girl in the subway station." She sat down on the couch and reached for her glass.

"In the subway station? You don't mean . . . ? Oh, Christ, yes; of course. She lived in the Village, I remember now. And she was your roommate?"

Ann nodded.

"My God, Ann! Why didn't you tell me?"

"It isn't something I like to talk about very much, I'm afraid."

"Then we won't," Nick said slowly, his eyes on her face. "We don't have to."

Ann leaned to set her glass back on the table. "I'm sorry," she said. "I just—it still—"

The springs of the couch creaked as he sat beside her and put an arm around her shoulders. "Okay, okay. Don't say anything. We won't talk about it."

Ann listened to the music, a sweet mournful swirl of piano and horns, as palpable in the small room as the wet breeze blowing in through the open windows. At last she said, "Paul Griffith. That was the intern she had a date with, the night before it happened. Do you know him?"

"Yes."

"She was at the hospital—in the cafeteria—that night."

"Yes."

She felt the hard throbbing of his heart and the tension of his arm around her. She thought: He can't help it, no one can; they don't feel grief or even horror so much as curiosity. Here it is, the inside dope, what the newspapers didn't say . . . Oh, why didn't I put the damned picture away? She said, "Did you ever meet her?"

"No." After a pause he added, "I remember seeing her that night, of course."

"Why 'of course'?" she said, moving a little away from him so that she could see his face.

He shrugged, letting his arm fall from her shoulders. "I just meant that we all remembered seeing her the night before with Paul, when we heard what had happened."

"Oh. Yes," Ann said, looking away. "A lot of people remember seeing her. Everything was so completely normal and ordinary right up to the end. That's what I can't—what I find so hard to understand." She thought: After all, he is a doctor, with an experience of death. If I could talk to him without its being anything—personal . . . "The police said homicidal mania," she said. "Maybe they'll even get a confession some day from some poor idiot who doesn't know what he's saying, or care." She took a sip of her brandy; it was harsh and thin. Nick had paid a good price for it—something else he would have to learn.

"I take it you don't agree with the police."

"No. I don't. I can't."

"That seems odd to me. Unless you have a definite reason, I mean. I should think you'd rather believe the whole thing was—well, blind and sick and crazy." When Ann was silent, he said carefully, "Ann—I'm not sure I understand. Are you saying you think someone actually planned to kill your roommate?"

Ann said flatly, "It does sound melodramatic, doesn't it?"

"Frankly, it sounds a little hysterical to me."

"That seems to be the general verdict—hysterical female." She stared across the room at the shimmering polished shapes of the phonograph and the desk in its white alcove. "Look, let's just forget it, shall we?" she said quietly. "I'm sorry the subject had to come up at all."

She felt his eyes on her face. After a moment he said, "You're not going to forget it, though, are you, Ann?" His voice was curiously tight and regretful. He put a hand under her chin and turned her face toward him. She said nothing, avoiding his eyes. "Then I can't, either. Do you understand that? Not tonight or any other night." Holding her with his hand and his gaze, he went on softly, "I want to hear about it. I want you to talk about it. Tell me what happened—what you think happened, and why."

"No," Ann said. "I don't want to." She drew in her breath sharply as his hands moved to her shoulders, gripping them hard.

"You said something about a general verdict. Does that mean you *have* talked about it, about what you think, to other people?"

"Well, not other people at random. It's hardly something you go around broadcasting. I just meant the police and the detectives. At the time. Almost two months ago. Could I still be hysterical after two months?"

His grip relaxed, he turned away. "I suppose not," he said, and added as if to himself, "All along I've felt you were bottling something up, but I wasn't sure what it was."

There was a silence. At last Ann said, "Look—I don't have any dramatic new evidence, or anything like that. I guess it's mainly a problem of acceptance. I don't mean just of Bobbie's death, but of the way it happened. I've thought a lot about it, trying to figure out why I feel the way I do. I am a rational person," she said soberly. "I don't believe, I almost *can't* believe, in a fourth dimension. I can understand intellectually how such a thing could exist, but I can't believe in it."

He nodded.

"So—I don't believe that people go around sticking knives into other people for no reason at all. Not even homicidal maniacs. I mean, the reason may be an irrational reason—oh, that doesn't make sense; what I mean is, it might not seem like a reason to any normal person, but it would still be part of a pattern. You're always reading about, well, sex maniacs who attack fat women, or red-haired women, or children of a certain age . . ." She drew a breath.

Nick picked up his glass and took a swallow of brandy. He said, "Haven't the police been working along those lines, more or less?"

"Oh, yes, I guess so," Ann said. "But as far as I can see, all that means is that they're waiting for the same thing to happen again. And even if it did—well, I'm not sure I'd be convinced."

"But, Ann—"

"I know. But at first—at first they thought it might have been a planned killing, I'm sure they did. They kept asking questions about people she knew, and I suppose they talked to some of them. And they went through her things, too, mostly her letters."

"They'd have had to do that in any case, wouldn't they? As a matter of form, if for no other reason."

"I suppose so. Anyway, they didn't find anything, so they decided it was just a blind killing after all. A maniac." She leaned her head back against the rough plaster of the wall. "I call them once in a while to find out if they have any new leads. They're very polite. If only Bobbie's parents—"

"What about her parents?"

"Oh, they felt the way you say I should feel. They didn't want any reasons; to them the whole thing was just a gruesome, incomprehensible accident. They only wanted to forget about it. So they went back to Cincinnati, and that was that."

"You can hardly blame them," Nick said, frowning into his glass.

"No." Ann got up to turn the record over, and stood looking down into the street. It was still raining fitfully. The light from the window glistened on the taut black skin of a passing umbrella. "Bobbie was an only child," she said.

Nick was silent for a moment. Then he said, "Had you known her a long time?"

"No. We'd just been rooming together since November. The roommate she'd had before, up on the East Side, was a friend of mine. When she left to get married, Bobbie and I got together. I already had this apartment, and it was a lot cheaper than Bobbie's, so—"

"Not much room, though," he said.

"No. I got it as a single apartment." She shrugged. "I'd been on this independent kick ever since college—no more roommates, no more arguments about laundry and who buys the toothpaste. You know. But Bobbie and I were so different from each other that I thought we could manage all right, that our lives would hardly intersect. It worked out quite well."

"I take it you were very fond of her."

She turned quickly at something in his voice. "What difference does that make, for heaven's sake? Even if I'd disliked her, I'd still feel pretty appalled at what happened to her."

"Of course. I didn't mean it that way. But look, Ann"—he spread out his hands—"do you really think there's any point in all of this? Naturally you can't just forget it, at least not yet, but what will you accomplish by brooding over it this way? Maybe the police will catch the killer, maybe they won't; but would you get so much satisfaction out of seeing some anonymous nut locked up in an institution for the rest of his days?"

"Yes," Ann said.

"I meant personal satisfaction."

"So did I. Because he wouldn't be anonymous then, not to me."

After a moment he said, "You are vengeful, aren't you?"

"If I really believed it was that kind of a—nut, just some poor demented creature . . . But what if it wasn't, what if it was done as a cold-blooded, vicious extermination of a living creature, for whatever reason?" Ann went on slowly, pleating the hem of the orange curtain between her fingers, "You know, I used to think I was against capital punishment; in theory I suppose I still am. But when it happens—when murder happens close to you, you can't help feeling it's the only kind of justice that counts. Whoever takes a life must lose his own. Maybe that's primitive of me, and—vengeful, as you say, but I can't help it. If you'd known Bobbie—"

"All right," he said, rising, moving restlessly about the room. "Tell me what she was like—Bobbie." He leaned against the mantel, half turned from her.

"There's not a great deal to tell. It's not as if she was anyone out of the ordinary . . . I mean, nobody who knew her could say that her death was any great loss to mankind, or anything like that." She gave a helpless laugh. "In a way, that's just what makes it all so—terrible and bewildering. Bobbie was just going to get married to an ordinary man and have some children and join a committee or two. Decorations for the country-club dance. She was never going to do or say anything very intelligent or earth-shaking. She was just—pretty and gay and able to take things for granted. That people liked her; that nothing really bad could ever happen to her . . . Happy endings." She added with violence, reacting to some quality of skepticism or impatience in his averted pose, "But I don't see why I should have to justify her to you or anyone else. Isn't it bad enough that she trusted life, and then lost it, without even knowing why?"

"Without even knowing why," he repeated. "Would it have been better if she had known? For her?"

"Of course it would! If she'd been able to defend herself—"

"But if she had no chance, no time to defend herself—would you have wanted her to know what was going to happen?"

"Maybe she did. Maybe she knew she was being followed, or stared at, or whatever it was. Maybe he even spoke to her . . . Oh, Lord," Ann whispered, "you're right, I hope she didn't know. The police said she probably didn't, from the way it happened."

A siren had been howling in the distance as they talked, fading in and out, but getting louder with each renewed wail. Now, as Nick turned his head swiftly toward the window, it shrilled to a piercing crescendo in the street below, slid down the scale, and died.

"Fire," Ann said, leaning out. "But only one engine. It can't be bad. We can watch from here."

The fire truck had stopped in front of the apartment house across the street. A crowd was already pressing up against its glossy red fenders, staring expectantly at the windows of the building. But nothing seemed to be happening; there was no sign or smell of smoke. Two firemen had gone inside. The others waited at their posts, looking bored.

Nick reached for his raincoat. "You stay here, if you want to. I'd better go down. You never know." When Ann looked at him uncomprehendingly, he said, "I'm a doctor, remember?"

"Oh! Of course. I wasn't thinking. I'll go with you."

They hurried down into the street, into the vibration of the engine and a gathering murmur of voices. The rain had stopped; people stood loosening the crumpled collars of their raincoats and shifting their feet impatiently. A pair of small boys raced around the corner from Waverly Place, their sneakers thudding damply on the pavement, and skidded to a stop on the outskirts of the crowd, shrilling questions that nobody bothered to answer.

"Excuse me," Nick said, making his way toward the entrance of the building. Glances flicked at him and lingered. A boy in a sweatshirt and jeans ground out his cigarette with a dirty moccasin, deliberately blocking their way. "All in good time, mister," he said. Nick pushed past him roughly. "Hey, take it easy, will you?" the boy called after them in an aggrieved voice.

"Yeah," someone said, "where's the fire, anyway?" There was a small burst of laughter.

A policeman guarded the doorway. Nick said, "I'm a doctor, Officer, if you need one."

The cop studied him suspiciously. "You ain't got a bag," he said.

Nick said, "No. But I—"

"All right, all right, stick around if you want to," he said, seeing Ann. "Some dame with a hot plate, that's all it is. Maybe you could put a Band-Aid on her finger or something."

Nick ignored him, stepping forward into the deserted brown lobby, whose speckled floor was streaked with the day's wet footprints. Ann thought: He certainly takes his job seriously. Or himself. Young Dr. Malone. But she, too, was conscious of potential drama; her own muscles had tightened sympathetically in expectation.

There was a faint whine and thud behind the blank elevator door. Then it slid open and two firemen came out, grinning sourly.

"Guy's a doctor," the cop announced, jerking his head at Nick. "You need him?"

"Christ, no," said one of the firemen.

"A flaming dessert, for Pete's sake," said the other. "One of the kitchen curtains caught fire—size of a large handkerchief. Come on, Ralph."

"Crêpes suzette," the cop said with a knowledgeable private smile, taking out his notebook.

Ann said, "Maybe it was cherries jubilee."

The cop gave her a brief look and said, raising his voice, "Okay, okay, move along, everybody. Show's over, nothing to get excited about."

"Some show," a voice grumbled.

The people drifted away, shrugging their shoulders. The fire truck drove off toward Seventh Avenue, chased by the small boys. Ann and Nick recrossed the street.

"Well, you tried," Ann said.

"Sure. Put it on my record," Nick said harshly. "Service above and beyond the call of duty."

They climbed the stairs in silence. He really is annoyed, Ann thought; how childish . . . Her limbs felt heavy and sluggish; she wanted suddenly to be alone. It's after eleven, she thought, he will be leaving soon.

But Nick sat down again on the couch, draining the last of his brandy. He said, "Well, where were we?"

"I don't know. Nowhere in particular. I— Nick, really, I've said as much as I want to, for one night."

"You started to tell me about it. I think you should finish it."

She shook her head. "It's been a long day."

"Thanks," he said, getting to his feet.

"I didn't mean it that way."

"No?" He smiled brilliantly, humorlessly; then his face relaxed. "That wasn't a very graceful hint, but I'll take it anyway. Look —I have to stick around the hospital next weekend. Are you free any time during the week?"

"Well—"

"How about Wednesday?" he said as they walked through the kitchen to the door. "Maybe we could see a movie."

He spoke rapidly, eagerly. Ann thought: He doesn't want to see a movie, he wants to hear more about Bobbie. It isn't every girl who has a murdered roommate, a genuine ghost on the premises . . . Rejecting the thought, she said, "Why don't we have dinner here first? I haven't cooked a real meal in ages."

"If you're sure you want to. Yes, I'd like that very much. Oh, Ann." He put his arms around her. "Oh, if only—"

After a moment Ann whispered, "If only—what?"

He held her closer, shaking his head, and kissed her. Her breath caught, she trembled and turned her head away. He kissed her closed eyelids, pressing her back against the narrow strip of wall. The warm spreading shocks of pleasure beat up into her throat. She said desperately, "You'd better go, Nick. Please."

He stood motionless, his cheek against her hair. "Yes. Make me go."

"I can't. All I can do is say it. Please."

"You should have said it before."

She raised her head to smile at him, but he was not smiling. He dropped his arms. "I'll see you on Wednesday, around seven. Goodnight, Ann."

He left quickly, closing the door behind him. Ann leaned against the wall, looking up at the blank cupboard door above the sink which a moment ago had tilted crazily behind Nick's head, so that she would not have been surprised to see it swing open, raining cups and plates upon their heads, while the rest of the world fell away into roaring darkness. Love among the shattered china, she thought with a shaky smile; love among the ruins, and I his virgin victim . . . but why that word, why victim? Because all virgins are? What a shockingly primitive pre-Freudian thought.

She reached accurately for the hanging light cord and in the white glare began to measure out the coffee for her breakfast, keeping her mind carefully wordless, clean and blank.

FOUR

Saturday morning was
hot and hazy, metallic with reflected light. Ann and Carlo took
the subway to the Bronx Zoo and spent the morning in the
reptile house, inhaling the vegetable odors of artificial jungles
while a loudspeaker played "Clair de Lune" and the pythons
writhed in their glass cages. Outside, even the delicate shapes of
antelope and deer looked dusty in the white light that drained
color from the plumage of birds and the starched dresses of little
girls, and poured glassily onto the painted metal top of the table
where Ann and Carlo sat at noon, drinking root beer through
limp straws.

"It's too hot even to eat peanuts," Carlo said irritably.

"For the people or the animals?"

"Both. Oh, the elephants try, all right, but you can see it's an
effort . . . You look tired," he added. "Late night?"

"Not very."

He looked away, drumming his fingers on the table top. "Lucky
you. I got involved in a party across the hall. You met the Forrests,
didn't you, Sue and Alan? It was going on till all hours. I decided,
what the hell, if you can't lick 'em, join 'em. But the girls were
terrible. What's more, they drank up all my booze when the
Forrests' ran out." He sighed. "Ambitious young lawyers shouldn't
try to live in the Village. Too hard on the nervous system. And

oh, yes—who should I find in my bed at three A.M. but George Henderson and one of those awful girls. I felt like Baby Bear."

Ann made a face.

"I couldn't agree with you more," Carlo said. "Still, I always thought George was something of a queer, and I was damn glad to see the girl, believe me."

Ann said, "I wish you wouldn't tell me things like that, Carlo."

"Oh, look, Ann—"

"No, I mean it. I don't care who goes to bed with whom, but I hate all this—sloppiness. The least people can do is find a room of their own and be quiet about it."

"So who wants privacy? This is the age of Togetherness, in more ways than one." Carlo tossed his paper cup at a trash basket, missed, and got up to retrieve it. "You're right," he said, sitting down again and lighting a cigarette. "The whole atmosphere stinks. Half the people I know brush their teeth about once a month and never change their socks. I keep telling myself these things don't matter, I ought to get rid of my bourgeois prejudices, but I go on brushing *my* teeth and changing *my* socks, so I guess it's hopeless. Do unto others . . ."

"You ought to get out of that place," Ann said. "Find a room in a brownstone or something."

"I know. I will, one of these days, when I get bored with the nuthouse. *If* I get bored with it. I can't help it, the place amuses me. Besides, what would they do without me? I'm the one who picks up the beer cans and balances their checkbooks and raises bail when necessary. And I'm their audience—anybody writes a poem, I read it; anybody acts in a play, I see it, I practically sell tickets on the street. Last week I even went down to somebody's loft to watch Cheetah—that's the hairy girl from Albany, remember? her real name is Julie something—do her weaving that she's been telling me about all summer. They had three enormous looms in this place. I just sat and drank this awful Spanish wine and watched Cheetah weave. Very instructive."

Ann shook her head. "I don't see how you can work so hard and then turn around and waste so much time."

"It's a cultivated schizophrenia," Carlo said amiably. "The mind-like-a-steel-trap lawyer and the helpless sucker. They can-

cel each other out . . . Do you want to go look at the polar
bears again?"

"No."

"Well, look—let's go down to my parents' apartment. I have to
pick up my laundry, and maybe Mom will give us lunch. There
are times when even I have to acknowledge the virtues of air-
conditioning." Carlo stood up, dropping his cigarettes and lighter
into the pocket of his pale blue cord jacket, which still held its
immaculate press despite the heat. His white collar hugged his
brown neck neatly, his silver tie clasp glinted against the striped
silk of his tie. Clean socks is right, Ann thought, smiling to herself.

"What's so funny?" Carlo said, eying her as they walked back
to the subway past the dry dun-colored grass of the African preserve. Ann shook her head. "All right, don't tell me." He scowled,
and added casually, "You've got quite an inner life these days,
haven't you, old girl?"

Ann said, "Oh, I wouldn't put it that way exactly."

"No? Something tells me you've been seeing your doctor friend
again. Could it have been last night?"

"It could."

"He still scare you?"

"Absolutely terrifies me," she said lightly.

"Honeychile, yo' got trouble," Carlo declared, and looked
thoughtful, but said no more.

Sophie Brunetti, Carlo's mother, had been a close friend of
Ann's mother; they had grown up together in Philadelphia, gone
to the same schools, roomed together at college, and shared an
apartment in Paris for a year, until Sophie met and married a
young musician named Louis Brunetti, who was studying there
on money his father had saved from a haberdashery in Milan.
Ann had always found it somehow difficult to believe in this
shared youth, though she had seen the photographs often enough
—the plump dark-eyed face and the austere blond one smiling
out from under the floppy white hats of the early thirties, a tennis
court in the background, willow trees . . . There was still the
money, to be sure, enough of it so that the amount didn't matter very much, and the trained singing voice that, speaking, still
held vestiges of a Main Line drawl. But—debutante parties, horse

shows, moonlight sails, croquet on vivid lawns? Aunt Sophie was a stout woman who always dressed in black and who looked from a distance like the old-fashioned popular image of the comfortable Italian or Jewish matron—Mama grown affluent, able to afford a maid and some good jewelry, but still most at home in her kitchen. Thus, strangers encountering the shrewd worldly appraisal of her glance were apt to feel momentarily disconcerted and even mistrustful, as though they had been the objects of some deliberate deception. It was true that Aunt Sophie was a good cook.

"I hoped you'd bring Ann back for lunch," she said now to her son, giving Ann a hug. "We haven't seen her in such a long time." Her eyes lingered on Ann's face for a moment before she added, turning away, "I'll just go see what Agnes is doing about lunch. Connie has a little friend visiting, so I'm sure there's plenty to go around." She went off toward the kitchen across the big Central Park West living room whose decorator, despite a fashionable insistence on ivory and chartreuse and old gold, had failed to triumph over the sheer quantity of furniture salvaged through the years from moribund family houses. Ann looked around, smiling, and said to Carlo, "I wonder if I could have felt so, well, daughterly with my own mother, if she had lived, as I do with yours. I've hardly seen her these last few years, but all I have to do is walk into this room—"

"I know," Carlo said, sitting down on a damask-covered love seat. "She creates this maternal atmosphere with people her own age, for Pete's sake. It's a kind of genius. Before you know it you're telling all."

"But I don't think I've ever even had a serious talk with her; not since I was a child, anyway," Ann objected, moving to the windows to look down at the dusty green expanse of the park. "Oh, odds and ends, but nothing really important."

"She'd be glad to listen," Carlo said, looking at her. "But she wouldn't give you any advice."

"I didn't say anything about wanting advice."

"I know. That's what I mean—that she'd just listen. It's infuriating at times, but surprisingly helpful. Mom would have made a good psychoanalyst." He reached for a table lighter, snapped it several times without success, and began doing something to the wick with a penknife.

Ann wandered around the room, picking things up and putting them down aimlessly, examining the latest photograph of Carlo's older sister Nina and her children. All at once she was overwhelmed by the restless Saturday mood of her childhood; she remembered fidgeting in just this way, often in this same room, waiting for the adults to complete some necessary ritual—lunch, a shopping list, a telephone call—while the afternoon lay bright and inaccessible beyond the windows. If she was at home in Gramercy Park, Mrs. Bekins, the housekeeper, would be puttering methodically from room to room, collecting the paraphernalia of their outing: her glasses, her knitting, an umbrella just in case, her lending-library novel, change for the subway, the navy straw hat in summer, the navy felt in winter, gloves for both of them. Ann would stand by the hat rack in the dark entrance hall, holding her jump rope or skates and envying the poor children of the city who tumbled unheeded on their dirty stoops and played gleefully in the yellow gush of hydrant water along the gutters, while the million noises of the city reverberated around them—

Louis Brunetti came in from the music room and shook Ann's hand firmly, but with reserved affection—a tall narrow man wearing banker's clothes and an expression of fastidious good humor. He was retired now from the Philharmonic, in which he had played a flawless oboe for several decades, and contented himself these days with a little teaching and composing—mostly chamber works for woodwinds, occasionally a small pure song for his wife's contralto.

"My dear, this is a pleasure," he told Ann. "You don't visit us as often as you should."

Carlo folded his penknife with a snap and slid it back into the pocket of his gray slacks. "She's a career girl these days," he said, getting to his feet. "Work, work, work."

"That I refuse to believe," his father said with a smiling shrug. "If she were teaching, or, let us say, serving as a missionary in darkest Africa—or even doing something political in Washington" —he looked thoughtfully at Ann—"then I would say, yes, her work absorbs her."

"You think I'm fit only for humanitarian causes?" Ann asked, laughing.

"Fit? No, it's not a question of fitness, my dear. I'm sure you do your work at the museum with great competence. But enthusiasm? Your instincts *are* fundamentally humanitarian, I should imagine."

"Oh, dear—and you don't think art is a humanitarian cause?"

"For some it is, undoubtedly. But for you?" He poured sherry from a decanter and presented glasses to them both.

Carlo said, "Oh, well, I guess we'd all like to find a cause. But in a complicated world—"

"There are complicated causes," his father said. "That does make an emotional difficulty, I agree."

Carlo studied his shoe tips. "Okay—suppose you're interested in politics; I could be, and not just as a game. But hell, after all that's happened in this country in the last thirty years, anyone with any brains at all can see that our political health depends on the—well, the interaction of opposing principles, and that if one set of principles holds sway for any length of time, the whole system is endangered."

"Yes. And so . . . ?"

"And so I for one can't even vote consistently, out of conviction. A man has two terms in office, and that's it; as far as I'm concerned, I don't care if he's a genius—out he goes. The most important thing is to preserve a dialogue of some kind, because the only truth is in the struggle itself. Can you see me running for office on a nice existentialist platform like that? Some cause."

"A very ancient one," his father observed. "The cause of freedom."

"Oh, sure. Freedom, freedom, rah, rah, rah. 'Allow me to introduce the Freedom candidate, Mr. Carlo Brunetti, whose slogan is: Folks, let a little anarchy into your lives, put a pinch of ambivalence in your orange juice in the morning—'"

Ann said, "Oh, Carlo—can't you see that everything's changing? The kind of dialogue you're talking about, conservative versus liberal or radical or whatever, it's already irrelevant, sooner or later it'll be obsolete. When a society gets as huge as ours, and the—possibilities of chaos become so endless, then it has to be run scientifically or collapse altogether, if only because people,

individuals, just can't cope emotionally with so much complexity."
Her voice had risen; she checked it and went on more calmly,
"They need to have it sorted out and arranged for them, to have
some logic imposed on the mass of details. Whether or not we
happen to like it personally, we're going to have government
planning on a vast scale, and party politics just aren't going to
matter very much, any more than personal actions or feelings."

"The possibilities of chaos . . ." Louis Brunetti repeated, and
looked at Ann gravely. "I hope you're wrong, my dear. In the
meantime, perhaps if enough young men like Carlo were to dedi-
cate themselves to something as quaint and old-fashioned as the
cause of freedom—"

"Oh, sure," Carlo said. "Like how? By doing what?"

"By helping to preserve its institutions, one would suppose."

"Papa, will you come out of the eighteenth century long
enough to take a good look around you? I agree with Ann as far
as that goes; after all—"

"The law, for example," his father said implacably, sipping his
sherry.

Carlo clapped his hands to his ears. "I can hear it all coming," he
groaned. "Why did you have to send me to law school, Papa? I
could have been such a happy barber or movie usher or forest
ranger—"

Louis smiled, but his glance at his son was troubled. He said,
"The world has always been complicated, but the young did not
always know it," and sighed.

"Yeah," said Carlo. "We finally wised up, didn't we? Not the
Silent Generation or the Anxious one, but the Savvy Generation
. . . Right, Kemo sabe?" He grinned at Ann.

"Hi-yo, Silver," said Ann.

Connie and her girl friend came banging into the room, shrieking at the sight of Carlo, and were sent back to take the curlers
out of their hair before lunch, which was leisurely and abundant.
Afterward Ann and Carlo took their coffee into the music room
to hear some new records and a tape of a clarinet quintet Louis
had composed some ten years earlier, which was to be performed
at a Sunday afternoon Frick concert in the fall. It was after three
when they emerged into the pale glare of the afternoon, Carlo
carrying his laundry case and Ann a loaf of fresh bread wrapped

in foil which Aunt Sophie had urged upon her; no one ever left the Brunettis' empty-handed.

"Where to?" Carlo said.

"Well—" Ann hesitated. "If it's not too much family for you, I'd like to stop in and say hello to Dad. I've been promising to for weeks, and I know he'd love to see you."

"You sure he's not in the country this weekend?"

"No," Ann admitted. "But at least I can say I tried. Anyway, there's a suit of Marge's there that she said I could have, and if it needs to be altered I ought to do something about it before the cool weather comes."

"Cool weather! Ye gods—women! Well, keep an eye out for an air-conditioned cab, since you're feeling so energetic."

"Oh, no, Carlo. Let's walk across the park and take a Fifth Avenue bus, the way we always used to. I've got flat shoes on—"

"Me and my laundry," Carlo said. "I hope you know a good doctor in case I have a heat stroke . . . but that's right, you do, don't you?" He took her arm, heading for the park. "Okay, the bus it is, for old times' sake."

"Your dad's home, Miss Ann," Howard told her as the elevator began its shuddering ascent to the fourth floor. "He had company till late last night, and I don't guess he feels like going anywhere in this heat. No, sir." He winked conspiratorially, his sparse gray hair stirring in the wind of the fan above his head. "You ought to look in on your dad more often, now he's a married man."

"I know," Ann said, smiling vaguely, as the elevator stopped and Howard, breathing hard, drew back the brass gate with a clash.

The apartment door was on the latch, but when they paused in the hall to call out, there was no answer.

"Howard's a nice old guy," Carlo said, setting down the laundry case and feeling for a cigarette, "but he always makes me feel as if he were hauling up the elevator by main strength, and I ought to help him, or at least cheer him on."

"He *has* to talk, too. Sometimes he drives me crazy. Of course, as a child I thought he was wonderful—"

"And now you're paying for it. Only fair," Carlo said, blowing smoke.

"Dad!" Ann called again. "Anybody home?" She started up the stairs. "Maybe he's taking a nap. Anyway, I'll go get Marge's suit before I forget."

But the bedrooms were empty, inhabited only by a smell of tobacco and a clock ticking in the master bedroom, whose double bed was neatly made. An array of shaving things in the adjoining bathroom, a plaid robe on a hook. Ann went into the small guest room where Marge kept her winter clothes in zippered bags in a dark closet that also held the Christmas ornaments and a box of old stuffed animals from Ann's childhood, marked for grandchildren or for charity. She was crossing the hall to her own room with the suit over her arm when Carlo called from the bottom of the stairs, "He's in the kitchen, Ann. Come on down."

Something in his voice startled her. She dropped the suit over the banister and hurried downstairs, through the dining room to the kitchen, where her father sat slumped at the old enameled kitchen table, a glass of beer untouched in front of him and a cigarette burning a long ash into a saucer, his face sagging with some recent grief or shock. Carlo stood uncertainly at his elbow.

"What is it?" Ann cried. "What's happened, Dad?"

Guy shook his head and waved a hand wearily.

"Dad, what is it? Is it Marge?"

"Yes," he said finally. "But she's all right. Thank God, thank God."

Ann sat down hard on a wooden chair while Carlo reached over her father's shoulder to stub out the cigarette. "Something happened, though," she said.

"Yes. They were in an accident. That damn woman!" Guy said with a violence that made them both start. "She only got what she deserved, and I hope she knows it."

"Who? What woman?"

He sighed. "Helen Carmichael. God knows, I've warned Marge about her. I told her specifically never to drive with Helen—morning, noon or night. The woman's an alcoholic, or the next thing to it, as I suppose you know."

With an effort Ann remembered Mrs. Carmichael, a widow who had recently bought the old Reagan house near the dairy—untidy gray hair, plaid shirts and slacks, a pleasant gravelly voice, a talent for flower arranging, or was it water colors? She said patiently, "But what happened, Dad? Was it a bad accident?"

"Of course it was a bad accident! With Helen Carmichael, what else could it be? The way I got it from Marge, she tried to pass a tractor on a hill, and then when she saw a truck coming down at her she just shot across the road and plowed into a tree and a stone wall and God knows what else." He picked up the glass of beer and drank off half of it with a convulsive gulp.

"Then you've talked to Marge."

"Yes, just before you came. She was calling from the hospital."

"But she's all right?"

"I guess so. Some bruises and a nice bang on the head, but no concussion, the doctors said. The car was completely demolished."

Ann put her elbows on the table and clenched her fists against the sudden trembling that had seized her. "How about Mrs. Carmichael?"

"Compound fractures, lacerations—the works, I gather. I don't mean she's going to *die*," he said, looking at Ann. "But she's going to be laid up a long time. Maybe it'll get her off the bottle, anyway. It's an ill wind that blows nobody good," he added gloomily, drinking his beer. His sense of the dramatic was returning visibly; he was conscious of Carlo, still standing gravely at his elbow, as an audience. He waved his hand and said, "There's more beer in the icebox, Carlo, help yourself."

Ann said tightly, "Are you sure Marge is all right, Dad?"

"Why, yes, I think so, honey. She sounded pretty shaky over the phone, but why wouldn't she?"

He reached across and patted Ann's hand. She stared down at his wrist, where the dark hairs curled over the leather strap of his watch. He wore an old cotton plaid shirt and faded blue denim slacks tied around his paunch with a frayed rope belt: standard summer attire. "I didn't mean to scare you, sweetie," he said. "It was just—well, after I hung up the phone I couldn't seem to pull myself together right away. Just thinking I might have lost Marge—" He shook his head and sat back heavily, thumbing a cigarette from his shirt pocket.

Ann said, "*Had* Mrs. Carmichael been drinking?"

"Hell, I guess so. They were on their way to Tanglewood for the afternoon. Marge gave her lunch at the house first, non-alcoholic, she said. But Helen was probably at it all morning, if I know her. Marge's car is at the shop, that's why they took Helen's," he explained.

"But you don't know she'd been drinking?" Ann insisted.

"Well, no, I don't know it for a fact. I don't suppose they bothered with any sobriety tests on the way to the hospital."

Carlo set a glass of beer in front of Ann and sat down with his own. The tall green bottles he had left on the counter glistened damply in the hot glow of sunlight from the small window over the sink. The fan above the pantry door sang rustily into the silence.

Carlo said, "Well, it could have been a lot worse, I guess," and drank, tilting his dark head.

"You're damn right it could," her father said. "Amen to that."

Ann said, "Is that all you can say—amen? And then go on drinking beer as if nothing had happened?" She pushed her glass away and stood up, shaking with a violent, painful anger. The two men stared at her.

"Take it easy, Annie," Carlo said.

"What else can we do except try to forget it?" her father asked in a bewildered voice, as though she had hurt his feelings.

"I don't know, I don't know!" Ann said, turning away. She slapped blindly at an open cupboard door whose latch had been broken since her childhood, and burst into tears. A chair scraped, her father's arm went around her shoulders, he said huskily, "It's all right, honey, nothing to cry about. Marge is all right, don't you understand?"

Ann nodded, but it was a moment before she could stop crying. Her father's arm tightened; she was squeamishly conscious of the fleshy pad of his shoulder under the thin shirt, of a faint acid smell of sweat. She took a step away, fumbling for the handkerchief in her pocket, and blew her nose. Her breath came in hiccups, like a child's. Finally she said, "I'm sorry. I don't know what's wrong with me."

She tried to smile at Carlo, who was looking at her as though he had never seen her before.

"Come sit down and drink your beer," her father said, pulling out her chair. "Shock," he said to Carlo. "I've seen it a hundred times—classic nervous reaction."

Ann gripped the back of the chair but could not make herself sit down. I am safe here, she told herself, looking around at the familiar room, at the wide shallow sink with its brass taps, the unmatched assortment of pots and pans—copper, aluminum, cast-iron—hanging from hooks on the yellow wall, the wooden spice rack whose original quaint bottles and jars had been lost or broken long ago. Marge's kitchen in the country was blue and white, with a complete set of Corning Ware and a garbage disposal, but with her usual good sense she had left this room alone.

Ann said rapidly, "I'm tired, I guess. I haven't slept much this week, what with the heat. If you don't mind my running out on you, I think I'll go back down to the Village. I really am all in, for some reason."

"Why don't you just take a nap here?" her father said. "We could all go out for dinner later."

"Well—I have some laundry and things I ought to do. I really think I should go. Thanks for the zoo and lunch, Carlo. Why don't you stay and give Dad a game of chess?"

"Great idea!" her father said enthusiastically. "We haven't had a game in ages, Carlo. You used to be pretty good. Legal mind, and all that."

Carlo stood up. "Thanks, sir, but I think I ought to see Ann home. If she isn't feeling well—"

"I feel fine," Ann said quickly. "Seriously, I'm just tired, and there are a few errands I ought to do. You stay here."

"That's going to be an interesting rest, what with all those errands," Carlo said.

Ann laughed and said, "Well, you know what I mean," and kissed her father on the cheek. "Let me know if you hear anything more from Marge, Dad."

Carlo followed her through the dining room into the hall. "Don't forget the suit," he said. "After all, that's what you came for."

Upstairs, in the coolness of her old room, Ann sank down onto the padded seat of the dressing table and stared unseeingly into the mirror, hoping that Carlo would get tired of waiting for her and go back to talk to her father. But he was still standing by the mail table when she came down again, turning over the pages of a *New Yorker*.

"I'm going to see you home," he said. "I can play chess with your father some other time."

Ann shook her head. "No, please, Carlo, I'd rather you didn't."

He caught her hand and held it. "What's wrong, Ann? Can't you tell me? It's not like you to get so upset over an accident, something you can't do anything about."

Ann was silent. "I don't know," she said at last. "I don't understand it myself. I just feel so—scared and trembly inside, all of a sudden. As though anything could happen . . ."

Carlo said roughly, "You mean violence? Sudden death, shattered bones, blood? Is that what can happen?"

"Yes."

They were almost the same height. They stared into each other's eyes, standing motionless and tense in the shadowy hallway. Behind Carlo the hat rack raised its arms in grotesque embrace.

"All you can do is live with it when it comes," Carlo said. "Don't anticipate, don't remember. Save yourself."

"No," Ann said. "Not if there's something you can do. Like seeing that Mrs. Carmichael never takes another drink, or—"

"Bobbie," Carlo said. "You're still thinking about Bobbie, aren't you?"

"Still?" Ann cried. "What do you mean, still?"

She wrenched open the heavy door and half ran down the corridor to the stairway, whose cement walls echoed loudly with her descending footsteps. The lobby was deserted except for an unfamiliar doorman, who nodded politely as Ann brushed past him into the glare of the street. At the curb two cabdrivers leaned arguing from their windows, their faces red and congested, their mouths twisted with rage. As Ann hurried away toward the subway, their voices seemed to rise behind her with all the other voices of the city in a single furious whine of self-assertion and hostility.

How do we live with it? she wanted to cry. Why should we have assumed that it is better or even safer not to fight back? And oh, God, how could I have prided myself on my own sanity, my self-possession, my capacity to remain normal and unscathed amid the stuff of blackest fantasy, nightmare hallucination? In such a world, what is normal and who is sane? Save myself, Carlo said. But what self would I be saving?

FIVE

Nick's **manner**
during dinner was abstracted and even formal; as though, Ann
thought, he shared in some way her own mood of suspension
before a decisive act. When she had cleared the table and poured
coffee for them, she sat down a little away from him on the couch
and said, "Nick—do you mind if we don't go to the movies, after
all?"

"After that meal, who can move? I'll never take you to a restaurant again. Don't you know it's a strategic error for a spinster to
learn how to cook?" But he set down his cup and looked at her
curiously.

Ann drew a long breath and clasped her hands tightly in her
lap. "Nick, I want to talk to you. I need your help. The other night
you wanted me to go on talking about Bobbie. I didn't want to
then; I was tired, and I thought maybe I'd already said more than
I should have. But I've changed my mind. You see," she said
slowly, staring at him, "I really do believe that Bobbie was murdered deliberately, with—what's the phrase?—malice aforethought.
I'm convinced it was a premeditated crime. I want you to help
me figure out who and why."

For a moment the room was utterly still; Nick sat motionless,
he hardly seemed to breathe.

In a low voice he said, "Why me, Ann?"

"For one thing," she said, "and I guess it's the main thing, you're the only person I—care anything about who's *wanted* me to talk about it; the only one who hasn't said I should forget it, either out of misguided concern for me or out of sheer laziness, or even cowardice." Her voice shook a little. "Nobody wants to think much about death. Anyone who does is morbid. But—well, you're a doctor. Your attitude is bound to be a little different."

He nodded. He did not look at her; his face was strangely bleak.

"Also—there's the kind of mind you have. Analytical, deductive. Cold." When he still said nothing, she went on with a small laugh, "Well, what it amounts to is that I'm inviting you to play detective with me. I know it's a strange request, to say the least. But I thought . . . well, maybe we could look at it as a kind of game, forgetting the—the personal side of it. A kind of puzzle, with hardly any clues and probably one chance in a million of coming out right."

"Or some very difficult form of solitaire. I had a maiden aunt who knew them all. When she had a stroke and couldn't move, we used to take turns moving the cards around for her on a board."

"Only it won't be solitaire, if you'll help me. Or do you mean . . . ?" Ann stopped, seeing his face. "I've just dreamed this whole thing up to pass the time, to get rid of my aggressions and so forth—is that what you think? A new sport for the frustrated female?"

He said, "I don't know. But you've got to admit it's a possibility."

Ann reached for the coffee pot. "All right," she said. "Forget it. I'm sorry I said anything." She filled his cup quickly and neatly, but spilled a little over the rim of her own. "What movie did you have in mind?"

Nick looked at her for a long moment. At last he said softly, "I'm only using my cold, analytical, deductive mind, Ann. You have a theory that I gather isn't supported by any definite facts. Then why the theory? What are the subjective reasons for your having it in the first place? That's where you have to begin."

"Subjective reasons?"

"Look," he said with sudden impatience. "You told me the other evening that you were basically such a rational person that you couldn't really believe in an irrational act—though I think what you really meant is that there are many degrees and kinds of rationality. The term 'irrational' denotes a very low degree, and I agree it isn't a very good term. But you were talking then about homicidal mania, at least I thought you were. Now you're talking about premeditated murder. Why? Why do you *want* to think your friend was murdered? Because that would involve a higher degree of rationality and thus give you something to think about —something to get your teeth into, to make *you* feel better."

"Yes, that's part of it," Ann whispered. "You're right."

"And then I also wonder whether, considering your fondness for your roommate, this detective idea isn't partly a way of keeping her alive a little longer. As long as you have an excuse for reconstructing her conversations, her actions, her friendships, anything that may reveal something in retrospect, you still have her with you in a way." He paused. His face was calm and thoughtful. "If she had been hit by a car, say, or killed in a plane crash, she would be—just gone. You would be forced to forget her, except as someone you had once been fond of."

Ann frowned. "Bobbie and I were friends," she said, "but if you're implying that I—that we—"

"Oh, well, I think there's always a sexual aspect to any close friendship between single women," Nick said easily. "Particularly women making their way in a man's world. There are bound to be emotional complications. I didn't mean anything overt," he added.

"Well, thanks. You're certainly nothing if not clinical," Ann said. "But actually it wasn't a 'close' friendship in the way you mean. We didn't see that much of each other, what with our jobs and Bobbie's being out so much. I did like Bobbie, nobody could help liking her, but—" She shrugged, reaching for her coffee cup. "Well, we won't argue about that, there's no point in it. Does that cover the possible subjective reasons for my wanting to play detective?"

"I don't know. It depends what the objective reasons are."

Ann played with the delicate handle of her cup, turning it in its saucer. She felt suddenly foolish, almost panicky. She said, "There's really only one reason, and I suppose it won't even sound

like one to you. It's just this: that if it was murder, it was a perfect one. Time, place, method—the kitchen knife, for instance,
the kind anyone could have bought anywhere in the city—all perfect, almost as though the whole thing had been planned. Only
not almost; I think it was."

Nick stared at her for a moment in astonishment. Then he threw
back his head and laughed. "The rational mind indeed! As Her-
cule Poirot would say, 'It is the very absence of clues that gives
me to think.' Isn't that it? I read Agatha Christie too." He
pounded a cushion with his fist, still laughing. "Honest to God,
Ann, is that what all this is about?"

Ann said nothing.

"Sorry," he said after a moment. "It's just that your logic is so
beautiful. It could have been the perfect crime, therefore it was.
Don't you see that you could say that about a hundred things
that happen in this city every day—every freak accident, in
fact?"

"I take it you don't think there's anything in it; except wishful
thinking, that is."

He shrugged. "There's everything and nothing, depending on
your point of view."

"All right. It even sounds silly to me, now that I've said the
words out loud."

"Conceding the game so easily?" Nick said with a strange smile.

She stared at him. "But I thought—"

"I'm accepting your invitation."

"You are?" She gave a baffled laugh. "But why? After what you
said—"

"There's the pleasure of your company, for one thing. How do
I know you won't find someone else to play cops-and-robbers
with if I turn you down?" He looked at his hands. "Also there's
the matter of your own convictions. You're going to have to be
proved wrong before you'll change your mind, aren't you? Right
now you're feeling a little foolish, but that won't last. You're too
stubborn."

Ann said slowly, "You're supposed to be on my side, you know.
At least that's what I had in mind."

"Was it? You must have known I'd be skeptical, to say the

least. In fact, I don't think you'd have brought the whole thing up at all if a part of you hadn't hoped to be proved wrong."

"Yes. That's probably true," she said after a pause. "At least in the sense that I need someone to test what I think as I go along. I mean, I'm not just trying to play Nancy Drew for the fun of it, obviously."

He let this pass. They were silent for a moment.

"Well, what now?" he said. "Where do we go from here? Your procedure, I mean."

She considered. "I think first of all I ought to just give you the facts about what happened that day—you know, as though you didn't know anything about it at all. Then we can go on from there."

He rose, loosening his tie. "Okay, shoot," he said. "In the meantime, let's get the dishes done."

In the small kitchen they stood side by side while Nick washed and Ann dried the dishes and put them away. She was sharply conscious of his body close to hers, of his muscular wet forearms, his hands that occasionally touched hers as he gave her a plate or a cup to dry. She kept her eyes away from his face, concentrating on giving Bobbie's story as factually and impersonally as she could.

"She went to work as usual that day, on the Sixth Avenue subway to Thirty-fourth Street. Her office was on Fifth Avenue between Thirty-sixth and Thirty-seventh—"

"Do you know she went to work that way?"

"Well—she was *at* work at the usual time. I assume she took the subway. I mean—"

"You didn't go with her."

"No. I left about fifteen minutes later, after I'd done the breakfast dishes. That was part of our system—she was supposed to do the dusting and straightening up when she got home in the evening, which was usually a half-hour or so before I did."

"Did anyone see her that morning?"

"I don't know. I don't know if they even checked on that. But she was at the office by nine o'clock, so—"

He said, "All right. I'm just trying to distinguish between fact and assumption, like a good detective." He ran hot water over a wineglass and handed it to her gingerly. "Now—her day at the office. What kind of work did she do?"

"She was a combination secretary and receptionist for a company that makes costume jewelry—Ultra Designs, it's called. It's not the ten-cent-store kind, some of it's quite expensive. They carry it at all the good department stores. This place is their showroom, with a small office to take care of the paper work. I don't know much more about it than that. Bobbie had been working there for about a year. I talked to her boss, Mr. Michaelson, at the funeral." Ann stared at the plate she was drying. "The memorial service, I should say; her parents had the actual funeral back in Cincinnati. Anyway, he said Bobbie seemed fine that day, not worried or upset or anything. They had lunch together, just a sandwich at the cafeteria next door, and then Bobbie went off to do some shopping, but she came back before the hour was up to retype a letter she'd made a mistake on. I don't think she was too efficient as a secretary"—Ann smiled faintly—"but she was attractive and good-natured, and the buyers liked her. Mr. Michaelson said everyone there was very fond of her."

"Mr. Michaelson in particular?"

"Oh—well, no, I don't think there was anything like that. At least not on her side. I mean, Mr. Michaelson is in his fifties and not exactly a romantic type, and Bobbie certainly had enough men on the string."

"Yes. Well, we can come back to that later. Did he say anything else about her behavior?"

"No, not really. This was at the service, as I said. We didn't exactly have a long detailed conversation. I could talk to him again, I guess."

"What about when she left the office?"

"That was as usual, too. She left at five with another girl who works there and they walked over on Thirty-fourth to the subway, only the other girl went on to get the IRT. She was the last person—I mean the last person who knew Bobbie—who saw her alive," Ann said, conscious of repeating the standard detective-story phrase. "All this was in the newspaper stories. I mean, I'm not adding anything—assumptions or otherwise."

Nick nodded. "Go on."

"Well—there were a lot of people on the subway, naturally.

One of the eyewitnesses—and there weren't many who stuck around; this *damn* city—" Her voice rose; Nick gave her a quick sidelong look and she went on, "One of the witnesses said he'd noticed Bobbie on the subway, standing near the center door and reading her newspaper—like a million other girls, he said, only with better legs than most . . . Well, the point is, he was just giving her the eye; there wasn't anything in her manner that made him notice her particularly. Then at West Fourth there was the usual rush for the doors, people changing trains or just in a hurry to get home. Bobbie was one of the first out. She got as far as the stairs, and then—she just fell. Everybody said not to move her, she might have broken something or had a heart attack. When they saw the blood they thought at first she'd hit her head. Then they saw the knife."

Nick pulled the plug out of the sink and watched the water drain away rapidly, leaving a torn rim of suds. He turned the cold water on hard and swished the dishrag around. "How was she lying?"

Ann swallowed. With difficulty she said, "There was a picture in one of the papers. Maybe you saw it." He shook his head, forcing her to go on. "It wasn't a good picture, just a blur—but she was lying crumpled up at the bottom of the stairs, on her side, sort of. You couldn't see her face, or the—wound. I have the picture somewhere, if you want to look at it."

He took the dishtowel from her and dried his hands. "Not now," he said, putting an arm on her shoulder. "I'm sorry I made you talk about it. But I had to know whether you could. If you couldn't—"

She looked up into his eyes, blue and somber under his frowning brows. "If I couldn't . . . ?"

"Then there wouldn't be any point in going on," he said, turning away. They went back into the living room. Nick sat down in the chair by the window, Ann on the couch. "All right," he said.

Ann said, "I could hear the telephone ringing and ringing as I came up the stairs that night. I remember feeling annoyed that Bobbie wasn't home—her clothes were strewn all over the place, as usual—and thinking it was probably she on the phone, calling to say she was going out to dinner or to the movies or something.

I'd stopped on the way to buy some chops for our supper and some of this awful pineapple yogurt she was always eating—and I was tired . . . Well, anyway, it wasn't Bobbie, of course, but the police, wanting me to come identify the body." She laced her fingers tightly together. "I'd rather not talk about that part of it, if you don't mind. I told them it was Bobbie, and then I called an aunt of hers who lives in Mamaroneck so that she could call Bobbie's parents. The police asked me a lot of questions—about her boy friends, whether I thought she had seemed depressed or unhappy or fearful lately . . . It was all so ghoulish, I couldn't take it seriously. I guess I still couldn't believe what had happened. Finally they said I could go, but they wouldn't let me come back here. They kept saying I ought to be where someone could take care of me." She shrugged. "I guess that's standard procedure —they wanted to go over the apartment, among other things. I said I could go up to Gramercy Park to my father's, so they drove me up there in a squad car, which I was grateful for when I saw all the reporters. I stayed with Dad and Marge for about a week. The museum gave me a leave of absence, with pay."

She closed her eyes and said tensely, remembering, "Everybody kept tiptoeing around, being solicitous and discreet, as though I had some unmentionable disease, when all the time—"

Nick was sitting forward in his chair, staring at the floor. "All the time—what?"

"I was so *angry* inside. I was in a sort of rage at what had happened. I wanted to do something, to act in some way, and I had this terrible feeling of urgency . . . but no one else seemed to feel the same way. I even thought after a while that my own feelings must be indecent or peculiar or something. But now—well, that's still the way I feel. The grief and personal sorrow I feel about Bobbie has nothing to do with it, in a way. It's something else entirely." She stopped.

"Death must be punished," Nick said.

"Death?" Ann stared at him. "No, not death—the murderer. Why do you say death?"

With an ironic smile he said, "Because it is the fact of death that is unforgivable, isn't it, and not the individual occasion of it? Never mind, go on."

"There isn't much more to tell. The police sent someone to talk to me again, but I had the feeling they weren't really very interested." She stirred restlessly. "It got to the point where Bobbie's parents were telling me not to brood about it so much—that they themselves just had to accept the whole thing as a tragic accident (those were Mr. Willis's words), and to concentrate on remembering Bobbie as she was, without thinking too much about her death. She couldn't have suffered, they kept saying, it happened so quickly . . . Think of all the people who die of cancer every day, or who drown or get burned alive. Think of the concentration camps, think of Hiroshima. The glad game," Ann said, her mouth trembling. "It was unbelievably grotesque. And they are such good people." She found her handkerchief and blew her nose. "Well," she said, "I guess that's it."

He stared out the window. "You've had a rough time. I'm sorry."

There was a silence, then a faint burst of laughter from the apartment overhead. Nick said, nodding upward, "Who lives there?"

"Oh, just a girl, Marion something—I don't remember her last name. I've only spoken to her a couple of times."

"What about the other tenants?"

She took up his matter-of-fact tone. "Two middle-aged women next door, not sociable types. The apartment downstairs keeps changing hands. There's a man there now, a writer, I think. At least I sometimes hear him typing in the evenings."

"So." Nick extended his legs, rubbing the palm of one hand along the arm of the chair. "Well," he said, "what now?"

"I'm not sure," Ann said. "I mean, there's no question about the how, when, or where of what happened. That leaves just the who and the why. Just. I suppose we have to start with the why. But—"

"But what?"

"I've tried, but I just can't seem to make the jump from the kind of person Bobbie was to the idea of her as a *victim*. I mean, the idea that she could have provoked something so—merciless."

"But that's exactly what you've got to do," Nick said softly. "Otherwise you won't get anywhere at all."

"I know." Ann hesitated. "It's just that none of the ordinary motives seem to fit. I keep thinking that it must have been something out of the ordinary, something accidental, almost—that Bobbie as a *person* wasn't really involved, if you know what I mean." When he didn't answer, she said, "Oh, I know that doesn't make much sense. I guess we should start with something more conventional and obvious. The crime of passion, for instance," she said with distaste.

"All right," Nick said, smiling faintly. "What about the crime of passion?"

"Well, my main objection to that is that the murder itself, if it was murder, certainly wasn't a very passionate act. In fact, just the opposite. I mean, if you're possessed with love for someone —or hate, for that matter—you don't just bide your time until you can stab them in the back and make a safe getaway. At least I wouldn't think so."

Nick said, "I agree. Still, if you'd been brooding about the thing for years, until you were slightly psychotic anyway, you might commit such an act in such a way—"

"Vengeance of some sort? Yes, I've thought of that. But wouldn't you want your victim to *know*—to see your face? What good would revenge be otherwise?"

"He might have written her a note—or let her know in some way that he was after her—"

Ann shook her head. "I'm sure I would have known about anything like that. Bobbie would either have laughed it off or have had hysterics, but she wouldn't have kept it to herself. Also," she said slowly, "there's the fact that she didn't suffer—that she wasn't intended to suffer. At least I gathered from what the police said that she would hardly have known what was happening. She might have felt a sort of pricking sensation between her shoulder blades before she keeled over, but nothing more. It was all very—clinically done."

"Yes," he said. "Well, do we eliminate the romantic angle then?"

"No," Ann said, standing up. "I don't want to eliminate anything yet." She went to the desk and took a folder from a drawer. "Here," she said, handing it to him. "I've made a list of the men in Bobbie's life. And there are some letters—mostly old ones from people she'd lost touch with but who could have been in the vicinity; also some from current out-of-town boy friends."

Nick opened the folder. There were several notebook pages

covered with Ann's clear, rounded handwriting, and a sheaf of letters with a few photographs attached. "Good Lord!" he said with a startled laugh. "You have been working on this, haven't you?"

"I just do things methodically," Ann said. "I can't help it. Anyway, I wish you'd look through it. Maybe you'll find something I've missed."

Nick pulled the floor lamp closer to his chair and spread the folder open on his knees, examining the first page intently. Ann stood looking down at him for a moment. Then she went into the kitchen and took two cans of beer from the refrigerator. Punching the triangular head of the opener into the metal, which gave softly under its pressure like butter, she was aware of a sudden sense of exhilaration and release. I've done something at last, she thought; I've made someone else think about Bobbie. Even if nothing comes of it, we will have done as much as anyone could do—more than the police or any detective; because whatever answers there are must be here, in the place where Bobbie lived, and in the mind of someone who knew her and can remember.

She set Nick's beer can on the window sill at his elbow and sat down again on the couch, glancing at her watch: nine-thirty, still so early? She looked at Nick's bent head, his face expressionless with concentration, and thought: I was right to tell him; even if it is only a game to him, he will play it as well as he knows how, for its own sake.

Nick scanned the last of the letters and laid it aside, shaking his head.

"I know," Ann said. "None of it's serious enough, is it?"

He glanced back at the top sheet. "There's this one guy, Patton —you mention an argument she had with him, and then phone calls—"

"He got engaged the other day—I should have added that. Anyway, Chuck is such a joker, I don't think he could keep a grudge for more than an hour at a time. The fight was probably about something like whether Bobbie would go away for the weekend with him. At least the last time he called, Bobbie said something about how impossible he was and how she wished he'd leave her alone—but she didn't sound really mad or upset. And he didn't call again. Oh, I don't know," Ann said with a sigh.

"The whole thing is, most of Bobbie's men were either jokers like Chuck or nice hard-working boys from Cincinnati who wanted to marry her. Bobbie didn't take any of them very seriously, and as far as I could tell they didn't take her seriously either. I don't mean she might not have married one of them, but as if she were choosing her date for the big dance or the house-party weekend or something. She wasn't really a very passionate person, I don't think; men who were too serious or intense didn't interest her, and she didn't interest them."

Nick nodded. "Well, how about jealousy? Sometimes these frivolous types like to play one guy off against the other just for the hell of it. Could there have been anything like that?"

"Oh, no, I'm sure not. I mean, if you'd known Bobbie—well, maybe she was too frivolous," Ann said, swallowing an irrational anger at the word and the way he had used it, "but she didn't enjoy that sort of thing. Anyway, she had no sense of strategy; she couldn't plan ahead to save her life."

The words fell heavily into the silence. Nick smiled drily. He said, "Well, there's one other possibility. Any chance that she was pregnant?"

"I don't think so." Ann frowned, considering. "I've wondered about that—but again, I think she would have told me. Or I would have guessed that something was wrong, I'm almost sure of that."

"They didn't do an autopsy, I suppose?" Ann shook her head. "Well, then, we just don't know. It's not a very pleasant possibility, but if she was badgering some guy to marry her or to give her money for an abortion, and he got desperate enough—"

His tone was objective, noncommittal; Ann tried to match it. "That would make sense in one way," she admitted. "The anonymous, cold-blooded way the thing was done—I mean, it does fit better than the crime of passion idea. But still . . . I can't help being sure I'd have known if something like that was bothering Bobbie. And then again, the men she knew—I can't imagine any of them being that desperate about something that happens fairly often, after all." She leaned back, plucking at a cushion. "The joker types like Chuck Patton wouldn't have had any trouble borrowing the money and finding the doctor—and any of the others would have proposed marriage on the spot."

"But if there was some kind of complication . . . Suppose she wanted to marry the guy, but there was a fiancée in the picture, even a wife, and she threatened to tell all or bring suit for paternity—"

"Oh, that's fantastic!" Ann said. "You can't—"

"Can't what? Look, Ann," he said softly, "this is murder we're talking about. Who knows how complicated and fantastic the reason for it might be?"

They stared at each other. Outside, a bus whined to a stop, exhaling gaseously; they heard the thud of its doors opening, and a woman calling, "See you next week, Maureen!"

Nick said, "Also, I think you should remember that it's easy to think you know a person when all you may really know is one side of them. There's a—marginal area of reaction and behavior for each of us that we ourselves can't predict with any certainty." He leaned to set the folder on the floor beside his chair. "Maybe you've never told a lie in your life, but when telling one becomes crucial for some reason, you may find yourself managing it like a pro."

Ann nodded reluctantly. "All right. I grant it's a possibility— that Bobbie was pregnant. But how on earth do we proceed from there?"

"First things first," Nick said, drinking his beer. "Can you remember—can you make yourself remember—whether or not Bobbie had a period in the month or so before her death?"

"Well—ordinarily I wouldn't have known one way or the other. I mean, she never had cramps or felt sick or anything." She hesitated, trying to overcome a sudden distaste and sense of intrusion. It's a little late to be thinking of Bobbie's privacy, she told herself.

"Then she wouldn't have said anything like 'Thank God, another month's grace,' or whatever girls say when they've been playing around some? At least I gather her habits weren't exactly virginal," he added as Ann stirred uneasily.

"No, I guess they weren't. But she never talked about her sex life to me. Not in detail, anyway. I suppose she was afraid she'd shock me."

"And would she have?" he asked with a smile.

Ann shrugged. "Probably. But it was also—well, I think in a way she wanted my respect. Not that she was ashamed of anything she did, but she knew our outlooks were, well, different, and that I didn't want to hear about whom she'd been to bed with and how many times. I think she thought of me as a kind of older sister, even though I'm not—I wasn't that much older. She didn't want me to disapprove of her."

"Yes," Nick said in a strange voice. "I don't imagine your disapproval would be an easy thing to live with." He turned his head away, looking down into the street, so that she could not see his expression. Almost absently he said, "Communications. That's something we might be able to check."

"Communications?" Ann said blankly.

"If she was in trouble, she was probably using the telephone quite a bit, one way or another. But what telephone? Not the one here, if she didn't want you to know about it, and certainly not the one at the office. Where's the nearest pay phone?"

"Well, I guess the hamburger place around the corner. But how . . . ?"

"Did she go in there very often?"

"I don't think so. She was always dieting, for one thing—yogurt and cottage cheese and all kinds of strange vegetables. When she wanted to splurge she'd go to Howard Johnson's for a sundae."

"Well, that should be easy enough to check. Three or four places around here, the ones near her office building . . . If there's a phone in the lobby the elevator man should be able to help. I guess it's worth a try. At least if we find she was making a lot of pay-phone calls we'll know there was something going on that she didn't want people to know about."

Ann stared. "You mean—actually go to these places and *ask* about Bobbie?"

He said evenly, turning his head to look at her, "You can't stay in your armchair forever, you know. Not if you're really serious about this thing."

"But that's impossible! There are a hundred telephones she could have used. Why, she could have gone into Altman's or Lord & Taylor, for instance—there are lots of booths on the main floor, and nobody would notice her if she came in every day for a month."

"True." Nick shrugged. "I admit the odds are poor. But you

were the one who was talking about a chance in a million. If we're going to explore this possibility at all—"

"Yes, but what would we say? I mean, you can't just walk up to a total stranger, some clerk or whatever, and start asking questions. At least *I* can't."

Nick said relentlessly, "Oh, yes, you can. Look—you go into the cafeteria next to the office building at an off time of day and you get talking to the cashier. You mention that you were an acquaintance of the girl who got stabbed down in the Village, and didn't she use to work around here, and wasn't it a terrible thing? Also you heard she was pretty chummy with the boss— did they ever come in here? People love to talk about these things. If Bobbie was using the phone a lot, you'll hear about it sooner or later."

Ann said, managing a smile, "You sound terribly—professional." He shrugged again, watching her. "Well, I don't know if I can do it, but I guess I'll have to try."

"Good," he said. "I can check the places around here, if you want. Better for me to do it than you. One other thing, I don't suppose you still have any of her stuff—handbags, for instance? If she was looking for a doctor, she might have been carrying a name or at least a phone number around with her."

"No," Ann said. "I mean, I do have her stuff. All of it. And there isn't anything like that; I've looked."

She had surprised him. He said sharply, "You've kept it all?"

"I know it sounds weird. But I kept thinking there might be something—"

"For God's sake, Ann! What have you been doing—ripping linings open, looking in the soles of her shoes?" He gave a short incredulous laugh. "You really have got this thing on the brain, haven't you?"

Ann stood up abruptly, the light folds of her skirt brushing against the coffee table. "I thought it might be evidence," she said.

He rose too, and stood close to her, so that she could hear the shallow intake of his breath before he said quietly, "I'm sorry, Ann. I didn't mean to hurt your feelings."

"You didn't."

"It just never occurred to me—"

"I said it was probably ghoulish of me. But it seemed logical too—I mean, if I was going to find out anything—"

"Yes, of course."

"No, maybe you're right; maybe I am hysterical or morbid or . . . Oh, God, Nick!" she said in sudden anguish, turning to him. "Why do we do the things we do?"

He put his arms around her, pulling her head against his chest. "It doesn't matter," he said. "It doesn't matter."

He began to kiss her in a slow, certain, leisurely way, taking command. He said, "I've been thinking of how we could seal our bond—our partnership. This is the one thing that will mean enough. Yes," he said as she stiffened against him. "Yes. It's what you want too." He kissed her again, finding the back zipper of her dress so that in a moment his hand was caressing the naked curve of her back between her bra and half-slip. Ann sighed and trembled as his fingers slid under the elastic of her slip and pants onto the swell of her buttocks, where no man's hand had ever touched her before.

"No," she said, but automatically, with none of the old urgency of defense or revulsion. It's true, we have made a pact together, she thought. Haven't I known all along what the terms might be? He slid the dress from her shoulders and released the firm hooks of her bra; she felt the fullness of her breasts against his chest, her breath seemed to splinter in her throat. Was all the rest of it only for this, to make this possible? He was unbuttoning his shirt, holding her a little away from him. When their flesh met at last she heard herself sigh with the unimagined bliss of naked contact, his smoothness against her own. When he said, "That's good, isn't it, Ann?" she could not answer; and she felt the muscles of his jaw tighten in a smile.

But even in the midst of their love-making on the narrow bed, even as he lay beside her with his mouth upon her breast and his hands caressing her into readiness, a small part of her mind noted and remembered his own self-possession, the attentive care with which he built upon the delicate structure of sensation. Only after he had entered her and begun to move did his own breath rise to meet hers; when he gave the long shudder of his climax she was perversely conscious of a shock of surprise and resentment, as though he had cheated or deceived her in some subtle way.

The curtains at the single window swung inward on a cool breeze, pale streamers in the half-darkness. Ann reached down to draw up the sheet, feeling all the long smooth shape of Nick's body against hers. Her breath quickened; she kissed his shoulder and rubbed her cheek against it softly, trembling a little as he stroked her thigh lightly in response. But after a moment he rose on one elbow to look down at her, smiling, and said, "It's late, and I've got to be at the hospital in a few hours. We'll do this another time, all right?"

"All right," she whispered.

"Better for you to wait, anyway."

"Yes, Doctor."

He gazed down at her for a long moment, and seemed about to say something more. But he only kissed her quickly on the cheek and swung himself out of bed. She saw his tall body briefly against the light before he went into the living room, and heard him pull down the shades before he began to dress. At least that's one thing he forgot to do earlier, for all his efficiency, she thought drowsily.

She must have dozed; when she opened her eyes he was leaning over her, fully dressed, tucking the sheet around her shoulders. The end of his tie hung down, tickling her nose.

"You forgot your tie clip," she said.

"In my pocket. Do you want the window closed a little?"

"I should get up and brush my teeth. And whatever else—"

"No need. Forget about your teeth and go to sleep. I'll turn off the lights as I leave." He bent and kissed her on her mouth, which felt sore and a little swollen, like the rest of her body. "I'll call you soon."

She listened to the snap of a light switch, the muffled click of the latch, and a moment later the dry rapid sound of his footsteps on the pavement below, going away toward Sheridan Square in the quiet night. She turned her face to the pillow then and slept, dreaming that Bobbie was waiting for her on a deserted subway platform while a subterranean wind blew great sheets of newspaper down the tunnel and she, Ann, dropped token after token into a turnstile whose heavy wooden arms would not budge, until the sound of Bobbie's laughter vanished into the roar of an express train that flashed by without stopping; and when she looked, Bobbie was gone.

SIX

There was no telephone booth in the lobby, after all; only the impersonal rectangles of elevator doors and display cases, on one of whose satin beds Ann was shaken to see a large gold sunburst pin like the one Mr. Michaelson had insisted on giving her the day of the service, because it had been Bobbie's favorite. She liked the modeling, he had said with a sad smile, it was the part of the job she liked best, and no wonder, such a pretty girl.

Ann turned away. The cafeteria next door was a small seedy-looking place with an urn of plastic gladiolas in the window under a sign announcing a 99¢ Meat Loaf Special. It wasn't crowded at this hour, but the interior was noisy with the thrumming of an ancient air conditioner and the clatter of crockery being violently washed by hand somewhere behind the scenes. A thin man in a dirty apron was drearily mopping up a rusty pool of coffee beneath a coffee urn with a dripping spigot. Ann saw with relief that it was not a modern cafeteria with the cash register at the end of the counter; instead you were given a check and paid at the door. She took a piece of cherry pie and a glass of milk and sat at a table near the wall, rehearsing her part. The cashier was a fortyish redhead with blue eyelids and silver fingernails which clacked against the keys of the register whenever she rang up a check and which she examined broodingly in moments of repose before picking up her cigarette and blowing another stream of smoke at the stained ceiling.

The pie was gummy and sweet, a pink mucilage. Ann made herself finish it and drank the milk to take away the taste. She picked up her check and took it over to the register, pretending to fumble for change in her bag. "Thirty-nine," drawled the redhead, looking at her fingernails.

Ann put down a quarter and a dime and began looking for pennies. She said in a preoccupied way, "Excuse me, you wouldn't know where Ultra Designs is, would you? I know it's somewhere around here . . ."

"Ultra who? Oh, yeah, the jewelry company. Right next door."

"Oh, good—thank you. I should have written down the number, but I don't know, I'm always so nervous when it comes to job-hunting—and I don't have an appointment, but I did hear they were looking for a receptionist, and I thought . . . Excuse me, is something the matter?"

"Huh?"

"Well, I mean, you looked so sort of—funny, when I said that."

"I did?" She shrugged. "I must have been thinking of something else. That's thirty-*nine*, miss. One more penny."

"Oh, I'm so sorry," Ann exclaimed, and dug down into the bag again, waiting, feeling the woman's eyes on her face.

"Uh—look, honey," she said with a sigh, making up her mind, "if I was you . . . I mean, maybe before you go in there about that job, you should know about the girl that used to have it." Ann looked up, wide-eyed. "Well, see, she got herself killed. Down in Greenwich Village, in the subway—stabbed to death. It was all over the papers for a while."

"Oh, how terrible! Yes, I remember reading about it . . . but I never thought—I mean, it never occurred to me—"

"Yeah, that's the one. Used to come in here all the time, I recognized her from her picture. Gus said she was in here the day it happened, but I wouldn't know, after a while you stop looking at the faces. Anyway, these girls, they're in and out, fruit salad and a cup of tea, and then off in a big hurry to spend their paychecks." She rested a plump elbow on the rubber mat and patted the red curls behind her ear. "They could come in every day for a year, I still wouldn't know 'em from Adam, you know how it is. But like I said, I remember her from her picture. Real cute, good figure, but snotty; that type, you know what I mean, wouldn't give you the time of day." She stubbed out her cigarette, her thin mouth drawn down at the corners. "But Jesus—in the subway like that, right at rush hour! I'm telling you, I ride the bus these days, I don't care how long it takes me."

Ann said, "And she was the receptionist at Ultra Designs?"

"Isn't that what I've been telling you? I mean, a job's a job, honey, but you could say some jobs are luckier than others." She laughed harshly. "So it's none of my business—but I says to myself, what the hell, she looks like a nice kid, somebody should at least tell her before she goes in that place."

"Well—yes. Thank you, I appreciate it."

"I mean, it could be kind of a shock, not finding out till later, know what I mean?" She swiveled back to the register as another customer approached, and added out of the side of her mouth, "Anyway, you still want the job, I hope you get it, honey."

Out on the street, in brilliant sunshine under a cloudless sky, Ann hugged her arms and clenched her teeth to keep from shivering. Oh, horrible, horrible! she thought, blindly dodging the passers-by, crossing Thirty-sixth Street inches ahead of a swerving cab. Why am I doing this, and what does it prove?

She found herself in the glittery gloom of Altman's, staring at the bank of phone booths, listening to the doors thump open and closed as the shoppers put through their urgent messages to sitters and maids, husbands and mothers . . . How innocently the receivers hung on their hooks, repositories of a thousand confidences, yet unmarked by the grip of the thousand hands; cool smooth plastic retaining no heat of anxious flesh . . . At last she remembered a health-food restaurant Bobbie had mentioned several times, and after a long search through the yellow pages of the phone book found it listed on a side street nearby.

The place was tiny and clinical-looking, with charts pinned to the walls and a long case filled with mysterious mud-colored foods in plastic cartons; evidently it served as both restaurant and delicatessen. The girl behind the counter was about Ann's age, with a serene olive-skinned face and thick braids looped up

behind her ears. She said, "May I help you?" in a voice so mild
and gently accented that Ann abandoned her concocted story
and said simply, "Yes. I was a friend of the girl who was killed in
the subway station, down in the Village. I think she used to come
in here quite often."

"Yes. Bobbie. It was a terrible thing," the girl said softly.

"Then—do you mind my asking you something? Did she ever
use the telephone here?"

The girl turned her head; Ann followed her glance. The telephone was on the wall, next to a shelf stacked with cereals and
special grains and flours. Hardly the place one would choose to
arrange an abortion, Ann thought, and began to laugh wildly
inside.

"Well, of course she may have," the girl said wonderingly, looking back at Ann. "I don't remember her using it as a special thing.
You see it is not a very private one, if that is what you—"

"Yes. I'm sorry, I can't explain. There's just one other thing.
Did she seem—depressed or frightened to you, any of the last
times she was here?"

The girl shook her head, smiling a little. "That would be impossible," she said. "Not Bobbie. Angry, yes, sometimes, if she
was kept late at her office or one of the salesmen tried to—how
was it she said?—oh, yes, tried to get cozy with her; but if you
ask me," she said with a twinkle, raising a finger, "Bobbie herself might have invited that, just a little. Oh, yes, Bobbie was just
a little bit flirtatious, I think! But you know, the next minute she
would be laughing and talking of something else. She was here
just, let me see, oh, just two or three days before this dreadful
thing happened, and she was not serious at all. Oh, no! She was
eating seaweed—she never would eat it, you know, only that one
time when I persuaded her, it was a joke we had—and making
these faces, and everybody was laughing . . ." Her eyes filled
with tears; she looked away. "What is the world coming to? I
ask myself. To be struck down like that . . . Still, we must keep
our spirits up," she said, nodding at Ann. "We must have faith."

"Yes," Ann said. "Thank you very much."

The clear weather lasted for several days and then progressed
by stages to a withering desert heat, each day like an overexposed

photograph of the one before, paler and more light-struck. Ann's stepmother Marge came into town for a week's shopping, hurrying energetically over the blazing pavements in her elegant city shoes, collecting clothes and linens at the August sales. Marge in the country was apt to look a little plump and careless, her springy brown hair always on end; the city had the effect of simplifying and stylizing her, emphasizing the jaunty set of her head and the startling blue light of her eyes. The jaded glances of city-dwellers rested on her in wonder and faint hostility.

On Saturday afternoon she persuaded Ann to join her in a tour of Saks and Bonwit's, where Ann bought a pair of gloves and some stockings on sale while Marge tried on expensive blouses and silk raincoats. Afterward they settled down in the cool gentility of the Palm Court at the Plaza for iced tea and a talk.

"I love this place," Marge said, looking comfortably around as she took off her gloves. "It always makes me feel so deliciously *fin de siècle*, and quite homesick for San Francisco. Please, Ann, don't let me eat any sandwiches. I've never understood why the English aren't all enormously fat, what with having tea every day. Maybe because the rest of their meals are inedible."

Marge loved to eat, and joked that she had lost her figure for good on the day she met Guy Claremont in San Francisco, where he was doing a restaurant article for *Esquire*; behind the joke, Ann knew, was her sadness that the marriage had produced no children, only a miscarriage in the first year which Marge never spoke of. She must be in her mid-forties by now, though you'd never know it, Ann thought, and leaned her elbows on the cool marble table top while Marge gave their order to a waiter.

Marge turned back to her with a frown of mock severity and said, "You know, you really are impossible, Ann. A pair of gloves indeed! I bet it's been six months since you bought a dress. You'll wait till an old one falls apart, I suppose, and then go and buy another Ann Fogarty."

"Well, they fit me and I'm used to them," Ann said mildly. "And they never fall apart."

"Some day I'm going to buy you something black and slinky and terribly expensive, whether you like it or not. Now how's that for a stepmotherly remark?"

"I don't go to black and slinky places," Ann objected. "Not if I can help it, anyway."

"Oh, well. I guess I should be glad you haven't joined the leotard set, at any rate. Though some eye make-up wouldn't be a bad idea on you, if you could grit your teeth long enough to give it a try." She studied Ann's face and laughed. "All right, I know it's hopeless. You have your own style, sweetie, and it's beautiful, so don't pay any attention to me. The only thing that puzzles me is—what do you do with your money? You don't spend it on clothes, your rent can't be much, you haven't taken a trip in ages or bought a car—"

"I'm saving it," Ann said, peeling the paper cover from her straw.

"But what for, darling, if you don't mind my asking? With the income from the trust you have enough money to travel whenever you want, you know—enough to spend a year just basking on a Greek island or wherever, if you count your nickels and dimes."

"I know. But I'm trying to live just on my salary—and anyway I don't want to go anywhere right now . . . Actually, I've been thinking what I'd really like to do is start buying some pictures, in a small way—not for a serious collection, just things I'd like to hang in my own house some day. I've shopped around a little in the Village, but it takes time and so far I haven't bought anything." She stirred her tea, listening to the pleasant clink of the ice cubes.

Marge lit a cigarette. "Good idea. And a good thing to do now, before you do have your own home and family and have to buy boring things like refrigerators and washing machines and garden furniture."

"That's what I thought."

"Ann—" Marge hesitated. "This is undoubtedly a silly question, and one I shouldn't ask; but—well, I know I must seem rather frivolous to you sometimes in money matters. To tell the truth I don't even know myself where half the stuff goes. Your father is terribly generous with me, and I admit I love it." Her sturdy brown hand, short-nailed but immaculately manicured, played with a silver cigarette lighter and then pushed it aside impatiently. "The point is, most of it *is* your mother's money, and

I can't help feeling that it really belongs to you. I wouldn't blame you if you sometimes resented seeing it spent on things that you consider stupid or trivial."

Ann stared at her stepmother in surprise and embarrassment. "For heaven's sake, Marge!"

Marge shrugged. "Well, it suddenly occurred to me when we were in Saks, after I'd bought that ridiculous blouse at that ridiculous price—something I'll probably wear three or four times a year and end up by giving away . . . I had the feeling you might well be thinking about starving Hungarians or crippled children or whatever, and of course you'd be right. I ought to send the stuff right back where it came from."

She looked so glumly at her pile of purchases that Ann couldn't help laughing. "Oh, Marge—you were the one who was thinking about the Hungarians, not me! You're just having an attack of conscience, and I don't think it has anything to do with me at all; I'm just an excuse." When Marge didn't answer, Ann said earnestly, "Look, Marge, except for my trust fund, Mother's money went to Daddy with no strings attached. Her own life wasn't exactly ascetic, you know; she would have been the last person to criticize a love of luxury. I admit my own tastes are different, but the money has nothing to do with me, and I've certainly never worried about what you spent or how you spent it, except to approve of the amount you *do* give away—much more than Dad ever would on his own, whatever you say."

"Oh, it's just that he's so erratic about money," Marge said defensively. "You know—three hundred dollars for some musicians' fund one week and a dollar for the Heart Association the next. Oh, hell," she said, "I wish I was even sure I believed in private property! Do you want another pastry, darling?"

They laughed. Marge blew cigarette smoke at the ceiling, and said with a sigh, "Oh, dear, I am such an ass at times. I apologize for embarrassing you by talking about money, even though it is a fascinating subject in its way, at least for those who weren't born with it. I guess I'll have to content myself with giving you an enormous wedding present one of these days. And of course an absolutely fabulous wedding."

"Don't worry about it," Ann said, smiling.

Marge put out her cigarette and sat back in her chair, crossing her tanned legs under the crisp silk of her skirt. "Maybe I *should* worry," she said. "You never even mention a man these days. What happened to that Yale advertising genius, or whatever he was?"

"Oh, Marge—that was two years ago, and it never did amount to anything."

"And Carlo?"

"A good friend, as always."

Marge smiled into Ann's eyes. "All right then, *you* tell *me*. Doctor, lawyer, merchant, thief? Soldier, sailor—"

"He's a doctor, as a matter of fact. Does it show that much?"

"Well, something shows, at any rate," Marge said, observing Ann's blush. "Have you known him long?"

"No. A month or so."

"So it's not a question of how long, but how well?"

Behind them the string trio struck an introductory chord and began to play a languid waltz. The music stirred the room like a soft wind; even the waiters seemed to sway lightly under its influence, and conversations became at once more formal and more leisurely.

Marge said, "I don't want to pry, Ann dear. I realize that we—your father and I, the kind of life we lead, to say nothing of the Palm Court on a Saturday afternoon"—she waved her hand in a light, ironic gesture—"must seem terribly detached from the life you've made for yourself these last years. I was a working girl myself for a good long time, as you know. Not that that explains at all what I mean—but I do know how *different* things can be; how different you must feel yourself to be from me at this point in our lives." She looked down at the table. "Also, you've had the business about Bobbie, as if dealing with your own life weren't enough . . . Well, anyway, I'm *not* asking about your man because I feel you've rejected me or because I'm trying to close a gap that's entirely natural and inevitable. No, it's really the gap itself"—she gave Ann a smile—"that made me think you might like to talk a little about him."

"Dear Marge," Ann said.

"Dear Marge *does* confess to a little wholesome curiosity, however. For instance, what's he like, and are you in love with him?"

Ann laughed, but hesitated a moment before she said, "I don't really know, to tell the truth. "We've spent—well, quite a lot of time together, and yet he's still a stranger to me in many ways. I never seem to be able to predict his reactions, or . . . well, it's hard to explain."

"And that intrigues you," Marge said.

"Yes, I guess it does. But it bothers me, too. You know me—I like to know where I stand with people, more or less."

"More or less. But curiosity!" Marge looked thoughtfully at her stepdaughter. "There are marriages of curiosity, you know. In fact, it seems to me most people get married either because they already feel like soulmates and marriage is simply the natural, *comfortable* thing to do—you know—or because the opposite is the case: they don't know each other, and the only way to satisfy the passionate curiosity they feel is to live together and see what happens . . . Of course there's always Love," she said with a chuckle, "but somehow I can't help thinking of love as a separate force—a source of energy and momentum, *sine qua non*, to be sure, but still somehow exterior. *If* you know what I mean . . . Good grief, listen to me sounding philosophical before I've even had a cocktail. Your father would have a fit."

"Marge," Ann said abruptly, "could I bring Nick in to meet you sometime soon?"

"Of course, any time you like. I'm going back out to the country tomorrow night, but I'll be back in town again for a longer stay in a week or so. In the meantime, maybe your father—"

"No," Ann said. "I'd like him to meet you and Dad together." She stared at a solitary woman a few tables away who was sipping a daiquiri and doing a crossword puzzle with a gold pencil. "We went to a party in the Village a few nights ago, some people I met through Carlo. It was all wrong. Nick almost had a fight with a man who made some reference to socialized medicine—just mentioning it in passing, you know, and taking for granted that everybody there was a good liberal or at least had an open mind on the subject. Nick got furious. I had no idea how conservative he is in some ways. Anyway—well, I realized how isolated we'd been together, and how little he knew about my background and—oh, atmosphere, I guess you'd call it. Yet I feel he understands me completely in other ways."

"Has Carlo met him?" Marge asked matter-of-factly.

"No. I don't think they'd like each other."

There was a pause. Marge said, looking at her watch, "Well, sweetie, I hate to run, but I've got dinner guests this evening, and not an hors d'oeuvre ready. Friends of Helen Carmichael."

Ann said, "How is Mrs. Carmichael? I meant to ask before."

Marge shrugged. "Still in the hospital, poor thing, and I guess it'll be months before she can get around without crutches or a cane or something. But at least it means she's on the wagon. In fact, one reason I've invited this couple tonight is that the woman's A.A. and thinks she might be able to help Helen at long last—be waiting for her outside the hospital when she gets out with a thermos of black coffee, or whatever it is they do. Anyway, it's worth a try."

"Then she *was* drunk that day you had the accident."

"I suppose she was. With Helen it's hard to tell sometimes."

Ann said, "And of course since alcoholism is a disease, we can't hold her responsible for her actions, can we?"

Puzzled by her tone, Marge said, "Why, no, I don't think we can. Not morally, anyway." The waiter returned with the change. She reached for her gloves, but hesitated when Ann made no move to rise, and asked, "What's the matter, darling?"

Ann shook her head. "I don't know. I guess I'm just feeling a bit—confused about a lot of things these days."

"It won't last," Marge said lightly. "You're not the sort of person who can stay confused very long."

"Yes. Well, maybe that's one of my troubles."

Marge sat back in her chair and looked at her searchingly. "Ann, what's bothering you?"

"I can't explain it all, Marge—not now . . . But it has something to do with—well, with trying to find something simple and definite and fixed, in a world where maybe nothing *ought* to be simple and definite, so that it's wrong, or an evasion at least, even to want such a thing. Oh, I know I'm not saying it properly, but—"

" 'Ah, what a dusty answer gets the soul, when hot for certainties in this our life!' " Marge quoted. "Is that what you're afraid of? I don't know, Ann," she said, looking down at the table, smoothing her gloves. "It has seemed to me sometimes that you tended to be less—flexible than you might be; that some day you might break when you ought to bend. But most of us do far too much bending as it is—I, for one—and God knows we need people like you to give us some sense of direction . . . to fight our battles for us, I suppose. The only thing is—don't judge too much, too quickly, Ann. You can demand whatever you want of yourself, but remember that other people . . . oh, God," she said, looking across the room, "there's Sally Frost, of all the people I don't want to run into, but what a stunning dress . . . Anyway, darling, all I want to say is—be sure you don't start seeing things simply, in nice neat black-and-white, just because you want them that way. On the other hand, *don't*—please—get all bogged down in self-analysis just because it happens to be part of the atmosphere these days—you of all people."

"You mean it's not my style."

"No," Marge said firmly. "It is not. Now come on, sweetie, give me a hand with these things and let's find a cab while we still can. I really must fly."

Ann followed her stepmother out into the terrible shimmer of the street. Standing at the curb in the hot wind of the traffic that hurtled past so fiercely and imperviously, she was assailed again, as she had been on the day of Marge's accident, by a sense of the terrible vulnerability of human flesh. Rock, paper, scissors—she thought of the game of her childhood: the rock wrapped by paper, but the paper falling away under the bright blade of the scissors, the scissors smashed by rock . . . On the battlefield the naked soldier advanced, bending his helmeted head beneath the mortal rain of steel and rock, forced to acknowledge beyond doubt or argument that the only security possible for the fragile, complex structure of his body—of his life—lay in the wielding of more metal, more rock.

The telephone rang twice on that hot Saturday evening. A friend from the office wanted the name of a Village restaurant. A drunk with a wrong number began telling her a long story about the treachery of a girl named Carol. "Just hang on a minute, will you, I got to get some more change," the voice was saying as Ann put down the receiver. "You sound like a sweet kid, I really mean it, you wouldn't hold a few drinks against a guy, not like that little bitch Carol—"

She opened a can of tuna fish and made herself a salad and sat eating it at the table, listening to the Saturday night sounds beginning in the street outside: voices unsteady with laughter, the slam of car doors, a distant beat of jazz beneath the sweet voluptuous slither of a tenor sax . . . At last she drew the curtains and put on a short cotton nightgown because it was the coolest thing she could think of to wear and began furiously scrubbing the bathroom floor, scouring the chipped tiles until her hands were gritty with soap powder and the sweat was streaming down her neck and the backs of her legs.

You were right, Marge, she thought, confronting her own pale image in the steamy mirror above the basin as she wrung out the sponge for the last time. I always expected it to be simple. I thought that was how you recognized love when it came. I never knew you could love someone who withheld so much of himself, even in the act of love itself. All this time I have been waiting—yes, not hiding but waiting—for the man to whom passion might be a key, a way of knowing: a man who did not already stand revealed in the ordinary light of sociability, conversation, the conventions of the date, the evening out . . . But there can be doors within doors; a single key is not enough.

She stripped off the gown and got into the shower and stood soaping herself, watching the water sluice off her arms and breasts, shining firm and beautiful in the greenish light of the shower curtain. Yes, she thought, I know that my body is beautiful, though he has not told me so, if only because he would not touch one that wasn't. He would be surprised if anyone accused him of arrogance in this; taking his own physical superiority for granted, he assumes as a matter of course that it must be matched in his women—leaving the others, the lesser animals with their blotched skins and clumsy limbs, to seek out partners among their own kind.

Well, she thought, and am I any different in this? Willing enough to please a boy, a man, to give him sympathy and liking, to enjoy his company in turn, but shrinking inwardly from the goodnight kiss for no more reason than a pocked cheek or a damp hand, never able to overcome this terrible fastidiousness of the flesh. Yet at the same time unable to yield to flesh alone without the attractions of personality and intellect: the handsome dull-eyed athletes I dated for a while at college, for whom I was never submissive enough anyway, incapable of sustaining the flirtation their vanity demanded. Whereas Nick—yes, Nick, on whose face I could read in an instant some knowledge of the rites of love (oh, I was waiting for that, too), a skill mastered, however incidentally, along with so many others—Nick—

Ann's mind made a sudden picture; she had to clench her teeth against an outcry of pain, a reflexive movement of her whole body, as though she had touched a hot stove. So this is jealousy, she thought in surprise and humiliation: this sense of physical outrage, scalding vision of his body lying so against another's, his long flat-muscled arm outflung across another's flesh in the aftermath of love . . . But in the past, surely in the past! she told herself, closing her eyes beneath the cool rain of the shower. Not tonight, when I am here waiting, when I know that he loves me, whether he says so or not, whether he comes or not; that in some way I do not understand, he loves me in spite of himself.

SEVEN

The Sunday morning streets of the Village were hazy and quiet, almost deserted except for people going out early to get their newspapers, wearing rain-coats over their rolled-up pajamas and yawning painfully on street corners. Ann lingered by the newsstand on Sixth Avenue, reluctant to go back to the apartment; ordinarily, when it was this early, she bought a carton of coffee and went over to Washington Square to read the paper on a bench under the trees and later watch the Sunday folksingers gather around the fountain with their guitars and mandolins and gutbuckets and harmonicas, while their friends stood around looking hung-over and restless and small boys cut in and out of the throng in self-absorbed games of tag and follow-the-leader.

But Nick might call. Ann walked slowly back to Christopher Street. The first-floor tenant, a paunchy man wearing a plaid shirt over his pajama bottoms, was methodically stacking beer cans in the hall outside his open door, through which Ann had a glimpse of a wall almost completely covered with old yellow maps; he nodded politely at Ann as she went past him to the stairs. Either he gives very quiet parties, she thought, or he drinks an awful lot of beer over his typewriter. She paused at the land-ing to look down into the small courtyard, where a woman lay reading on an aluminum deck chair and a baby in plastic pants crawled around on the patchy grass.

Her little living room was still cool and full of the peaceful light of the morning. Ann warmed some coffee and settled down by the window to read the paper, conscientiously plowing through the News of the Week in Review and giving herself the current events test (her score was only Fair this week) before she went on to the theater and book sections. On one of the society pages she saw the engagement announcement of a Friends School class-mate she hadn't seen in years but who would probably invite her to the wedding, which was bound to be a big one with a reception at the Cosmopolitan Club. She cut out the announce-ment and addressed an envelope to a friend in Denver and wrote an accompanying note asking for news of the friend's two children and new house, adding that this year she really did think she might get out to Aspen for some skiing after Christmas. She put the envelope, neatly stamped, against the copper bowl on the mantel where she would not forget it, and tried to think what other letters she ought to write. So few of her old friends seemed to be able to manage more than two or three letters a year now, occupied as they were with husbands and babies. It was this last year that had made the difference, Ann thought, the third year out of college. Suddenly the ranks had thinned, and the girls with whom she had occasionally lunched and bought theater tickets lived now in Westchester or Connecticut, or spent their time at Macy's and Bloomingdale's choosing fab-rics for their new apartments on the East Side.

She opened the door of the closet and stood trying to think of some small chore that needed doing. After a moment, almost ab-sently, she began again the search she had made so many times of Bobbie's clothing, slipping her hands into the empty pockets of coats and dresses that were already beginning to smell a little musty and stale. I'll get rid of them soon, she told herself, I might as well. The Salvation Army or something. I suppose beneficiaries of the Salvation Army, even the children, are used to wearing the clothes of the dead . . . But there's still a chance I might have missed something—a number, a name—

Probing the pocket of an old coat, her fingers brushed against a crumpled bit of paper and then lost it again—a hole in the

lining, she thought, looking around for her scissors. Quickly she
cut the thread of the hem and pulled it until the lining came
free. A penny rolled onto the floor and then the stub of a pencil
and finally the tiny ball of paper, which skittered under the
couch so that she had to get down on her hands and knees to
retrieve it. She smoothed it out with tense fingers. "Martin R.
Tolliver for State Senator" said inch-high black letters above a
smudged photograph of a bespectacled man wearing a cautious
smile. "Progress in the Public Interest! An End to Waste in
Government! Albany Needs This Man, and So Do You!"

Ann stood up slowly and dropped the pencil, the penny and
the leaflet into the wastebasket by the door. Then she took her
sewing basket from its place on the closet shelf and sat down to
repair the lining of the coat, working swiftly and mechanically.

"Anybody home?" said Nick's voice. Ann started violently,
pricking her finger, and turned to see him leaning against the
jamb of the kitchen door behind her, blond and smiling, his blue
shirt open at the throat, his light jacket hooked over one thumb.
"I didn't mean to scare you," he said.

Ann's heart still pounded absurdly in her throat. She said, "De-
layed reaction. I mean, I knew it was you, but my nervous system
couldn't seem to catch up with my mind."

"Well, I should have called first, but I thought I'd take a chance
on finding you home." He sat down beside her on the couch,
stretching out his legs, and watched as she stuck the needle into
the lining and pushed the coat aside. "I must admit the last
thing I expected to find you doing on a day like this was sewing
—and on a coat, of all unseasonable things."

"It's Bobbie's coat," Ann said, a little defiantly. "I *have* been
looking through linings, just as you predicted. I thought I'd found
something—but it turned out not to be anything after all."

"In that case, may I ask why you feel it necessary to sew it up
again?" Nick said lightly; but she saw that at the mention of Bobbie his face had lost its ease and humor.

She said, "I don't know. I just didn't think I ought to leave it
that way. I mean, it's a perfectly good coat. Somebody ought to
be able to use it."

After a moment he leaned down to kiss her on the cheek, and

said, "I really meant to call you last night, but I got tied up at the hospital for a couple of hours unexpectedly."

"Some kind of emergency?"

"More or less, from my point of view. I was arranging to get hold of some autopsy material from pathology. A patient with multiple sclerosis was shot to death on the West Side. Some sort of gang fight, and she got in somebody's way, I guess. Anyway, it was prime stuff—she died instantly, no shock to complicate the picture. So many of these people die from falls or burns, or get knocked down by cars," he explained.

"Oh."

"Until we can get enough good data from pathology on enough cases, we can only go on theorizing. I'll say this for the great Beddoes—he's got that pathology department terrorized to the point of cooperation." Nick gave a short laugh. "If he can find some sucker to take care of the routine clinical stuff for him, so much the better. Why should I complain if a genius wants to stand on my shoulders?"

Ann said uncertainly, "But you must be learning a lot from him. I mean, if he's as good as you say he is—"

"Oh, sure, sure. Hell, it's the system. The only trouble is, I happen to be a genius too," he said matter-of-factly.

"It's quite an honor to get a fellowship before you've had a year of residency, isn't it?" Ann said. "Especially under someone like Dr. Beddoes. I mentioned you to a doctor friend of my father's, and he was quite impressed."

Nick said quickly, "Who was that?"

"Dr. Leighton, Henry Leighton, I think it is. He's a pediatrician."

He nodded, losing interest. "Oh, as far as the fellowship goes, it was just a combination of circumstances."

Ann waited. "Meaning . . . ?"

He gave a short laugh. "Meaning—meaning I happened to be in the right place at the right time. The guy they were giving it to couldn't take it at the last minute. I was number two on the list."

"Should you have been number one?"

He looked at her. "Yes. Except for the year of residency, which the other guy had. Even then. And Beddoes knew it," he said harshly. "In spite of the way he stalled around till the last possible minute, hoping I'd fall over a cliff or something—"

"But why?" Ann said. "I mean, if you were the most qualified candidate, why shouldn't he have wanted to have you work with him?"

"Dislike. Or personal antipathy, to give it a more dignified name. Not helped by my calling his bluff a couple of times as a lowly intern—seeing a few things he'd missed, questioning a diagnosis here and there . . . It just isn't done, my dear. Not with the great Dr. Beddoes."

"Still, you got the fellowship."

"Yes, I got the fellowship. Never let it be said that the great Dr. Beddoes ever let himself be influenced by anything remotely resembling a personal consideration . . . Oh, I'm the fair-haired boy, all right. You might as well know it, because eventually you'll run into some colleague or ex-classmate of mine who hates my guts. I've been lucky some of the time, and smart most of the time, and I haven't been above polishing the old apple when I thought it would do some good."

He gazed at Ann with a faint smile, expecting some comment. But she said thoughtfully, "You know, it seems funny that I've never even seen your apartment, the place where you live, or met any of your friends—except the people at that first party, I mean."

Nick shrugged. "Well, that was about it, as far as friends go. Guys to talk shop with, have a beer with. I don't do much fraternizing. In fact, I've spent more time away from the hospital this summer than I ever have before; or could, for that matter, when I was interning."

She said, "I guess men don't keep in touch with each other as —compulsively as girls do. They're probably right. So many of my friends are married and starting families, and—oh, I don't know, no matter how *intelligently* interested in their children they are, if you know what I mean, it's still boring to have to hear about them." Nick smiled. "Even if they're not married. My college roommate is working for IBM out in California. She comes East a couple of times a year and we have a good time talking for the first few hours—but we don't share the same life any more, and it all seems kind of pointless and forced. You know, like these couples that meet on their honeymoon and go on seeing each other once a year just because they thought it was a great idea way back when over a bottle of champagne."

Nick said, "Don't tell me you haven't got a Best Friend! I thought that went along with the hockey and the Shetland sweaters and Ivy Day, or whatever it is at Wellesley."

"Naturally," Ann said. "But *my* best friend married a man who thinks the United Nations is a Communist-front organization and collects antique cars. She spends her weekends polishing hubcaps or something. Twice a year they drive hundreds of miles to an antique-car rally—twenty-five miles an hour in veils and goggles and God knows what." She giggled. "They really are a pair of complete asses."

Nick pulled her across his knees and kissed her, mussing her hair. "Laugh some more," he said. "I like to see you looking disheveled and grubby on a Sunday morning."

"Grubby!"

"Well, look at those shorts you've got on. Which war were you in, anyway?"

"Putney. Softball games in the mud," Ann said, laughing against his shirt front. "It gets terribly muddy there in the spring."

"And you've never bought another pair since."

"Oh, yes! You should have seen me at college. A pair of Bermudas for every occasion. Very soignée."

"I'll bet. Hey, listen—"

"Yes?"

"I said *listen*. Why don't we go out for lunch somewhere?"

"Now?"

"Well, not quite now. I meant afterward."

"All right," Ann said with a sigh. "Afterward."

But strangely their love-making had at first a strained abruptness that left her damp and unsatisfied, oppressed by a vague sense of nightmare. Oh, God, what is happening to me? she thought, pushing the heavy hair from her forehead. Lying sprawled here like a—a hussy, on a beautiful Sunday morning when other people are going to church or taking a walk or listening to Brahms . . . But Nick's hands were beginning their slow caresses once more, and this time an unexpected wave of ecstasy broke over her and swept her out of reach of his hands and voice, to lie stranded and slack upon the rumpled sheets under the square yellow eye of the window, whose shade Nick had remembered to draw.

Later, when they had showered and dressed and Nick had put on the tie he had kept neatly folded in his coat pocket, they walked through the quiet Sunday streets to the Fifth Avenue Hotel and sat down in the sun at one of the outside tables. It was still early; only a few of the other tables were occupied. A sleepy-looking waiter served their drinks and then retired to the shade of the awning. Above them the sky blazed blue and clean, free of weekday smog.

"You don't even notice the soot after the second martini," Nick said, stretching his legs.

Ann sighed. "Let's stay here all afternoon and get pleasantly drunk, shall we? I've never really *been* drunk except once at a Williams house party, but then I didn't even feel high; I just blanked out for a half-hour. I was terribly upset about it for months afterward—the lost half-hour of my life. And everybody acted so peculiar about it, I didn't know what on earth I might have done or said. But they were just teasing me. I guess."

"You guess."

"Please don't get me started on it again!" Ann said. "It still bothers me, to tell the truth. I never went out again with the boy who was my date that weekend, I was so afraid I'd find out I'd been to bed with him or done a strip tease or something—which was certainly unlikely, since when I came to I was just sitting at the bar drinking beer like everybody else. Oh, dear," she said, "it's awful to be such a prude."

"Oh, I don't know. Is there anything more fascinating than a beautiful prude, when all is said and done?"

"Well, when *all* is said and done—"

Nick smiled. "Who would have thought you'd take to a life of sin so enthusiastically?"

She smiled back, and the lazy air between them sharpened with desire. An elderly gentleman passing along the sidewalk on the other side of the hedge glanced at them and tipped his hat unexpectedly at Ann, startling her into conversation.

"Well," she said, settling back in her chair, "I really think we ought to talk about something, don't you? School integration, or admitting Red China to the UN—"

"Or our murder," Nick said casually. "I did my homework this morning on my way to your place—that was another thing that held me up."

"Oh," Ann said. "You did?"

No, she wanted to say, not now, not here! Bobbie herself would never have intruded at such a time and place, she thought resentfully—Bobbie, of all people. Couldn't he understand that? But of course; she thought suddenly, meeting his calm gaze. He understands it perfectly well; he is deliberately juxtaposing—what? himself and Bobbie?—in order to make me see how grotesque it all is, in order to make me choose . . . No, she told herself, that doesn't make sense. He agreed to help me, didn't he?

He said, "Maybe you'd just as soon forget the whole thing."

"No," she said sharply. "I don't want to forget it. Do you?"

"Just thought I'd ask," he said easily.

"I'm sorry. You're right—there are times when I'd like to forget it. I mean," she said with a helpless laugh, "here we are just having a drink and talking like anyone else, and suddenly you bring up the subject of murder—and nothing seems quite normal or real any more . . . as though we'd cut ourselves off from the rest of the human race or something." Her voice trailed off; she watched a boy and girl argue laughingly about which table to take, leaning away from their joined hands like figures in a dance, and felt that she was on the verge of tears.

Nick said in a harsh voice that drew her eyes back to his face, "What is normal, Ann? What is real? Isn't each moment we spend without the awareness of death unreal? We are dying, both of us, as we sit here; each minute brings us closer to the minute of our own deaths. Until we acknowledge that fact our lives are a lie."

They stared at each other; the waiter, setting another drink in front of them, looked at their faces and withdrew hurriedly, as though he too saw something to be shunned. Nick looked down at his glass and remarked in a light, pleasant voice that held no vestige, no memory of the thing he had just said, "Well, this martini looks real enough, and I suppose you're right. This isn't an appropriate moment for playing detective."

Ann whispered, "Is that really what you believe? But I couldn't live that way, no one could. The thought of my own death is so terrifying that it paralyzes me. If I had to think about it often, I would just—dissolve. The blackness . . . just the thought is like a black pit, and I can feel myself slipping on the edge of it, and falling down and down into the blackness, and nothing to stop me ever, no way to get back . . ." Her fingers clenched the edge of the table; with a violent effort she fought her way up again to the bright surface of the day, to the familiar assertive glitter of glass and metal in the sunlight, the murmur of conversation and the slam of a cab door at the curb. Nick's blue eyes watched her curiously and almost regretfully as he said, "Take it easy, sweetheart. I was only stating a well-known biological fact, after all."

Ann pushed her glass aside with a trembling hand and said, "I guess I shouldn't drink martinis in the middle of the day. Can we order a sandwich, please? And I would like to hear about your phone-call research."

After the waiter had come and gone once more, Nick said, "Well, there isn't really much to report. The cashier at the hamburger place remembered her all right, but just that she used to come in for a snack once in a while. Oh, yes, and she used to flirt with the chef, a big black guy."

"Yes, I remember."

"The people at the other places were pretty vague. Claimed she was a faithful customer and all that, but it was obvious they didn't really remember her."

Something in his voice, or perhaps just the way he was pointedly meeting her eyes, convinced Ann suddenly that he was lying—that he had not been to any of the other places, or at least no more than one or two, that he had certainly not made the methodical check he had suggested to her. Oddly, she felt no anger, not even surprise. Why should I blame him? she thought, relaxing in her chair, letting her body go comfortable and nerveless in the sunshine. I suspected all along that this particular idea was just a concoction of his, nothing he took seriously—his way of making me feel better, and at the same time of showing me how hopeless the whole thing really is.

She said lightly, "Then that's that, I suppose. I don't really see that it proves much of anything."

"No, it's something," Nick said. "We've partially eliminated the possibilities of one part of one hypothesis, to be exact. That's standard scientific procedure, uninspiring as it may sound."

"But we have no way of testing it any further. Have we?" When he shrugged, Ann said, "Oh, well. It wasn't a theory I really believed in, anyway."

He looked at her sharply and seemed about to say something when the waiter arrived with their sandwiches. The tables had filled up since their arrival; looking around at the bare-armed women and the men in their light summer jackets drinking gin and tonic or cloudy rum cocktails, Ann thought idly that they might all have been sitting on the sundeck of a country club or resort hotel, their eyes shaded against the leaping glitter of the sea instead of the flash of glass and metal. Across the street a doorman stood like an attentive lifeguard beneath his scalloped green awning, one hand on his silver whistle.

Nick stirred cream into his iced coffee and said, "To return to the subject at hand—what about blackmail? I've been thinking about that as a fairly likely possibility."

"Blackmail," Ann repeated, swallowing a mouthful of chicken sandwich and stifling a hysterical desire to laugh. She said, "You mean something other than the pregnancy business?"

"Yes. Some kind of knowledge she was using against somebody."

"Using? You mean for money?"

"Money, clothes, a better job—it could have been something quite trivial, as far as the payment went; she might not even have thought of what she was doing as blackmail. You scratch my back, I'll scratch yours—that kind of thing."

Ann nodded, feeling an unwilling surge of interest. "It's a possibility, I guess. Something Bobbie might have thought of as a sort of joke, but that was serious to the other person. Like—" She thought a moment. "Well, like kidding one of the buyers about his expense account. Not that people commit murder over an expense account—and anyway, that would be common knowledge . . . but, oh, I don't know, saying something like, 'I'm going to tell that nice wife of yours about the gorgeous redhead I saw you having lunch with the other day.' If the man's whole future depended on his wife's not knowing about the redhead—"

"His wife was an heiress, and would divorce him if she found out that he had been unfaithful—"

"And he adored his children and would do anything to keep from losing them. And his boss was a strict Catholic who never kept a divorced man on his staff—"

"And in the first place the redhead was the boss's wife," Nick finished, and they both laughed.

"I suppose it's hopeless, in a way," Ann said, playing with the thin paper cover of her straw, "but I have a feeling it's the right idea. I mean, it's the kind of situation I can imagine Bobbie's getting into all too easily—making some kind of careless remark without noticing the effect it had, and then repeating it in a teasing way whenever she saw the person, just as a stock joke. Yes," she said, "that's just the kind of thing Bobbie used to do. She wasn't particularly witty, but she had a teasing way of saying things that made you wonder what she was really thinking underneath—when all the time it was just a mannerism, a trick she'd learned."

"A pretty-girl trick," Nick said. "Makes you think they're more intelligent or sophisticated than they really are. Refined to an art as they grow older—you know, the drawl and the well-timed pause that somebody always fills with a laugh, whether or not they've said anything funny."

Ann smiled at his society-voice imitation and said, "Well, I don't think Bobbie would ever have been that bad, but I know what you mean. Anyway—"

"Yes, anyway. There's the actual blackmail part of it to consider. The payoff." He leaned back, squinting thoughtfully into the sunlight. "What would Bobbie have done if, say, the man embroiled with the redhead—just to stick to one story for the moment—had come to her and said, 'Please lay off,' or words to that effect?"

Ann considered. "She would probably have given him a hard time about it, in a kidding way. She'd say something like 'Aha, a guilty conscience, just as I thought!'—and she'd want to know why it was so important to him. Not that she'd have any intention of causing trouble, just that she'd want her curiosity satisfied."

"And if he told her why?"

"Well, if it was something really serious, I think she'd have been embarrassed; she wouldn't even have wanted to hear all of it. She'd apologize and tell him that of course she wouldn't say anything more, and that would be that as far as she was concerned."

Nick said, "Yes. And suppose he didn't believe her? Suppose he wasn't sure he could trust her? From what you say about her, he might have had good reason to worry that she would say something to the wrong person some day, or even tell the whole story to someone just for the hell of it, without thinking." He looked at Ann; she nodded, thinking: How quick his instinct is, how accurate. No wonder he bothers so little about other people when he finds them so easy to diagnose and classify—even people he has not known. "All right," he went on, "let's say some time goes by; the guy can't stop stewing about the thing. Finally he approaches her with an offer of some kind—say a discount at his store, if he's a buyer, something fairly innocent that could be construed as just a favor between friends . . ."

Ann said promptly, "Bobbie would have been completely taken aback. And furious, when she realized what he was getting at—not just because he wouldn't trust her, but because she was really very moralistic in some ways, especially about money. Also, there's the fact that I certainly saw no evidence that she was being—paid off in any way. I mean, she didn't suddenly start buying a lot of clothes and jewelry, or taking trips to Mexico or wherever; isn't that the sort of thing the police always look for in suspected blackmail cases?" she added with a faint smile.

"All right. Suppose she wouldn't take anything—that she told the guy his secret was safe with her, and that she didn't want anything more to do with him. Do you think that would reassure him for any length of time?" Ann stared at him; her fingers tightened around the icy cylinder of her glass. He went on in the same dry tone, "Or—given his desperate situation, whatever it was—would he come to the logical conclusion that the only way he could be sure of his safety was to get rid of her, to kill her, and hope that the connection between them would never be uncovered."

"Logical conclusion!" Ann repeated. "That would be a madman's logic, maybe. But for an ordinary person in an ordinary amount of trouble—"

Nick glanced down at the check and drew a bill from his wallet, nodding over his shoulder at the waiter. Almost impatiently he said, "Yes, madman's logic. What's one of the legal definitions of insanity—'irresistible impulse'? Or take the concept of monomania, an overwhelming obsession. Isn't every murderer a madman in that sense? The instinct of preservation overwhelms every other consideration at the moment when he commits his crime; what for most people is an 'ordinary' and healthy instinct becomes an unbearable pressure."

Ann said slowly, "Every murder is an act of self-preservation—is that what you mean?"

"Basically, yes. Even suicide, the murder of self, is a defensive act, a final way of saying no to the world. Isn't that where all conflict comes from? Your primitive sense of self against your sense of everything that is outside, exterior."

Ann said, "But what about the conflicts we feel inside ourselves?"

"Well, what about them? To love or not to love—"

After a moment Ann nodded, but did not return his brilliant, ironic smile. She reached for her purse and said slowly, "I see how it could be—that Bobbie could have been killed in the way she was for the reasons we have said, or something like them. But what about us? What can we do? How on earth do we go about tracing a connection, a relationship, that maybe no one else was even aware of? Oh, I don't know. I guess in a way this whole thing *has* been just a game to me; and now that I feel we're on the right track, I see how hopeless it is."

Nick shrugged, smiling faintly.

"And you knew it all along," Ann said with a flash of anger. "That's the only reason you've gone along with it—because you knew it would come to nothing in the end."

"That's not fair, Ann," he said evenly. "I'm willing to go as far as you want me to." There was a silence. "Anyway," he added, "I disagree with you about its being hopeless. Isn't there someone at Bobbie's office you could talk to—some friend of hers who would know something about her relationships there? And in particular about any teasing or repartee that went on as part of the routine; that's the sort of thing people are apt to remember."

Ann said slowly, "There's one girl, Stephanie something, a colored girl—she was the one who walked Bobbie to the subway that day. She used to take over the switchboard for Bobbie or something; I think they were together a lot at the office. Stephanie Harris, that's it. I've met her a couple of times—very sleek, but intelligent and probably quite observant. Yes, I guess I could talk to Stephanie. But how—I mean, what reason can I give her for asking a lot of odd questions? Oh, I don't know, maybe the thing to do is actually hire a detective, if we could find one who'd listen."

The waiter was eying them restively as strollers paused beyond the hedge, looking for empty tables. Nick rose and said, "Why can't you just tell her the truth and swear her to secrecy, at least within the office? She'd probably find the whole thing rather glamorous, and she'd certainly tell you more than she would any detective. Invite her down for dinner or something, have a nice long sociable chat."

"And avoid the office so that if the murderer *is* on the premises he won't be suspicious? Sorry to sound so melodramatic, but—"

"Why not? But as far as that goes, using a detective to ask questions wouldn't improve your own position much. The murderer would be pretty sure he'd been hired either by you or by Bobbie's parents, and that wouldn't be hard to settle."

"In other words, I'm sticking my neck out anyway."

"Isn't that what you wanted? Such a lovely neck, too," he added, brushing it lightly with his fingers as they turned to go.

The holiday sun burned down. They walked southward toward Washington Square, whose triumphal arch bulked dingily against the sky, casting a short thick shadow in which a barefoot child stood cooling the soles of his feet for a moment before dodging off into the sunshine again. Through the arch drifted a desultory sound of music; somewhere a woman shrieked piercingly, whether in laughter or pain it was impossible to tell.

EIGHT

"Ultra Designs,

Incorporated, good morning."

"Stephanie Harris, please."

"Speaking."

"Oh," Ann said, startled. "Stephanie—this is Ann Claremont. I don't know whether you remember me or not: Bobbie Willis's roommate."

"Yes, of course. How are you, Ann?" Stephanie's voice was cool and unsurprised. "Are you still working at the museum?"

"Yes. Look, Stephanie—I'd like to see you about something. Do you think you could come down to the Village and have dinner with me some night this week?"

"Tomorrow, maybe," Stephanie said after a pause. "I just got back from my vacation, and my mother will give me hell if I'm not home tonight."

"Tomorrow night would be fine," Ann said, and added politely, "Where did you go on your vacation?"

"Chicago. My brother lives there." Stephanie did not elaborate. She said, "You still living in the same apartment?"

"Yes, on Christopher Street. Do you know where it is?"

"I'll find it." She added, "I meant to write you a note or something about Bobbie, but I never did. I came to the service, though."

"I know," Ann said. "I saw you."

"Well, I'll see you tomorrow, around six, okay? I've got to go, the switchboard is going crazy." As Ann hung up she heard Stephanie's voice repeating metallically, "Ultra Designs, Incorporated, good morning."

She sat back at her own neat desk, feeling a little shaken, as though by acting in her own character, no longer anonymously, she had at last committed herself. But did she really expect to learn anything from Stephanie? If it hadn't been for Nick's pressure, would she have ventured in this direction at all? He has taken control, she realized, thinking back to yesterday's conversation, rather as if I were a not too bright patient to be steered gently in the direction of proper hygiene; or perhaps a hypochondriac who can be convinced only by a series of impressive tests that her imagined brain tumor is in fact nothing more than a neurotic headache.

Her boss, Miss Polk, thrust her narrow beaming face through the doorway and said, "*Newsweek* wants more on the Tanguy show, friend, so get busy. They're in quite an arty mood, and we might even get a cover story if the Russians don't drop a bomb this week and nobody discovers a cure for cancer, et cetera. Alvin Dressler will be here at ten-thirty, when I will be conveniently detained in conference, so he's all yours."

"Oh, Ruth! Not Alvin Dressler! All he ever wants to do is stand around talking about how his brother knew Jackson Pollock, and pawing through all the photographs."

"Well, better the photographs than you, sweetie. Just give him a bibliography and get rid of him. There's a woman from Bloomingdale's I want you to see later."

"Bloomingdale's?"

"Windows. Picasso clowns for Christmas, or some damn thing; you figure it out." She whipped off her gilt-framed glasses, grinned at Ann, and went off humming "Yes, We Have No Bananas."

Ann sat staring down at the Tanguy file and thinking about Stephanie and her Chicago vacation. Well, what would a Negro office girl do with her vacation these days, anyway—go picket a Woolworth's or join a sit-in somewhere and get arrested? Not Stephanie, Ann thought; or at least not unless there was a good

chance of getting her picture in the paper. Stephanie worked for
Stephanie, period, and why not? Bobbie and Stephanie. Was it
possible, even remotely possible, that Stephanie . . . ? No, Stephanie had gone home on the other subway, the police must have
checked on that. But violence, racial violence—something as
simple as a black man with rage in his heart against the forbidden white flesh of an unknown girl—

The telephone rang. Ann reached automatically for a pencil;
but it was only her father. He said, "Sorry to break in on you at
work, honey, but Marge made me promise to call you about a
party she's giving a week from Thursday. You and your young
man are invited; and if he can't make it she'll change the date."

"Thanks, Dad," Ann said, smiling. "I'll call and let you know."

"Okay," Guy said absently. "Hey, the damndest thing just happened to me. You know the Manufacturers Trust building on the
corner of Fifth and Forty-third? With all the glass and the pachy-
sandra, or whatever it is? Well, I was just in there cashing a check
a few minutes ago, and a guy robbed the bank. I'm not kidding,
he walked off with ten thousand dollars in his coat pocket. I was
practically standing next to him while he was talking to the teller
—this nice-looking young guy, no hat pulled down over his eyes
or anything like that. I thought he was just passing the time of
day with the teller, or asking who he should talk to about a loan
or something."

"Didn't anyone try to stop him?"

"No. He claimed he had a gun; maybe he did. Anyway, they
said they'd have photographs and they'd catch him sooner or
later, they didn't want any violence. I figure they just didn't want
to mess up their beautiful bank with a lot of blood and gore. But
the stupid guy—why didn't he wear a stocking over his face or
something?"

"Maybe he plans to grow a beard," Ann said.

"Yeah. Or maybe it's one of these hard-luck deals—you know,
his kid needs an operation, never mind what they do to him afterward. Half the people there didn't even know what had happened. Just my luck to see a *tame* bank robbery," Guy said regretfully.

Ann looked at her watch. "Well, I'm glad no one was hurt."

"Sure. The guy had plenty of guts, I'll say that. If I ever saw him again, I'd look the other way, believe me."

"Dad! Would you really?"

"Sure I would. Only he'd probably recognize me, too—he looked straight at me on his way out. Poor guy, he'll probably be having nightmares for weeks about running into me. I mean, unless he expects to be caught anyway. I ought to put an ad in the paper: *Bank robber, relax, I'm with you.*"

"Dad, you're terrible. It's your money, too, you know."

"He's welcome to my share, all ten mills of it. Well, sweetie, I've got to go beat up my agent. I'll call you soon—"

"—and maybe we can get together some day for lunch," Ann finished with a laugh. But she hung up thoughtfully, looking down at the piece of paper on which she had been doodling a jagged Steinberg face with staring eyes. "Recognition?" she wrote beneath it in heavy block letters—and tossed the paper into the wastebasket as her buzzer rang to announce the unwelcome arrival of Alvin Dressler.

Tuesday was humid and dull, with intermittent drops of rain squeezed out of the air by the pressure of a sky clamped like a lid on the city. Nonetheless Stephanie was as cool and impeccable as Ann remembered her. Over sherry Ann explained awkwardly what it was she wanted to know, and Stephanie, as though she had surmised something of the sort, complied with a concise fifteen-minute account of Bobbie's office acquaintanceships, while Ann took dutiful notes in a small loose-leaf notebook. Stephanie's tone managed to be both expressive and impersonal; she might have been a secretary presenting a report to an eccentric employer.

Ann put the notebook aside and said, "You won't mention this to anyone, will you, Stephanie? It might be terribly important."

"Naturally." Stephanie lounged gracefully against the cushions on the couch, her hands clasped around her drawn-up knees. Her smile, a narrow white gleam in her dark face, said: You don't really have to give me dinner, you know, now that you've got what you wanted; but I won't embarrass you by offering to leave.

Ignoring the smile, Ann said slowly, "What do you think, Stephanie? Was Bobbie killed deliberately, or just because she—happened to catch the eye of some maniac?"

Stephanie remained motionless. After a pause she said, "I think she was probably killed on purpose. From what I read, it was a pretty clean job, wasn't it? I know something about knives. I would suspect that whoever stuck that knife into her knew exactly what they were doing. But," she added drily, "I don't think you'll find it was one of her office pals."

"Neither do I, really. I've got another idea. It's a needle in a haystack, but—"

"I don't want to hear about it," Stephanie said flatly. "This is a hell of a big haystack, this town. If I were you, I'd forget your idea, whatever it is. I knew Bobbie; you don't think *she'd* be doing any Sherlock Holmes bit if this had happened to you, do you?"

"No," Ann admitted. "But I'm afraid that doesn't make any difference to me."

The smile glimmered again as Stephanie reached for her glass. "Well, just as long as you understand that. I liked Bobbie, but she was no Joan of Arc, that's for sure. In fact, in her own way she was almost as selfish as I am, which is saying a lot."

"Oh?" Ann extended a small wooden bowl of nuts; Stephanie shook her head. "What are you so selfish about?" she said with a smile.

Stephanie shrugged. "I've got her job, you know."

"Whose? Bobbie's?" Ann said in surprise.

"They put me on it temporarily, and then when they found out how good I was they let me keep it. Not at Bobbie's salary, of course, but pretty near it." Her smooth eyelids closed over a flicker of triumph. She added, "It was the chance I needed."

Ann said as casually as she could, "Oh, well, the law of the jungle and all that," and got up to go to the kitchen.

"Or: it's an ill wind blows nobody good."

Ann turned and looked at the other girl. She's asking me to dislike her, she thought; but why should I? She said, "Look, Stephanie, I'm glad you got the job. I'm not career-minded myself, but I know the importance of getting the breaks when it counts."

"Do you? How is the museum, by the way?"

"Fine," Ann said from the kitchen, ladling cold soup into two earthenware bowls. She carried them out to the table.

Stephanie had risen and was walking slowly around the room, one hand on her hip and her sleek head tilted to one side—a model's pose, except for the cold appraising stare she gave Ann as she said, "Do they take Negroes here, do you know? A place like this would suit me to a T."

"I'm not sure," Ann said, disconcerted. She added quickly, "There aren't any vacancies now, but the downstairs apartment seems to change hands fairly often. I could speak to the landlord; I mean, unless you—"

"By all means," Stephanie said, sitting down across from Ann and picking up her napkin. "Lay it on the line. The indirect approach just wastes everybody's time."

"The only thing is—well, it's pretty expensive for what you get."

"How much?"

"One-twenty a month."

Stephanie crumbled a saltine between her long fingers and said thoughtfully, "I could manage that. Maybe I could even find me a white roommate down here in this advanced part of the world." She looked up at Ann and smiled. "I don't mean you, honey, don't worry. I'm sure you've had it with roommates for a while, and anyway, I don't think we'd hit it off. But—I don't know. I'm still living with my family up in Harlem, and it's a fight, let me tell you. I've been thinking about the Village ever since I got the new job, and it helps to have an in."

"You're welcome to it, then," Ann said, eating her soup.

"A closet," Stephanie said dreamily. "A mirror you can see your face in. Being able to arrive at the office without wondering if you smell of somebody else's BO. It's almost worth a hundred and twenty a month."

Ann looked at the beautiful, smiling, feline face, and said quietly, "I can see that it might be."

Stephanie said, "I could have killed Bobbie, couldn't I?"

"What?"

"I didn't, but I could have. If she'd gotten in my way. Do you see that?" Stephanie reached across the table and grasped Ann's hand in her own hard fingers. "Listen, Ann, there are lots of other people like me. You aren't ever going to understand them, but there's one thing you ought to know: if one of them killed Bobbie, he's not going to let you get in his way, either."

Ann said lightly, "Oh, at the rate I'm progressing, I don't think

I'm exactly a threat to the murderer, whoever and wherever he may be."

Stephanie picked up her soup spoon, her dark gaze on Ann's face. "I hope not, honey. For your sake, I certainly hope not."

After Stephanie had left, Ann sat for a long time by the window studying the notes she had made. Nothing, as Stephanie had said, except for one incidental addition to Ann's already voluminous record of Bobbie's love life—a weekend spent in the Catskills last spring with a buyer from Syracuse. That must have been the weekend Bobbie said she was visiting the college friend and her husband in Rye, Ann thought, with a small retrospective twinge at the deception. The buyer was young, unmarried, attractive, Stephanie said. Bobbie had hoped to see him again.

Ann listened to the hiss of tires outside on the oily street. What had he felt when he heard of Bobbie's death? she wondered. A superstitious horror at the mutilation of her flesh that had once lain against his own in a rented hotel bed? Or disappointment, shock, even grief, as the shutter banged down on a vision of the future, still tentative and unformed but alight with possibility? Or had he, like Nick, merely thought to himself that we all must die?

She turned to a blank page of the notebook. It's a crazy idea, she told herself; and yet— She wrote a date across the top of the page, and paused. The week before Bobbie's death—but if she was on the right track, the thing she was looking for might have happened two weeks before, or six, at any time, in fact . . . Still, she had to begin somewhere; and probability, at least, would favor a date immediately preceding the murder. What was one probability more or less when you were acting on the wildest supposition to begin with?

"Theft," she wrote in her neat rounded script.

"Assault."

"Accidental Death."

"Kidnaping, Disappearance, etc."

She thought for a moment, the gleaming nib of her fountain pen poised above the page. Then she added with a shrug: "Miscellany."

She would go to the public library in the morning.

NINE

Ann arrived at the Gramercy Park apartment for Marge's cocktail party feeling tired from the day's work and unrefreshed by the lukewarm shower she had taken in the late-August heat of her own apartment. Nick was coming straight from the hospital; later they would go out for dinner with Marge and Guy. Helping Marge arrange hors d'oeuvres in the kitchen, Ann was annoyed at her own nervousness. Nick is nothing if not presentable, she told herself irritably, and anyway, what does it really matter to me what anyone else thinks of him? But she felt a thrill of resentment when the Brunettis arrived, calling out from the hall with the ease of old acquaintance. I suppose Marge invited Carlo too, she thought, kissing Aunt Sophie's plump soft cheek. Nothing like a casual evening with all the old family friends on hand to pass judgment on Ann's young man.

She sat down next to Mrs. March, an elegant woman who had no children of her own and who had always made much of Ann, even to offering to take over the arrangements for the debut Ann had declined—Marge hadn't yet appeared on the scene—a favor for which Ann supposed she ought to be grateful. They talked about a play Ann had seen the week before until the Frieburgs' arrival shifted the guests into new groups and Ann found herself hearing all about last June's Wellesley reunion from Maggie

(Armstrong) Ramirez, pregnant and shiny-nosed, who had taught Ann to roller-skate when they were five and seven respectively in their navy reefer coats and berets, and who had made an unlikely marriage to a Brazilian millionaire with four children by a previous marriage. Maggie's conversation centered these days on the comparative virtues of assorted schools and camps, and on the problems of transporting her household from one latitude to another as the seasons changed. "My marvelous maid Lupe absolutely refuses to come to New York with us without her drunken husband," she told Ann with a world-weary sigh. "He spends most of his time in a horrid little bar on Second Avenue and has to be carried home twice a week by these weird Hungarian drinking companions who can't understand a word he says, anyway. Once they arrived in the middle of a dinner party, ambassadors and whatnot, very decorous—my dear, I was *never* so embarrassed—"

Then Nick was in the room, tall and smiling at Marge's elbow. Ann watched her stepmother make the introductions with a slightly flustered formality, and smiled to herself: so he made Marge nervous too, with his good looks and his air of ironic reserve. He waved at Ann across the room, but stood for a while with her father in front of the fireplace, listening calmly to some tale of travel, with its inevitable hard-boiled tag line: "Listen, boy, don't let anybody give you this crap about the high-minded Indian politicians, all this neutralist idealism. Guy I knew was an Oxford buddy of Nehru's, he told me confidentially . . ." Nick said something in response that sent Guy into one of his rocking laughs; he clapped the younger man on the shoulder and went off to mix fresh drinks.

Nick turned and smiled at Ann, so that she lost the thread of whatever mild little Mr. Frieburg was saying and had to apologize. When she looked again, Nick had made his way, with accurate instinct, to Aunt Sophie's side on the couch. Ann saw how her shrewd dark eyes examined Nick's face above her faint habitual smile which did not, Ann thought, necessarily express amusement or even liking, but was a sign of patience, a willingness to wait until you had revealed yourself in some way, by answering inadvertently the questions—whatever they might be—which she would never ask directly. Gradually their conversation became serious, they glanced briefly in Ann's direction without really seeing her—meaning I'm the subject under discussion, Ann thought, but without feeling much concern until she saw that Nick was no longer looking at Aunt Sophie, that his hands were playing restlessly with the heavy Ronson table lighter, that he looked strangely ill at ease and even—Ann saw with alarm—angry.

To distract herself, she turned to Uncle Louis. "Where's Carlo these days?" she asked. "I haven't seen him in ages."

"Perhaps he is aware of the nature of his competition," Uncle Louis said with his grave smile. "Your doctor looks like the very model of the competent medical man—you don't mind my saying so? One would say that he must either be a doctor or a very skillful actor impersonating one. A loss to the performing arts, if a gain to science." He chuckled at his own whimsy, and added, "The fact is that you have some competition yourself where Carlo is concerned, my dear. He is seeing a good deal of a young harpist of my acquaintance to whom I rather slyly introduced him some weeks ago."

"A harpist?" Ann said, restraining a smile.

"A student at Juilliard, extremely talented, I am told. She has quite a pleasant singing voice as well. Carlo has even been persuaded to resuscitate his ancient tenor for the sake of some family madrigal sessions. The other day we actually managed to sing through one of those fiendishly complicated little canons I composed in my youth; perhaps you remember them."

"I certainly do," Ann said with a laugh, remembering long-ago evenings around the worktable in Uncle Louis' severe little black and white music room: another life.

He was glancing at his watch. "I'm afraid I must carry Sophie away from your doctor in a moment or two. We are meeting Carlo and Moira at Town Hall to hear a jazz concert by a group which calls itself the Modern Jazz Quartet; Carlo assures me I shall enjoy it. I understand that it does not include cellos or flutes or English horns, at any rate, which will be a relief. I fear my taste in jazz is sadly primitive and unenlightened—I would rather listen to Louis Armstrong blowing a hot trumpet than to Pablo Casals himself performing variations on 'Sweet Sue' or some such ditty." He patted Ann's hand and got to his feet stiffly. Ann thought in surprise and consternation: Why, he's getting old;

Uncle Louis is almost an old man. In his presence she herself
could never be anything but a chaste and respectful sixteen-year-
old, a second soprano faltering under Uncle Louis' stern and
courteous eye.

Nodding across the room, Uncle Louis asked, "Is Dr. Sheldon
a music lover, by the way?"

"No," Ann said. "He doesn't care for music. At least that's what
he says."

"Indeed?" He gazed thoughtfully at Nick. "Then there is probably some music he could care for very much, except that he has
not heard it yet. I find that is usually true in such cases. And I
commend the young man's honesty in this era of cultural exhi-
bitionism." He gave Ann a dry precise kiss on the cheek. "It's
always a pleasure to see you, my dear." With a smile he added,
"Now I shall go receive the full report from my wife."

The Marches were leaving too, and in the stir Nick crossed the
room to Ann's side. "That's a formidable woman," he said, looking after the Brunettis. "Old family friend, I gather?"

"Aunt Sophie? Yes. Though I've never thought of her as formidable, exactly."

"Impressive, then."

Ann ate a smoked oyster from a toothpick and said casually,
"What were you talking about all that time?"

"You, for a while. And then—oh, I was telling her about a new
educational program that's been developed for some types of
brain damage. Seems she's done some work with retarded children, the usual half-trained volunteer kind of thing that I suppose does more good than harm." He smiled coldly. "I thought it
might interest her, but apparently she didn't like my tone of voice
or the color of my tie or something. It was not a successful conversation."

Ann said, "Aunt Sophie has done that sort of work for years.
I know she's had some training and hopes to get more when
Connie—her youngest daughter—goes off to college. She's a very
intelligent person. I can't imagine her not being interested in
something new in the field."

Nick shrugged. "At any rate, she didn't like me much. And I
can't say that I go for these warm maternal types with the cast-

iron egos. Especially the ones who consider themselves infallible judges of character."

"That's very unfair!" Ann said angrily. "Aunt Sophie is one of the kindest people I know; and if there's one thing she's not, it's a hypocrite. If you knew her better—"

"I hope I won't have to."

Ann stared at him. Without thinking she said, "Why, you're afraid of her, aren't you?"

He tensed; she was aware that she had struck home, even before he said harshly, "Maybe I am. I said she was formidable." He added, "There's a son in the picture, isn't there? An old boy friend of yours? You can't blame Mama for feeling a little hostile toward a newcomer who's succeeded where her precious boy failed. And in more ways than one. I suppose she figured that out, too."

Ann gave him a furious look and turned away without a word. She found herself in the hall saying goodbye brightly and automatically to the Frieburgs while a calm voice inside her head repeated: You knew how cruel he could be, will always be, whenever he feels himself threatened in any way. But what made me say that about Aunt Sophie? And why did it anger him so—only because it was an absurd and insulting thing to say? Or because in some unimaginable way it is true?

They hardly spoke in the cab on their way down to Charles with Marge and Guy. Sensing some strain, Marge exerted her social charm until Nick relaxed enough to respond, looking grave and handsome in the spacious high-ceilinged gloom of the old restaurant. It occurred to Ann suddenly that he was sitting exactly where Bobbie had sat on that other evening at Charles—surely this was the same table?

Her father was telling a series of stories verbatim from the pages of last year's book on the Greek islands. He did this unconsciously, Ann knew, having little power of invention and an indiscriminately photographic memory. Half listening, she thought of the sunlit balconies of her childhood, the long restless mornings spent gazing down on the noisy street scenes of Mexico or Naples or Bali—any place where the sun shone and every day was Market Day—while her father transcribed the latest anecdote, the latest scenery from his shorthand notebook to his typewriter in the shuttered darkness of their hotel room. Ann felt now that she had hardly traveled at all, that she had seen the world through an eye as restricted as that of the camera lens she had learned to train obediently on each new discovery of her father's —the white-washed alley narrowing to a sliver of sky, the mountain or lake in its frame of bamboo or hibiscus, the children posed on donkeys and camels and elephants, or playing in the dust and gazing at the camera with eyes made huge and photogenic by hunger.

Nick said, "Ann showed me the book you did on the Caribbean, sir. I wanted to ask you—"

"Oh, yes," Guy said comfortably. "Matter of fact that's one of my next projects, revising that thing. The area's changed so much, new hotels and airports, new islands for that matter, practically rising out of the sea overnight. We're going down in December. Christmas in Martinique, hey, Marge?" He drank off his wine and grinned at his wife. "Then we'll beat our way back up, take a look at the Leewards, some of the smaller places I missed last time—"

"Only if we can fly," Marge said firmly. "I am *not* getting on some native fishing boat with no bathroom and a lot of goats, Guy."

"Lots of new airports," Guy repeated expansively. "Anyway, doll, you can always settle down in a Hilton somewhere and drink rum punch with the other Yanks while I go off on day trips exploring."

"And you'll never be gone more than a week at a time," Marge said with a sigh. "I know."

Nick said surprisingly, "I'd like to get down there myself sometime. I've never traveled at all; in fact, I've never really had a vacation."

Guy swallowed a forkful of wild rice, shaking his head emphatically. "Europe," he said. "You've got to start with Europe. No two ways about it."

"I'd want at least a month in Europe," Nick objected politely. "Right now I couldn't manage more than a week or two. The Caribbean seems like a good place to start, particularly if you wouldn't mind giving me some advice about where to go and what to see."

"Sure, sure," Guy said enthusiastically. "I'll have all the latest poop when we get back. Just give me a call any time."

Nick would be a good traveler, Ann thought: efficient and tireless, impatient with the spurious and trite, bearing himself with an intelligent wariness which would earn him the respect if not the liking of the people he encountered, and which would in the end be far more productive than her father's amiability. People liked Guy and therefore told him only what they thought he wanted to hear. He had been laughed at for his gullibility by more than one reviewer in the past. This wounded him, Ann knew, but he had no more idea than a child how to defend himself, beyond adopting a child's transparent toughness of manner and speech.

She smiled at her father affectionately and said, "How long will you be gone, Dad?"

"Oh, a month, six weeks. I want to go back down in June or July, see what the off-season facilities are now they're making such a big pitch for summer tourists."

"Sounds like a nice life," Nick said.

"It is, boy, it is. You professional types don't know what living is, believe me!" Guy lit a cigarette and lounged back comfortably in his chair. "Now, what you ought to do is go down, look around the American Virgins, say, start a practice in St. Thomas or St. Croix. More and more people living there the year round, they need doctors and dentists and lawyers, and they'll pay for them. Of course, during the season—"

"Nick is a specialist, dear," Marge said.

"Well, hell, they need specialists too. Seriously," he said to Nick, "a bright young guy like you could clean up in a place like that. Get out of the New York rat race, away from all the pressure. I tell you what you do—"

"I happen to like the pressure," Nick said.

"Aah, that's just because you've never known anything else. Am I right? And what does it all add up to, in the end? Americans don't understand the art of living, that's what it amounts to. Guy I knew, Andy Drummond, one of the best damn cardiologists in the country—"

"Dad," Ann said.

Nick said with a cold smile, "The kind of work I intend to do requires facilities of great refinement and complexity. There are

only a few places in the world where I can find them, New York
being one. Also, the idea of escape has never appealed to me
very much."

"But that's just it!" Guy exclaimed. "Which is the escape, anyway—a life of leisure and contemplation, or a life of frantic ac-
tivity? Work, work, work, and then you never have to take time
to sit down and learn to live with yourself. That's what people are
afraid of," he declared, slapping his hand on the tablecloth. "Self-
knowledge! It scares them. Why, our whole twentieth-century
technology is just an attempt to escape from ourselves. The self-
alienation of modern man."

"But, Dad—there are other things—" Ann began helplessly.

Marge said in her firm voice, "You can't turn back the clock,
Guy. And I don't think romanticizing the past helps anybody's
sense of alienation, if that's what we're all suffering from. As for
myself, I seem to have eaten entirely too much. Are we having
dessert or not?"

Guy said triumphantly, "But you *can* turn back the clock!
That's my whole point. You can go back a hundred, even two
hundred years on some of these islands that are just a few hours
away by plane—"

Nick smiled, and Ann and Marge began to laugh.

"All right, all right," Guy said. "The old man getting philosophical in his cups. I know, I'll shut up. Say," he said, grinning
at them, "this is a hell of a lot of fun. We ought to do it more
often."

"Yes, dear," Marge said. "Let's order dessert. We've got a lot of
glasses to wash at home, and I'm sure Ann and Nick can find
something better to do with the rest of the evening."

They stood on the curb outside the restaurant, watching the
retreating red taillights of Marge and Guy's cab. The air was still
hot and sultry, smelling of exhaust fumes and sweaty cotton.

Nick said, "Okay, take it easy, Ann. I enjoyed your father and
stepmother very much, and I'm sorry about Aunt Sophie. We
just rubbed each other the wrong way, I guess."

"I'm sorry too."

"I'm always leery of motherly types, which I suppose has some involved Freudian explanation. Also, to be honest, I'm sure if she'd liked me better, I'd be singing a different tune."

"Really? The objective Dr. Sheldon?"

"Oh, the hell with it." He walked away from her, looking down the avenue for a cab.

Ann caught up with him and put a hand on his sleeve. "Please, Nick," she said miserably. "I don't know what's the matter with me tonight. Don't go."

"You just thought it was time we had our first fight?" he said.

"Something like that."

His face relaxed into a smile; but he looked suddenly tired too, Ann thought, as though her gesture had renewed in him a certain tension or strain of commitment. Didn't she feel something of the kind herself?

"Well—" He took her arm. "Where to?"

"I don't know."

At the thought of going back to the apartment, of their joined bodies clammy with love in the airless night, Ann felt her skin prickle unexpectedly with her old virginal repugnance. She said after a moment, "I feel like doing something completely—oh, corny and touristy. And cool. Like the Staten Island Ferry. Yes, why not? Oh, Nick, let's go ride on the ferry. I haven't been down to the Battery in ages, and it's practically my favorite part of the city. And it will be cool. And it's a weekday night."

Nick looked blank.

Ann said impatiently, "The lights—all the buildings. People working late on weekdays. Can we afford a cab? I don't think I could stand the subway tonight."

"Well, I don't know," Nick said. "If I have to spend a whole nickel on you for the ferry—"

"It does seem silly, doesn't it?" She smiled, feeling suddenly light-hearted. "We ought to take along a bottle of champagne or something extravagant, to balance things off. I wonder if they'd let you drink champagne on the ferry. Half the fun is getting there and all that."

"The whole fun, I should think," Nick said, flagging down a cab. "I mean, what is there to see on the other side, anyway? I've never ridden on the Staten Island Ferry."

"Really?" Ann said in surprise, getting into the cab. "You've lived in New York all this time—"

"I never knew anyone on Staten Island," Nick said, and looked nettled when she burst out laughing. "Well, for Pete's sake— what's supposed to be the point? Shuttling back and forth on some old tub in the middle of the night like a bunch of crazy schoolkids—I never could see it."

The cabdriver reached back and slammed the door violently, his face intent and businesslike.

"I was a crazy schoolkid once," Ann said.

"I wasn't."

"No. I don't suppose you were." The cab swung out in an il- legal U-turn; a horn blared in rage behind them as another cab swerved past their fender and dived under a red light. The cab- bie shook his fist after it. Ann said, "Anyway, it's more than that. It's a view of the city, and—well, I guess the sense of the city as an island, a port, that you tend to forget when you live in the mid- dle of it." She added a little defensively, "I used to love looking at old prints of Manhattan, and reading about the Revolutionary battles and all that. You know—meadows in Brooklyn, and sheep on Murray Hill."

"Turning back the clock like your father?"

She shook her head. After a moment she said, "You know what you said about people being simpler underneath than so- ciety has forced them to be on the surface?" Nick nodded, his eyes on the traffic. "Well, I used to feel the same way about the city. As if all the steel and concrete were part of a fantastic game we were playing, and if we could all just agree to *stop*, we'd find that other island still there underneath, waiting to be lived in— peaceful and beautiful, like the part of ourselves we'd almost for- gotten. The best part."

She laughed self-consciously. "Oh, well, there's nothing like symbolism when you're fourteen. I even wanted to paint a picture of all this, the two landscapes coexisting in some kind of surreal- ist composition. Only I was going to wait and perfect my tech- nique, and maybe do practice paintings of sections of the picture, and then when I was at the height of my powers—you know, by the time I was twenty-five or so—I'd rent a gymnasium or an armory or something and lock myself in for ten years with this gigantic canvas; and when it was finally unveiled, people would fall on their knees before it, overcome with longing and remorse . . . And the next day, I suppose, all the buildings would have toppled into the sea."

Nick said, "But in the end—"

"In the end," Ann said with a smile, "I decided I was never going to amount to anything as a painter, anyway; so I more or less lost interest in my Arcadian dream, seeing that I wasn't going to be able to help make it come true. That's the trouble with me," she added. "I can never find anything to do that's both practical and idealistic enough at the same time. Unless the old ego can be in there building Utopia with its bare hands, it loses interest."

Nick said with a shrug, "I suppose that's one of the virtues of science. It uses specific technical means to arrive at specific ends; your own ego doesn't have to get involved. Even if it does, it's irrelevant."

"Irrelevant?" Ann stared at him. "But I should think— Well, in medicine, for instance, the personal decision to practice in one place rather than another, or to go on in a line of research no one else believes in, to say nothing of the decisions that have to be made about the use of new discoveries—all those things involve people and their egos, don't they? I've never really understood this business about science being an impersonal process. I don't see why it isn't as much involved with motives and reputations and whatnot as any other field."

He said carelessly, "Sure, but those are just the externals. The actual work *is* a process—a series of steps based on what is known objectively about various physical and chemical relationships. Whereas a painting—"

"A painting is a process, too, only the artist is dealing with a different set of relationships—light and color and mass instead of cells and reflexes and whatever. And anyway, what you call externals are really terribly important, because they control the process—don't you see?"

"I'm no moralist," Nick said impatiently. "It's obvious that the means are never going to be as pure as the ends until the millennium, anyway. In the meantime, it's the work that counts."

"Is it?" She looked away. "Oh, well—I can think of about a million things to say to that, but I guess I won't."

"Don't," he agreed, putting his arm around her. "I've heard them all anyway, and they've never convinced me."

"What does convince you?" she said softly.

He stroked her bare arm gently. "This. Physical fact, reality." She stirred uneasily; he laughed. "All right, can't you see I'm just trying to shut you up long enough to kiss you?"

They stood close together at the stern railing of the ferry, watching the towering lights of the city recede across the oily water.

Nick said, "The trouble with you is that you really belong in the country. Raising horses, or possibly dogs. I can see you making rounds in an old pair of slacks with a scarf on your head, ministering to sore paws and giving distemper shots, accompanied by a devoted hired hand."

"Don't laugh," Ann said. "As a matter of fact, it was one of my childhood ambitions to be a veterinarian."

"On the other hand"—he looked down at her smiling face in the dim light from the cabin behind them—"you would make a decorative hostess and efficient mother of handsome blond children, who in turn would want to be veterinarians when they grew up. Or missionaries. Or maybe even doctors."

Ann looked away. After a moment she said, "There's the Statue of Liberty."

"Really? I never would have guessed," he said, mocking her evasion; but he moved a little away from her, his hands in his pockets. Ann gazed across the liquid darkness at the gauzy lights of New Jersey on the horizon, and found that she was thinking about Bobbie for the second time that evening—Bobbie, who floated now in her own darkness, pale fingers swollen and nerveless, drowned empty eyes . . . She fought away the horror, feeling Nick's presence at her side. I am using her as my defense against him, she thought clearly, just as I have been using him as my defense against her. Why? And why should I feel in my imagination this almost personal antipathy between them, as though they had actually known and disliked each other?

She glanced at Nick, who was staring down at the slick black swell of the water; he had the slight frown of someone doing a calculation at once abstract and practical. She forced herself to speak. "I haven't told you about Bobbie—about what I'm working on now."

Swiftly he turned his head to look at her. "Working? I didn't know you still were."

"I know. I didn't mention it because—oh, it's just such a wild guess in some ways."

"Then why are you telling me now? Have you found something?"

"No," Ann said, taken aback by the sharpness of his tone. "It's only that the more I think about it, the more sure I am that I'm on the right track. I thought you'd want to know, that's all."

Nick was alert, his eyes on her face. "And . . . ?"

She said, "It occurred to me that Bobbie might have seen or known something she didn't even know she knew. I mean, when we talked about the possibility that she was killed because she had some kind of information that was terribly important to someone, we assumed that she must have known the person and talked to him. But what if she didn't actually know him at all? What if she was just a witness to something—something—"

"Like what?" Nick asked, staring at her. A bar of light from the cabin fell diagonally across his face from temple to cheekbone, leaving his eyes in shadow. Except for the beat of the engines and the hiss of the water against the broad flanks of the ferry, the deck was very quiet. A couple who had been murmuring amorously on one of the dark benches against the cabin wall had moved away, and now a man smoking a forbidden cigar by the port railing snapped the glowing butt off into the night and strolled yawning into the cabin, letting the heavy door thump after him.

Ann gripped the railing, full of a strange tense certainty. She said, "I don't know what. How can I? But I'm sure that's it. It fits, somehow; it explains why Bobbie didn't seem at all worried or preoccupied or anything except normal . . . and the method, too, literally cold-blooded, because she wouldn't have been anything more to the murderer than an impersonal threat of some kind."

"Of some kind?" he repeated. "But surely the murderer must have been convinced that she would use what she knew. Otherwise, why bother to kill her?"

"Of course," Ann said impatiently. "But he might have been mistaken; or maybe the situation, whatever it was, seemed completely innocent to Bobbie at the time, and he only killed her on the chance that she might put two and two together some day. Or—well, anyway, the important thing is that he *thought* she was a threat to him, whether she actually was or not. And so he killed her. Yes," she said in a low voice, "I know that's it. I can feel it."

"Feminine intuition," Nick said lightly; but Ann saw how his hand gripped the railing beside hers. Did he feel the same excitement she had felt? When he spoke again his voice was curiously hard and toneless. "Of course, it's impossible to investigate a theory of that sort."

"No," Ann said. "The newspapers."

"Newspapers?"

"I've been reading them at the library, on microfilm—working back day by day from the time of Bobbie's death. I spend an hour or so there in the morning before work, taking notes."

"What kind of notes?"

"Don't you see?" she said. "There's a whole category of things, crimes of various kinds, that take place more or less in public and that it could be dangerous to see accidentally. It sounds melodramatic, I know, but—"

"For instance, she saw the bank robber as he raced to his getaway car, and he saw her and took down her name and address on the chance that he might want to do away with her sometime? Or maybe she just happened to be looking in the window when the butler slipped the arsenic into the old lady's teacup."

Ann shook her head and leaned forward against the railing, trying to shield her sense of certainty from the sound of his voice. As she did so, Nick grasped her arm above the elbow with a sudden and startling pressure that forced her forward against the rail. She stiffened reflexively, her body straining back against his, so that for an instant they stood tightly locked together by their mutual tension. But for an instant only; in the next moment he was pulling her around to face him, his other arm was around her shoulders, he was holding her close against his chest. She could feel his rapid breathing.

She said shakily, "Do you often have that kind of impulse?"

"What kind?"

"You know."

"You were leaning over too far. I wanted to pull you back."

"No," she whispered.

He rested his cheek against her hair, still holding her tightly. "Ann," he said, "Ann. I love you."

"No," she said again.

"Yes. Please." After a moment, standing motionless, he said, "Don't you believe me?"

"I don't know."

"I love you. I need you."

"Do you? I wonder if you need anyone, Nick."

"You don't know. Oh, God, Ann. Listen to me: I want to marry you. I want to know that you belong to me."

"And would you belong to me?" she asked, raising her head to see his face.

She saw the sudden bleakness in his eyes before he bent his head to kiss her. After a moment she turned her face away, putting her arms around him tightly out of a strange impulse to reassure or comfort him. Without warning she felt herself pierced by a physical excitement so pure and intense that she had to hold her breath to keep from crying out with it. "Nick," she said.

"Yes?"

"You must know that I'm in love with you. But marriage—I need time to think about it. Can you wait?"

"If I have to." She felt him smile, relaxing. "You're surprised, aren't you? You didn't think I was the marrying kind. Well, neither did I." He kissed her again, saying urgently, "Don't think, Ann. Just feel. If you do what you only think is the right thing, whatever it is, you'll regret it. It's feeling that matters, for you."

"Are feelings so much simpler than thoughts?" she asked softly.

"Yes," he said, stroking her breast under the thin silk of her dress. "You know they are."

She gave him a gentle push and drew away. The ferry was approaching its slip; there was a grinding shudder beneath their feet as the engines were reversed, and a yaw before she slid heavily into her berth. Car horns brayed, there was a violent clanking of metal on the lower deck. As Nick stood aside to let Ann precede him down the stairway she saw his face clearly under the lights and was startled by his look of exhaustion: his mouth was drawn, his cheeks hollow beneath their sharp bones. She came back up the steps she had descended and took his hand and held it to her lips.

He smiled painfully. "All right," he said. "Just don't take too long making up your mind."

"I may have to," Ann said. "I mean, I may feel I ought to."

He stared. "As a matter of principle, you mean? Oh, Lord. Of course—I should have expected that, from you." He laughed, propelling her down the stairs. "A long engagement too, I suppose."

"Naturally," Ann said over her shoulder. She added scrupulously, "But we're not even going to talk about that yet."

"Okay." He looked around with a sudden restless gaiety. "Well, now what do we do? Line up somewhere and pay another nickel to get back on this thing?"

She thought: Yes, let him think that—that I'm just stalling on principle, as he says. And what other reason is there, after all? What other reason could there be?

"Come on," Nick said, taking her arm. "I don't propose to spend the rest of my life on Staten Island, even with you."

But she stood for a moment with her face lifted to the night sky, where a half-moon now glimmered behind a film of clouds. Does he know what he is asking? she thought. My life! Ah, dear God —can I give him my life?

TEN

"All right,"

Marge said over the phone. "If you won't, you won't, I guess. Is it just masochism, may I ask, or romance? I'm afraid your father would be upset if I put you and Nick in the same bedroom, but Lord knows there are plenty of haystacks around, if you want *that* kind of privacy."

"Thanks," Ann said with a smile. "But Nick really does have to work on Monday, and we'd barely get up there before we'd have to turn around. We thought we'd rent a car and go out to Jones Beach on Sunday if it's a nice day, so it won't be as grim as it sounds."

"Jones Beach on Labor Day weekend? You're absolutely mad, sweetie. Why don't you call up someone in Southampton and go out for the day? The Halleys are back from Europe—I know they'd love to see you."

"Oh, there'd be parties and things," Ann said vaguely.

"All right," Marge said, "go your proletarian way. Poor Nick, I don't suppose he'll ever meet *anyone* at this rate."

"Nick doesn't want to meet anyone."

"I didn't say he did. But let's be realistic, dear, and admit that your social connections *could* be very helpful to a young man in his position."

Marge's tone was matter-of-fact; Ann wished she could see

her face. She said calmly, "Nick isn't going to be a society doctor, Marge. He's a specialist in a very sophisticated field."

"Even specialists need patients," Marge said. "Well, I'm sorry about the weekend, sweetie; maybe you'll take a rain check before I close up the house in October. It's been ages since you came up to the country—not since last spring, if I remember."

"No. I've wanted to, but—"

"I know. It's a little disorienting, isn't it—if there is such a word. Everything so pastoral and relaxed"—Ann smiled, thinking of Marge's country regimen of gardening and horseback riding and parties—"and then you come back to the city and it's at least Wednesday before you can even believe in the place again, much less live in it. And of course, this summer there's been Nick. I think he's terribly attractive, by the way, if frightening."

"Frightening?" Ann sat very still.

"Well, of course, that's part of his attraction, isn't it? Oh, I don't mean the obvious tough-and-sexy kind of thing; it's something much more subtle. Very masculine," Marge said musingly.

"I've got to get to work, Marge," Ann said, looking at her watch. "Have a good weekend if I don't see you, and give my love to Dad."

"All right, darling. Have fun at Jones Beach. It really is a *very* nice beach, even by California standards."

But it rained on Sunday. Nick had spent the night at the apartment for the first time, and by the time they had finished a late breakfast and read the paper he was beginning to look restless, pacing about the small room and staring down through the streaming windows at the empty street. Finally he said, "I think I'll go back up to my place for a while, if you don't mind. There's some reading I ought to catch up on, and a patient I want to look in on later at the hospital. I'll come back down around four or five, we can have an early dinner and see a movie or something."

"Or something."

"You don't mind, do you?" He looked at her.

"Oh, no, I guess not." Ashamed of her tone, she came to stand at the window beside him. "Damn this rain, anyway."

"I know. You could have been in the country this weekend, too."

"You mean I should have gone? Without you?"

"Ann." He put his arms around her shoulders. "You know I didn't mean it that way."

"But you do have other things to do."

"Yes. My work."

"I know," Ann said. After a moment she leaned her head against his shoulder and added, "I'm sorry, Nick. I hate possessive women, but I guess I also hate the idea that you can feel bored when you're with me."

"You mean *you* hate feeling possessive," he said with a smile. "The independent Ann Claremont. But as for being bored—well, maybe it's not very romantic of us, but you can't just sit around doing nothing any more than I can, and you know it. What you need is a project of some kind."

Ann laughed. "All right, you win. Any ideas?"

He shrugged. "Well, if you'd only agree to marry me, you could start planning your trousseau or your hope chest, or whatever it is."

"Hope chest! Heaven forbid."

"Well, why not? After all, we'll need towels and things."

"Oh, you get those at showers. Along with all the phony oohing and ahing, and that stupid business of tying the ribbons together . . . I guess I've just been to too many of them," Ann said with a sigh.

"I'm beginning to think it's the business of getting married that you're resisting, rather than the idea of marrying me," Nick said. "Encouraging thought."

Ann said lightly, "Maybe so. Anyway, if we do get married, we're going to a justice of the peace and be done with it."

"That I doubt, having met your stepmother. Anyway, you're being selfish. A society wedding is just what the old career needs. It all adds up, you know," he said coolly, ignoring her look of surprise. "You didn't think I wanted to marry you just for your beauty and charm, did you?" He kissed the top of her head. "Well, if I'm going to go at all, I'd better go now. And I've thought of a project for you."

"What?"

"Getting rid of Bobbie's clothes." When Ann said nothing, he added gently, "Don't you think it's about time? You haven't found anything, and all they're doing is reminding you unnecessarily of something you're going to have to try and forget sooner or later."

"I don't have to forget anything," Ann said, turning her face away.

"Yes. For my sake you do."

The rain blew against the windowpane. Ann shut her eyes against the command in his voice. It was chilly outside, the end of summer. She thought of the fields of New England lying yellow and green under the rain, and then of the seacoast: boats swinging at their moorings, shuttered beach cottages whose chimneys sighed in the wet sea wind. At last she said, "I have no place to put them—her clothes."

"I'll get you some boxes if you need them. But she must have had suitcases." Ann nodded slowly. "You pack them and I'll take them when I leave tonight. There are Gray Ladies at the hospital who are always collecting clothes for some organization or another."

The clothes of the dead, Ann thought. She said, "All right. It would help if you'd dispose of them for me. I guess that's one reason I've put off doing anything about them. Having to telephone some place . . ."

He touched her shoulder lightly and turned to get his coat. Still standing at the window, Ann saw the door of the grocery store on the corner of Waverly Place swing open on a rectangle of yellow light, and a young man run, leaping puddles, across the street, his bare dark head bent beneath the rain. "There's Carlo!" she exclaimed.

"Who?"

"You know, the Brunettis' son."

"Coming here?"

"I guess so."

Ann looked quickly around. The bed was made, the breakfast dishes put away. Nick saw the look and said drily, buttoning his coat, "So we meet at last. I hope it won't be awkward for you."

"No, why should it be?" The buzzer sounded. "Heavens, when did they get that fixed?"

"I notice you haven't been in any great hurry to introduce us," Nick said, adding, "Here, I'll get it." He pressed the button on the kitchen wall just as Carlo opened the door and called, "Anybody home?"

"Evidently," Nick said. "Come in."

"They've fixed the buzzer, but the lock still doesn't work. A step in the right direction, anyway," Carlo said. "Hi, Annie, have you got a towel or something? It's really coming down outside."

Ann reached around Nick for a dishtowel and said, "Nick, this is Carlo Brunetti; Carlo, Nick Sheldon."

"Dr. Sheldon, I presume? Glad to know you," Carlo said. They shook hands.

"I'm just on my way out," Nick said, turning up the collar of his coat. "Maybe I'll see you later."

"I just dropped in for a minute," Carlo said, looking at him.

Ann said quickly, "Can't you stay for a little while, Nick?" She laughed self-consciously. "Anyway, we don't all have to crowd into the kitchen like this, as though we were playing sardines."

"Sardines," Carlo said, going into the living room and throwing his wet coat onto the radiator. "I always thought that was a hell of a funny game. I wonder who invented it. Sounds vaguely 1920-ish, like something Benchley might have dreamed up for a *New Yorker* piece. For instance, you can learn a lot of good word games from reading Thurber."

"I'll see you later," Nick said to Ann, kissing her on the cheek. "Nice to have met you," he added over his shoulder to Carlo, and went out.

"Coffee?" Ann said briskly, listening to Nick's diminishing footsteps on the stairs. Why must she always listen this way, with such anguish, as though she might never see him again?

"Sure, if you've got some made." Carlo sat down in the chair near the fireplace and lit a cigarette. "Is he always so friendly?"

"Carlo—"

"Okay, okay. It just looked so damned domestic, that's all." When Ann said nothing, busying herself with the coffee pot, he said, "This lousy weather. I was going to a double-header this afternoon, but I guess they'll have to call it at this rate."

"With Moira?" Ann said, bringing him his coffee.

"Moira? Hardly," Carlo said, laughing. "No, just some guys from the firm. How do you know about Moira?"

"Your father."

"Oh, yeah. Dad's nuts about her—thinks she's a good cultural influence on me, or something. Anyway, she's not the ball-game type."

"I know," Ann said, sitting down on the couch opposite him. "The ballet. French symbolist poets. Horseback riding. Sews beautifully but doesn't knit."

"I don't know about the knitting," Carlo said. "It's been too hot to knit." He scowled. "You're pretty sharp these days, aren't you?"

"You gave me the same treatment about Nick, remember?"

They grinned at each other. Carlo stretched, looking out at the rain. "Labor Day. I was thinking on my way over here about all the places I've spent Labor Day weekend. It seems to me it was always raining."

"No," Ann said. "But I know what you mean."

"Northeasters, usually," Carlo insisted. "Everybody reading best sellers by the fire and drinking bourbon. Or playing Scrabble and drinking bourbon. And periodically making noble excursions out into the elements to look at the beach or the lake or neck in the boathouse—"

"Or go to the grocery store," Ann said. "I was always getting stuck with the groceries."

"And then back inside to drink more bourbon and eat spaghetti or goulash or something," Carlo said dreamily. "Remember the time at the Vineyard when we made Mrs. Murphy's chowder with the caretaker's overalls?"

"It's funny," Ann said. "I was thinking about the same thing, sort of, just before you came."

There was a pause. "God, we sound about a hundred years old," Carlo said. "But I had this—I don't know, this terrible feeling of nostalgia suddenly, for no good reason." He stirred his coffee, his face intent and puzzled.

Ann said, "I know. The feeling of a place like that comes back over you with a terrible rush. The smells—"

"Wet wool. When I write my Proustian reminiscences, they're going to begin with the smell of wet Shetland wool. And oilcloth." He looked around for an ashtray, and finally tossed his cigarette through the open bathroom door into the toilet. He said, "You going to marry this guy, Ann?"

"I don't know. Are you going to marry Moira?"

"Oh—" Carlo shrugged. "It's not that serious yet, at least not on my side." He added suddenly, "We're not very good for each other, are we, Annie, right at this point? Just seeing each other reminds us of so many things, and makes anything—anyone—else seem alien. At least I can't help feeling that way."

Ann said, "Yes. I feel it too. But I think it's a good thing. Seeing you sort of—well, renews my sense of what my life has been and meant up to now. Do you know what I mean? And I need that now. I need to make this decision with my whole self, not with just a part of it." The part of it that loves Nick, she had been about to say.

"So you're pitting me against Dr. Sheldon? I'd say the outcome's a foregone conclusion, from all appearances."

"Oh, Carlo, you know that's not what I meant. Although there are so many things about you that I—value very much, that Nick doesn't have. In that sense, I suppose, I *am* trying to test him by you."

"You mean trying to decide if you can live without these things, whatever they are? If I may be so indelicate as to ask—"

"Most of the virtues," Ann said, smiling at him.

"On that note I'd better leave." He stood up and looked around for his coat. "Hey, I almost forgot," he said, taking something from his pocket. "Toffee. I saw the kind you used to like when I was buying some cigarettes."

"Oh, Carlo, thanks—I haven't had any in ages," she said, taking the tin.

"A *madeleine* of sorts, only don't try dipping it in tea. Thoughtfulness is one of my many virtues, needless to say. Well, I'll leave you to devour it in solitude while I go tackle Sunday dinner with my parents. Unless you'd like to come along."

"I wish I could, but there's something I have to do. And Nick's coming back later on."

"Cheer up," Carlo said, patting her shoulder. "I'm sure he's counting the hours too."

Ann followed him to the door. All at once she wanted to talk about Nick. "His work is so important to him," she said, "and I feel so little connection with it. He hardly ever talks to me about it, and when he does I can tell he's talking down to me and it bores him."

"Well, Annie, what do you expect?" Carlo said gently. "I certainly don't sit around discussing my latest briefs with Moira; she'd have to know a good deal of law to make it worthwhile." When Ann was silent, he added, "I know—you'd like to be a farmer's wife and work in the fields beside your husband and be entitled to your own opinions about the crops and weather. But unless you're planning to go to medical school, I don't see how you can really share in Nick's work. You've just got to accept that."

Ann sighed. "I guess so. But if I could just *see* him at work sometime—"

"At the hospital, you mean? Well, why not? You can go up there any time."

"Nick wouldn't like it."

"Why not?"

"I don't know. He just wouldn't."

"Well, he wouldn't even have to know you were there, as far as that goes. Look sweetie"—Carlo held out his hands—"I'm sorry I can't stay and talk but I've got to get going or Papa will have all the booze locked away again by the time I get there. I was drinking stingers last night, and my stomach's still lurching around. I'll call you soon."

The wind thudded against the windows, stirring the strips of orange curtain.

Ann went into the bedroom and pulled a suitcase from under the bed. Keeping her mind carefully blank, she tugged open a bureau drawer and plunged her hands into the soft mass of Bobbie's sweaters and scarfs, as strangely warm to the touch as if they still held the heat of living flesh. She found that she was thinking about Nick, listening already for his returning footsteps on the stairs. Her movements came to seem to herself unnecessarily hurried, even stealthy, as though she were a burglar watching a clock. She thought: It's absurd to feel that this is a betrayal of some kind, when I know that the answer is somewhere else, not to be miraculously revealed in a coat pocket, a missing button. Nick was right, it was high time.

Bobbie's big wardrobe suitcase was wedged under the couch; she had forgotten about it. She dragged it out and went to the closet for the coats and dresses. But there were so many of them that although she jammed them in as tightly as she could, she couldn't get the lid to close. She repacked the suitcase methodically, with the same result. A vague horror overwhelmed her; she found that she was shaking. She pushed the suitcase aside and went to the phonograph to put on a record, a Brandenburg Concerto whose vigorous rhythms pulsed through the room like rays of sunshine, dispersing shadows. When Nick came in at last, looking wet and cheerful, she was filling the last suitcase with the heavy things, shoes and handbags.

"Well," he said, standing over her. "Hard at work, I see. I thought you'd be through by now."

"I procrastinated awhile. I'm almost finished." She brushed a strand of hair from her forehead and said without looking at him, "Would you bring me that pair of ice skates from the closet?"

"Ice skates? Sure. They look brand-new," Nick said, handing them to her. "Couldn't you wear them?"

"No," Ann said, wadding newspaper around the flashing blades. "Not my size, and much too elegant. I'm strictly a Central Park skater. These are Rockefeller Center skates." She stared down at them, remembering Bobbie in a tight velvet jacket and skirt whirling over the milky ice beneath the brilliant pyramid of last year's Christmas tree. After a moment she said, "There are just a few more things. You could move the other suitcases out into the hall. I couldn't get the top down on one of them."

"Sure."

She went back into the bedroom to check the bureau. Bobbie's drawers were empty now, except for her jewelry case. An earring was wedged in a crack of the drawer; Ann pried it loose with a hairpin and opened the case to replace it. On top of the tangle of bracelets and necklaces lay the outsized gold pin that Mr. Michaelson had given Ann on the day of the service.

"Oh, dear. I wonder what I should do with this."

"With what?" Nick said from the other room.

"Oh, an Ultra Designs pin that Bobbie's boss insisted on giving me. It was one of Bobbie's favorites, and he wanted me to have it—you know. I didn't want to take it, but I couldn't hurt his feelings. I don't know . . . I guess I could send it to her parents. It's probably the kind of thing they'd appreciate."

He came to look over her shoulder. "Oh, yes, that thing."

Ann turned quickly in surprise.

He said, "I mean—she was wearing it the day I saw her."

She turned away again with an irrational, urgent sense that she must not let him see her bewilderment. As though her silence puzzled him, he said, "You could hardly help noticing it. Why do women wear these things, anyway? Those spikes must hurt like hell if you bend over the wrong way."

Ann said, "It was just a fad. Bobbie loved fads." She held the pin up to the light in the palm of her hand; it felt cold and heavy against her skin. Ask him, she thought. Why don't you just ask him? The back of her neck prickled with his nearness in the tiny room.

"Anyway, it's certainly not your type," Nick said.

"What is my type?" Ann asked. She began disentangling the strings of beads on top of the jewelry case.

"Oh—classic things. Pearls, and plain gold. Nothing jangly."

"What, no diamonds?"

"Well—small diamonds."

She forced a laugh. "I really am almost through," she said. "Why don't you go out and get us some beer? We've only got one can left. And some bacon for breakfast. I meant to ask you before, but I forgot."

"Stores open?" Nick said doubtfully.

"I guess the one across the street's closed now," Ann said, peering through the rainy window, "but you could try the place around the corner."

"Okay. Back in a minute."

She waited until she heard the slam of the door downstairs. Then she went to the refrigerator and took out one of the two remaining cans of beer and looked around swiftly for a place to hide it. But this is idiotic! she told herself, jerking open the closet door and staring at the row of empty hangers where Bobbie's clothes had hung. Concealing one thing—and why, why on earth didn't I just ask him?—and now having to conceal another, my excuse for getting him out of the apartment for a few minutes, like a character in a French farce. But I must have time to think. Of course there is some simple explanation, if I can only have a moment to think about it.

She dropped the beer can into a rainboot and shut the closet door. All right, she thought. He says he noticed the pin the time he saw her, that night at the hospital. But that's impossible, because Bobbie was only allowed to model the company jewelry during office hours; it had to be returned to the safe at five o'clock. Then Nick must be mistaken; Bobbie must have worn another pin, one like it . . . But there was no other one like it, Ann knew without looking. Bobbie loved fads, as she had said, but in her own way she was conservative with her money and seldom bought anything extreme if it was expensive as well. Still . . . Ann went back into the bedroom and dumped the contents of the jewelry case out onto the bureau. No, there was nothing here like the sunburst pin, nothing anywhere near its size; in fact, nothing that you would notice at a distance across a room full of people.

All right, then. She leaned against the bureau, forcing herself to think calmly and logically. Suppose Bobbie had gotten special permission to wear the pin that evening—suppose even that she had sneaked it out of the office somehow and had returned it the next morning. That wouldn't have been stealing exactly, and it was the sort of thing she could imagine Bobbie doing for an important occasion. But—important? A casual evening with a casual date, dinner in a cafeteria and a movie afterward for the few hours Paul was off duty? Ann piled the jewelry back into its silk-lined box with numb fingers, brushing a delicate shell earring to the floor, where it shattered into pale dust around its flimsy metal clip.

"Oh, yes, that thing," Nick had said. She listened to his voice again in her mind, re-creating its tone of light certainty as he stood looking over her shoulder at the pin. It was just the tone in which people did say such things, offhand and unconcerned. And anyway, what reason could he possibly have had for lying about it?

He had also said, ". . . the day I saw her," she thought. Not the night, but the day. Of course, people often said "the day" without meaning actual daytime . . . but Nick was always accurate in his speech, and the daytime would make sense if he really had seen Bobbie wearing the pin.

Yes, Ann thought. He must have seen Bobbie twice. It's the

only explanation that makes any sense. Once in the evening at the hospital, as he had said, and some other time. Or times. Ann moved to the window, waiting once more for the sound of his footsteps returning. Her mouth had gone dry. Why? she thought. Why should he have lied to me? After all the talking we've done about Bobbie . . . No, there must be another explanation, something I haven't thought of. If only I had more time to think!

But Nick was coming back, striding along the pavement below in the windy gloom, light from another window sliding briefly across his bright hair. Almost automatically, as if in some way her body had begun to act independently of her mind, Ann wrapped the pin in a piece of Kleenex and dropped it into a drawer of the desk: the drawer that held the notebook, the letters and the photographs . . . Then she packed the jewelry case into the space she had kept for it in the suitcase and forced the lid down. That was everything, except for Bobbie's few books and records, which she would keep.

The latch clicked noisily; there was a thump as Nick set the grocery bag down on the kitchen table. Ask him now, her mind said. Ask him! But her face, going to meet him, was calm and smooth; her voice said only, "Was the store open? I'm sorry to have made you go out in the rain again."

"I'll bet," he said, grinning down at her. "It's convenient, having a man around to run errands, isn't it? Maybe you can make it a habit."

He hasn't noticed anything, she thought incredulously as his arms went around her, pressing her against the damp cloth of his raincoat. Will he remember later and see his mistake? And then will he speak? I have never trusted him, she thought suddenly, turning her face from his kiss. More than that, in some perverse way I have never wanted to trust him. Oh, surely I can still resist him then, and let him think what he wants of my resistance.

But she could not; she could no longer resist. The time for that was past. When they went to bed together later, her involuntary tremor—of what? fear, panic, shame?—at his first touch became a series of helpless shudders, her tension transmuting itself into an exquisite sensitivity, her nerves turned to a new pitch of voluptuous response. Her hands fell away from him to pluck at the sheet. She heard herself moan as each thrust of his body brought forth a fresh gush of sweetness within the dark canal of herself, until the canal widened, becoming a pool whose least luxuriant ripple spread bliss through every nerve; and then the sweetness flooded her, her very bones were liquefying.

Dear God, she thought afterward, lying still beside him, waiting—waiting so long this time!—to possess herself again, to feel her body take back its familiar weight and definition in the darkness: What am I afraid of? Of him? Of myself? *I am afraid for my life!* she thought in a flash. No, how senseless, those are words that people read, not real words that anyone thinks, nothing to do with me.

The light from the street lamp burned upon her cheeks and forehead. She lay listening to the wet city night beyond the windows while Nick slept beside her, his face as pure and empty in sleep as the eyeless face of a Greek athlete, long dead.

ELEVEN

October came,
beginning the city's new year. At five o'clock the streets already crackled with the artificial light and energy of the evening; the resplendent skies of autumn supplied no more than a fitting canopy, it was felt, for a drama of such brilliance and moment. The island drew into itself, its defenses sure once more. Voices rang out above the rumble of the traffic with a new decisiveness, the clothes of fashionable women—furs and leathers of expensive glossy animals—gleamed in the rich light, everywhere there was a new density of texture and clarity of line. Above all, there was the renewed vigor of expectation, which gave to the most ordinary gestures of the people a certain nervous grace. Only those who were themselves moribund returned to the parks to mourn the death of the summer leaves, retracing paths abandoned once more to old people and children.

Ann Claremont moved unseeing through the shimmering days, doing her work efficiently and mechanically, speaking when spoken to, no longer looking into the faces of the people she met. Nick was working long hours in the laboratory now; his manner was often abstracted and self-absorbed. She refused invitations and spent the evenings when she was not with him reading or listening to music or sitting for long hours over her notebook—full now of newspaper jottings, of headlines, names and dates, a hieroglyph of miscellaneous acts of violence, mad and meaningless upon the sober white pages—doggedly willing her imagination to see what Bobbie might have seen so fatally. But she could see nothing; or everything and nothing, as Nick had said. Could someone else? Could he? She did not ask him. She asked him nothing at all.

Sometimes now she spent the night at his apartment, a monastic pair of rooms in an old apartment building off Riverside Drive. Its furnishings were cheap and functional: no prints adorned its sand-colored walls, the bookcase held only medical texts and a few paperbacks, there was no phonograph, only a portable radio on a window sill. The very absence of personal belongings seemed to Ann a kind of arrogance; when they made love there, she was frightened by the completeness of his possession of her, as though he had taken her to a strip of beach under an empty sky where not even a gull would hear her involuntary cry of pleasure and submission.

Miss Polk at the museum was puzzled and disappointed. She inquired gingerly about Ann's plans for the future. Ann replied that she had none. "I thought marriage might be in the air," Miss Polk said offhandedly. "We're bound to lose you eventually, I know, but I hope we can make it as far as the first baby. I can arrange a leave of absence for you any time, Ann, if it's a trip or a long honeymoon or something you're brooding about."

"Thank you," Ann said. "I don't have any immediate plans."

Miss Polk shrugged and went away, looking baffled.

On a Saturday morning in November, Ann woke to a gray winter sky and the sound of a violent quarrel in the street below. She sat up at once, her heart pounding. From the clock-radio on the bureau a bass voice said, "It will be a day of clashes between the giants of the Big Ten. The Buckeyes of Ohio State play host to the Illini at Columbus, where three inches of snow fell during the night. A crowd of eighty thousand is expected to be on hand as the Buckeyes take the field against the sensational quarterbacking of . . ."

Saturday. Ann's mind was suddenly clear and calm. She felt as if she had awakened after a long and inexplicable illness. Of course; she would do today what she had promised herself to do

weeks ago. She would go to the hospital and see Nick at work. Or
if she couldn't see him, if he was too busy, he would at least know
that she had been there—and might come again.

The nurse at the desk outside the clinic asked if she was a patient. Ann explained that she had come to see Dr. Sheldon and
would wait until he was free. "Is it anything urgent?" the nurse
inquired.

"Oh, no. I mean—I just wanted to see him for a moment. I'm a
friend," Ann said. "Miss Claremont."

The nurse frowned at this frivolous declaration, but said,
gesturing with her pencil, "Waiting room to your right. I'll tell
Dr. Sheldon you're here if I see him."

"Thank you." Ann turned away, conscious of the nurse's scrutiny and feeling that she was too smartly dressed in Marge's suit,
which she had worn mainly because it was heavy enough to wear
in cold weather without a coat. Black always makes me look
overdressed, she thought, sitting down in an alcove from which
she could see most of the corridor. Nurses slapped by on rubber
soles, orderlies combed their hair with pocket combs when they
thought no one was looking. Ann herself had been in a hospital
only once, years ago, to have her tonsils out—in Cairo, was it,
or Beirut? She remembered a sunny square of window, purple
flowers against a white wall, a drowsy foreign murmur of voices
beyond the bed screen.

A tall fair-haired doctor came hurrying along the corridor with
an intent frowning air, ignoring the greeting of a passing nurse;
he would have gone on past the desk to the elevators if Ann had
not called, half rising from her chair, "Nick!"

He spun around and saw her; and paused a moment before he
started toward her, smiling. In a painful wave of anger and humiliation, Ann thought: I will never forgive him that moment's
hesitation. "Ann," he said. "What on earth are you doing here?"

"If this is a bad time—"

"Well, no, I was just on my way to check some x-rays; I've got
five minutes, anyway." He laid his charts on the arm of a chair
but didn't sit down. "Why didn't you call me? I could have met
you for coffee somewhere."

"I wanted to come here," Ann said. "And you know I never like to call you when you're at work." He shrugged. She said, "Well, when you think of all the important calls that come into a place like this every minute of the day . . . I always feel I'm interrupting for no good reason—or rather for personal reasons, which I guess is the same thing."

"Oh, I don't think one telephone call is going to bring the machinery grinding to a halt," he said drily.

"Meaning I should have called?"

"I'd rather you had. Then I could have arranged to get away for a few minutes. As it is—" He gestured with distaste at the waiting room with its plastic upholstery and synthetic water colors.

Ann said, "All right, I shouldn't have barged in this way. I'm sorry," and reached for her gloves.

"Now, look, Ann, you know I didn't mean it that way. It just happens to be a rather hectic morning, that's all."

"You've never suggested that I come here," she said. "You've never offered to show me around, or to introduce me to the people you work with." She heard the childishness of her tone, but could not stop herself. "It's as if you'd put me in a separate compartment of some kind, marked 'women' or 'recreation,' or whatever my label is. You ask me to marry you, but it never occurs to you to share your professional life with me in any way, although it's obviously the most important part of you."

"Ann—"

"Well, there's some reason you don't want me here, isn't there?" she demanded angrily.

"What are you talking about?" Nick said, giving her a hard stare that made her catch her breath. After a moment he said tightly, "As far as my colleagues are concerned, we'll receive plenty of dinner invitations, when and if we're married, from the ones who count. The others don't interest me, and I can't see why they should interest you. And as for my work, it is not the kind of thing that lends itself to a dramatic ten-minute tour of the wards. I've tried to explain that to you. Of course, if you want to borrow some textbooks—"

"Maybe I will!"

"Ann, for heaven's sake—"

"Ann Claremont!" exclaimed a baritone voice behind them. "What are you doing here?"

Paul Griffith, the curly-haired intern who had dated Bobbie, stood in the corridor grinning at them.

"Hi, Paul," Ann said, relaxing her tense grip on gloves and purse and holding out her hand. What is the matter with me? she wondered despairingly, forcing a smile; I've never behaved this way in my life, making a scene like some cheap—

Paul said, "How is everything, Ann?"

"All right, thanks."

"About Bobbie," he said hurriedly, lowering his voice. "I was going to call or write a note or something." He colored a little under Ann's gaze. "Then I thought, well, what was the point, you probably had enough to handle as it was. Especially after some cop came and talked to me. I mean, I figured you probably had them camped on your doorstep."

"You two know each other, don't you?" Ann said, turning to Nick, aware of his silence. "Nick Sheldon, Paul Griffith."

"Sure," Paul said, looking from one to the other. "Hey, I heard you had a girl, but I had no idea it was old Annie here." Nick shrugged, smiling coldly. "What do you know?" Paul said, shaking his curly head. Nick glanced at his watch and picked up his charts as Paul said curiously, "How did you two happen to meet, anyway? You didn't know Bobbie, did you, Nick?"

"No."

"Not that I wouldn't have gotten around to introducing you sooner or later," Paul said with a grin. "But you know how it is, with a girl like that you can't be too careful." The grin died. "Sorry, Ann—I always seem to end up with my big foot in my mouth."

"We met at a party last summer, at Ken Brainard's."

"Oh, yeah, I never made that one but I heard it was a real blast. Well, well," he said, staring at Nick. "What a coincidence."

"Coincidence?" Nick's eyes returned sharply to Paul's face. "What's so coincidental about it? We both knew some of the same people, we were both invited to the same party. There's nothing exactly earth-shaking about that."

"No, I guess not," Paul said, looking at him.

"I've got to go," Nick told Ann. "I'll call you later."

"Tonight's the night we're going to the Brunettis'," Ann reminded him tonelessly.

"Yes. Seven o'clock, right?"

Ann nodded; he reached for her hand and held it a moment before he turned and strode away, the light tails of his coat floating behind him.

"Sounds serious," Paul said, looking after him. "If you don't mind my asking."

Ann said, "He wants me to marry him."

Paul looked at her in surprise. He said uncomfortably, "Hey, I wasn't trying to be *that* nosy." Ann said nothing. "Well, he's quite a guy," Paul said heartily. "I have to hand it to you—I would have said he'd wait until he was through his residency and at least three years established in practice before he'd even consider marriage. If then. Of course, I don't really know him."

"He's not exactly an easy person to get to know."

"You can say that again." Paul fingered his stethoscope, looking away from her. He said haltingly, "I don't mean that I don't admire him a lot. Everyone does. You know how it is—you sling a lot of bull around about how you're going to get a house in a good suburb and three weeks' vacation in Maine out of all this blood-sweat-and-tears; what the hell, a doctor's no vestal virgin, you're just as greedy and as fallible as the next guy, even if your brand of quackery is a little more advanced, et cetera. But underneath you can't help envying the guy who really does feel committed or dedicated, or whatever you want to call it. There's more in it for him, I guess, in the long run." He blew out his breath and said, "Wow! I really am wound up today. But anyway, what I wanted to say was—well, I'm glad Nick's marrying someone like you. It makes him seem a whole lot more—human, or something. He's not the most sociable guy in the world, and—oh, hell, all I'm really trying to say is congratulations and good luck."

"It's not settled yet," Ann said. "I mean, I haven't said yes."

There was a confused silence. Paul said, "Well, you can save the speech then, I guess. Or forget it." He sat down on the arm of a chair and stared at her. At last he said good-naturedly, "Do you go around making this announcement to everyone you meet? Somehow I don't think Dr. Sheldon would appreciate it very much."

"No. I guess that's why I said it," Ann said with a sigh. "I'm sorry, Paul, don't mind me. We were in the middle of a fight, that's all; I didn't mean to take it out on you."

"Oh." Paul looked relieved. "Good thing I came along, I guess?"

"Yes." Ann smiled at him.

"Hey, look," Paul said, staring down at his shoes. "About Bobbie. Really, I was so—so damned thrown by the thing, I couldn't function for a while. Being with her the night before, and then hearing what had happened . . . the senselessness of it. I don't know," he said, shaking his head. "Have they found the guy who did it yet?"

"No."

"It's funny," Paul said after a moment. "After the shock wore off, you were the one I kept thinking about. I mean, I had this impression of the kind of person you were, and how hard this thing must have hit you. I thought of calling you I don't know how many times this summer—but then I thought, well, you might think it was strange or something, one of her boy friends getting in on the act, white charger and all . . ." He laughed self-consciously. "Anyway, it looks like somebody beat me to it. More power to him. You look great, by the way, Ann—just great." He rose. "Well, back to the salt mines."

"Wait a minute, Paul," Ann said, putting a hand on his arm. "There's a—question you can answer for me. I don't know why I didn't think of asking you before." Yes, she thought drearily. Just a phone call. Why couldn't I make it? Would I ever have made it? "Bobbie had a pin," she said. "A big gold thing with spikes. When I was—going through her things, taking inventory for her parents, I couldn't find it. I don't know whether she lost it or whether it's still in the apartment somewhere. I thought I remembered her wearing it the night before—the night she had the date with you, but I wasn't sure."

"No," Paul said. "She was wearing pearls that night, and a light blue suit. I remember."

"If you're sure—"

"I'm no better about women's clothes than most guys, but I remember that night. How she looked and everything. She wasn't wearing any pin. I mean, a thing like that you could hardly help noticing."

"Yes. Well, it'll turn up, I'm sure," Ann hesitated, and added bleakly, "By the way, I'd appreciate it if you didn't mention this to Nick—my asking about the pin, I mean. He thinks this sort of thing is—well, morbid and unnecessary."

"Oh? Sure," Paul said quickly, as if no opinion of Nick's could surprise him. "Still, you can't blame her parents for wanting to get her things in order. Aah," he said softly, shaking his head, "the poor kid. What a world. Well, so long, Ann, I'll see you around, I hope. Don't make any rash decisions," he added with a grin. "And if you're ever available again, let me know."

Ann stood alone for a moment, listening to the noises of the hospital—the whir of rubber wheels on linoleum, the clatter of the lunch wagon, a distant burst of convalescent laughter. As she drew on her gloves, a big man in a camel's-hair coat brushed rudely past her and slumped into a chair, staring at the unlighted cigar in his hand. He began to curse under his breath, fluently and urgently; Ann thought at first that he was praying.

It was cold in the apartment. Ann took off the black suit—still a little tight under the arms—and put on an old sweater and skirt. She stood holding out her hands to the radiator, which was clanking and spitting to small effect. The street below was gray and empty except for the young man who ran the basement novelty shop across the way, returning unhurriedly from a long Saturday lunch hour. He was wearing a quilted parka and boots, and kept glancing at the sky as if he expected or desired snow. The door closed behind him, and a moment later the window gave out a pallid gleam of light behind its basement railing. Ann longed suddenly to follow him, to offer a pot of coffee in exchange for companionship; or for work, she thought, which was what she really needed. She could help him to clean up or unpack cartons or whatever you did on gray Saturday afternoons when nobody wanted to buy handwoven aprons or Japanese lanterns. In fact, she had been in the shop only once and had taken a mild dislike to the young man, who had weedy hair and an ingratiating smile . . . I could call Marge, she thought more reasonably. But she would be seeing Marge and her father that evening at the Brunettis', in a few hours; and Nick, too. What was it, in any case, that she wanted to say to Marge—that Nick had lied to her, and that she didn't know why?

No. I've put it off long enough, she told herself, and sat down in the chair by the window, hunching forward with her hands clasped tightly around her knees. She watched the ovals of her thumbnails whiten at the tips, and thought: He must have known all along who I was—that I was the dead girl's roommate. The business of recognizing Bobbie's photograph was a fake; I would have seen it if I hadn't been so nervous myself that second evening. And why the second evening? If it had really been a matter of simple recognition, he would have known at once or not at all, with the kind of memory he has. At the party—no, she thought, looking back at her face and Nick's through the noise and haze of the crowded room, he couldn't have known at the party; someone must have told him afterward. And the strain I felt that first evening when he came here, which I thought was only the inevitable strain of seeing each other again after the queer intensity of our first encounter, must have been partly his not knowing what to say, whether or not to tell me he knew about Bobbie. And—yes, of course!—when I said nothing, even after he had given me a natural opening by asking about the picture, he must have assumed that it was a closed subject, something I couldn't or wouldn't talk about. It would have been awkward then, almost impossible, for him to announce out of the blue that he had known Bobbie, however slightly.

And then—Ann let her hands fall to her sides with a shock of surprise and relief, seeing how smoothly the path of her narration ran on before her, no devious labyrinth after all, nothing to dread—then, when he found that he wanted to go on seeing me, he realized that he must clear the air about Bobbie somehow (just as I was deciding the same thing), and he allowed himself to recognize the picture. He must have sensed my horror of all the morbid interest I'd already been subjected to, and feared that if I found he'd known about the murder all along I would think he'd been attracted to me because of it—like the strangers who lay in wait for me that first week, outside the apartment door. And that's exactly what I would have thought, did think, about almost everyone I met for a while, until Nick came along. So he couldn't tell me he had known Bobbie; and it probably didn't

seem important anyway, at least not until we began—or I began
—our detective work.

The detective work—

Ann gazed out the window. Thin flakes of snow had begun to
fall, leaving a faint sheen on the pavement; the young man in
the parka had been right, after all. A tall gaunt woman in a dark
coat was standing on the opposite curb, staring up at Ann's windows as if demanding something from the squares of light. Even
from a distance her attitude appeared so fierce, so penetrating
and expectant that Ann found herself shrinking back absurdly in
her chair, her heart thudding. The woman turned away, sending
a last mad brooding glance over her shoulder.

An acquaintanceship, Ann thought, closing her eyes. It couldn't
have been more than that. If he had known her well, he would
have told me. She remembered Nick's questions about Bobbie—
would she have said this, done that, reacted in this way? No, his
ignorance was genuine, she would swear to that.

And so—and so it's all quite simple, she told herself, and not
mysterious at all. Or at least if there is a mystery it's a very small
one, the kind of thing that may always exist between two people
who have led such divergent lives before their meeting with each
other. No need to imagine such darkness in an unexpected revela-
tion, just because your own preference is for clarity and sunlight,
an unambiguous childhood landscape that never existed anyway, except by virtue of adult deception . . . She got up and
took a book from the shelf. Of course, I'll have to tell him sometime that I know, she thought, if only to satisfy my own curiosity.

Only later, as she was making her way along the blurry snow-
smeared pavements in search of a cab, did it occur to her that
when she questioned Nick, he would be bound to ask why she
had not spoken right away about the pin; and that she would
have no answer to give him.

TWELVE

Nick himself opened
the door of the Brunettis' apartment, which exhaled a warm breath of conversation and music, and the odor, bitter and earthy, of the bronze chrysanthemums heaped in a bowl on the hall table. At the same moment Carlo's younger sister Connie sauntered into the hall from the living room, carrying a small overnight case and noisily eating a potato chip.

Connie said, "Hi, Ann, everybody's here but you. Mama said I could go now. You know, pretending not to be kicking me out." She looked sideways at Nick under her black lashes.

"Don't you want a coat? It's freezing out," Ann said as Nick helped her off with hers.

"No, I'm just going down to Molly's to spend the night. Big deal. Her mother won't let her watch TV after nine, so there's nothing to do except play Scrabble or put on nail polish or something. Last time we painted the cat's toenails. Persian Pink," she said, giggling. "That's what made us think of the cat. Molly's mother made us take it off with polish remover, only the cat didn't like the smell and went charging around and knocked down this African mask they have in the den. Well, 'bye, nice to have met you," she said to Nick, and started out the door. As an afterthought she came back and whispered noisily to Ann, "Let me

know what you think of Moira, will you? If Carlo marries her,
I'll die!"

Nick grimaced as the door slammed after her. "Charming
child."

"She's thirteen," Ann said. "It's the worst age for a girl. At least
Connie has a sense of humor, which I certainly didn't at that
age."

"You couldn't have been anything but beautiful even then,"
Nick said, putting his arms around her as she stood at the mirror
smoothing down her damp hair.

"I was a militant Girl Scout, and fat." She met his smile in the
mirror. "Well, I was."

"Can I take you home later, Scout?"

Ann looked away. She said, "I take it I'm forgiven for trespassing this morning."

"Trespassing? Oh, that." Nick shrugged, releasing her. "I'm
never my social best when I'm at work, I'm afraid. I have to save
all my charm for the patients, and the head nurse."

There was a pause. Ann nodded toward the living room and
said, "Well, who's here?"

"Just your parents, and Carlo and his girl. A family party. Not
a bad time to announce our engagement, if you felt like it."

"Nick—"

"All right, it was just a thought. I promise not to make any
unexpected toasts."

He smiled down at her, but she saw with a pang how tired he
looked, how strained. Tonight, she thought. Why not? What is it I
want, anyway, except to give him a home like this one, and children—to see him less alone, to bind him to me insofar as he can
be bound?

"Ann dear," exclaimed Aunt Sophie, coming toward her with
outstretched hands. "I'm so sorry you had to make the trek up
here by yourself on such a miserable evening. I don't know why
my idiot son didn't pick you up on his way to Moira's."

"But it wouldn't have been on his way," Ann objected. "Doesn't
Moira live up on the East Side somewhere? Anyway, I have to
confess that I'm late only because I couldn't find anything but
a pink lipstick to wear with my new red dress, and I stopped at
a drugstore on the way."

"How frivolous of you!" Aunt Sophie said with a smile, and added to Nick, "I can see you're having a civilizing influence."

"Not at all," Nick said. "If I had my way she wouldn't wear lipstick at all. She looks much better without it."

"Really? Well, that's a fashionable point of view, anyway. When I think what a struggle I had with Louis when Nina, our older daughter, got to the lipstick-wearing stage . . . and now that Connie's the same age, we both find ourselves wishing she *would* wear lipstick instead of this awful eye make-up they all yearn for that makes them look like so many Hottentots." She led them into the living room, saying pleasantly, "Now, what can we give you two to drink?"

Ann saw with relief that Aunt Sophie's manner toward Nick would be determinedly noncommittal, but she felt the older woman's dislike of him like a thin impenetrable coating over her voice and smile. She thought defiantly: It is easier to dislike some people than to like them. Aunt Sophie indulges herself; Nick is right about that at any rate.

"Ye gods, Mama," Carlo said, pushing his plate away with a theatrical groan, "don't you realize Thanksgiving dinner is only a couple of weeks away? I can't afford to get fat at this stage in my career. People don't trust fat lawyers; at least not *young* fat lawyers."

Marge smiled at Nick across the table and said, "Does that apply to doctors too?"

Nick shrugged. "I guess it does, up to a point. You don't want to look too prosperous and well fed, for obvious reasons. On the other hand, if you're the lean and hungry type, the patient is apt to decide you're some kind of fanatic scientist who's only interested in him as a laboratory specimen."

Guy said, "Yeah, that's a damn strange thing, isn't it—this association of intellect with leanness and spareness? A Western thing, too; I mean, the Asians have the opposite tradition—Buddha, Confucius, the fat philosopher."

"Santayana was fat," Marge said.

"And Gandhi was thin," Carlo said.

"Well, hell, Gandhi didn't eat anything," Guy said. "Anyway, I'm not talking about ascetics necessarily—"

"We all use the same metabolic pathways," Nick said impatiently. The others looked blank. "A thin person may appear to have more nervous energy than a fat one, therefore more intellectual energy, at least in a certain kind of culture."

Aunt Sophie said thoughtfully, "A certain kind of culture. I suppose the difference is in our notions of intellect—what it is and what it does."

"Exactly!" Guy said triumphantly. "In the West intellectual effort is traditionally dynamic, progressive; in the East it's contemplative and self-contained. So it's not surprising that your men of genius in the two cultures are apt to be of different physical types."

Uncle Louis said, smiling at Nick, "Theoretically, then, an undistinguished fat man in our society—intelligent, let us say, but lazy and unproductive by our standards—might have grown up a philosopher instead of an automobile salesman if he had been born in India instead of New Jersey." He sipped his wine gravely.

Nick gave a polite laugh. Ann saw that he had lost interest in the conversation.

Carlo said, "Dynamism and energy, ha! Not from where I sit. The rule these days is moderation in all things, or at least the appearance of it. You may keep immoderate working hours or have a wildly immoderate love life, but your professional personality has to stay bland as rice pudding. It's damned dull. Even the big corporations have convinced themselves that they're really just dedicated public servants whose executives blush at the very mention of the word profit. Nice guys finish first these days," he added with a sigh.

Nick said shortly, "Only because niceness is easier to counterfeit than some other things. Efficiency, for example, or intelligence."

There was a pause as Agnes entered with the dessert. Moira, sitting next to Uncle Louis, gave an appealing little laugh and said, brushing the straight fair hair from her cheek with a slender hand, "Goodness, the musical world must be terribly old-fashioned. I mean, one's success or failure is still a matter of performance in the long run. Of course, it helps to know the right people, but—"

"There are fakes in any profession," Nick said.

Aunt Sophie said, spooning chocolate soufflé onto her Dresden dessert plate, "Gracious, you do sound disillusioned!"

"I had no illusions to start with," Nick said evenly.

Her dark eyes rested a moment on his face before she murmured, turning away, "That must have simplified your life greatly," and ended the general conversation by asking Guy a question about a mutual friend.

Why must he be so arrogant with her? Ann thought heavily, and said with an effort to Carlo next to her, "You haven't been over to see me in ages. I've missed you."

Carlo grinned. "Oh, well, between my immoderate working hours and my wildly immoderate love life—"

"No, seriously. I haven't even heard the latest stories about the flock."

"A collection of strays," Carlo said. "It was never a flock. Well, for one thing, I've moved. Just over to Perry Street, but the psychological distance is enormous."

"Moved! When?"

"A few weeks ago. Wonders never cease, eh? No," he added, following her quick glance at Moira, "I'm not living with Moira, sadly enough. She lives with her uncle and aunt, very protective types who aren't sure whether they approve of me or not. But I finally got tired of playing the good shepherd to all those clunks —it was getting too expensive, among other things—so I found myself a nice little bachelor apartment complete with fake oriental décor (you have to lie down to read, all the lamps are so low), and there I live in decorous splendor, passing out kimonos and paper slippers to my occasional guests. You and Nick must come join me in a cup of sake one of these days, before I forsake the Western world entirely to become a fat oriental philosopher."

Ann laughed. "Nick's too tall and Anglo-Saxon-looking; he'd make a very poor Japanese, even temporarily."

"Oh, I don't know," Carlo said. "He looks pretty inscrutable to me. And probably ruthless as hell—you know, just as soon run you through with his samurai sword as shake hands with you. All done with great neatness and precision, and no hard feelings, yes?" He hissed the "s" comically, giving her a slit-eyed grin.

Ann sat back suddenly, her spoon rattling against her plate. She set it down with care.

"All right, I'm jealous," Carlo said. "I admit it. But I have my consolations, anyway." He sent an amorous glance at Moira, who was listening earnestly to one of his father's anecdotes.

With the part of her mind that could still move independently, flickering around the cold stillness that had gripped her, Ann thought: Yes, and Moira's a little like me in appearance, except that her features and coloring are more delicate. That restrained, uncertain, feminine manner must be good for Carlo; no need to wear the armor he had begun to wear with me.

She willed herself to pick up her spoon and finish her dessert. Carlo had turned away to talk to Guy. On Ann's right Uncle Louis lit a cigarette, looking thoughtful. It seemed to her that he was gazing at Nick. She thought crazily: Of course, he sees it too; they must all have seen it except me . . . The candle flame tilted briefly in the draft from the pantry door as Agnes entered to remove the plates; at once the room grew darker and objects took on a new solidity, the conspiratorial solidity of objects in a dream at the moment when the sleeper fights for release, bruising himself horribly against the heavy oak of a locked door which his waking mind assures him is mere fantasy, illusion without substance . . . Ann stared fixedly at her plate, memorizing the pastel pattern beneath the random dark streaks of the chocolate, until Agnes' brittle old hand snatched it away. It left a faint circular print on the smooth damask of the cloth. No, she thought. It's impossible. Impossible! Don't even think it for a moment. Stop it; stop thinking.

Chairs scraped around her; the damask stirred heavily against her knees as Carlo stood up. She watched Uncle Louis lean forward to blow out the candles nearest him, pursing his lips, his thin neck straining over his old man's tendons. She sat still.

Oh, God. Oh, God.

"Come on, Annie, snap out of it," Carlo said, dropping a warm hand on her shoulder. "What are you doing—thinking up names for your six prospective children? I thought we might be getting the good word about you and Nick tonight."

She rose, keeping her face turned away from him. If he saw it he would know too. Carlo, she thought distractedly, I must get away from Carlo. No—Nick was the one, coming toward her now while the others moved into the living room for coffee, his gaze seeking hers possessively. She saw his expression change as he caught sight of her face.

"Everything all right?" he said, taking her arm.

Ann kept one hand on the back of her chair, consciously balancing the pressure of his touch. She said, "As a matter of fact, I'm not feeling too well. I think maybe if I could lie down for a few minutes—"

He frowned in concern, but not before she had seen the quick light of wariness in his eyes—a look she had seen so many times before, but which now seemed to tell her all she feared to know. Her mind leaped forward convulsively, searching, and paused. She said with an apologetic laugh, "It's just cramps. I took a pill before dinner, but it doesn't seem to have helped."

"Want me to get Mrs. Brunetti?"

"Yes, if you would. I'm sorry to be such an idiot."

The right lie—where had it come from? she thought as he turned away. For the timing was right, her period was due at any time, and Nick himself had seen last month how ill she could become . . . Already Aunt Sophie was coming toward her, looking capable and sympathetic. Nick lingered in the doorway, watching them.

"I'm sorry you're not feeling well, dear. What is it? Not flu, I hope." She saw Ann's face, rigid with calm, and said quickly, "Why don't you lie down in Connie's room for a while? It's Nina's old room—you know, at the end of the hall—and you can be as ill as you like in complete privacy; I always think that helps, don't you?" Talking, smiling her serene smile, she led Ann into the hallway, past the music room and the master bedroom to Connie's room at the end.

"There," she said, snapping on the bedside lamp and moving to the window to adjust the blinds, "you take your shoes off and stretch out. And here's the bathroom—we added it when we had the room done over for Connie." She opened the door and pressed a switch; the fluorescent tube above the mirror flared soundlessly as Ann sat down on the edge of the bed.

Ann said, "It's just cramps. You know what a time I have with them sometimes. I just suddenly felt—"

"It must be hereditary," Aunt Sophie said, busying herself with towels. "Your mother used to be absolutely prostrated every time

—couldn't eat, couldn't sleep, just lay on her bed staring at the ceiling and memorizing things. Irregular verbs, geometry theorems, dates . . . she claimed she never forgot anything she learned that way. When we first roomed together in boarding school, I thought—oh, dear, it still strikes me funny—I thought it was some sort of religious seizure; I thought she was *praying*, really I did! She certainly wasn't particularly devout the rest of the time, as far as I could see, but once a month she would go through this strange performance—complete with fasting, you see. I would tiptoe around, feeling quite awed and not daring to say anything." She chuckled. "Oh, dear, girls are such idiots about these things; or used to be, anyway. Connie's generation seems to have gone to the opposite extreme. All these ghastly little clinical talks about sex at age thirteen—one feels they might as well be discussing home permanents, for all they get out of it."

She looked over at Ann, who had turned down the thick chenille bedspread and was lying on her side with her eyes closed, the skirt of her red dress bunched around her knees. "Do you want to take something, Ann? Connie has all sorts of things here in the medicine cabinet."

"I took a pill before dinner, thanks," Ann lied mechanically. "I'd better wait a while."

"Well, I'll stop rambling on and leave you, if there's nothing I can do. Just call if you want company."

Ann said, "Marge. Would you ask Marge to come in, Aunt Sophie?"

"Of course."

She left, closing the door softly behind her. Ann thought: Of course, Aunt Sophie never rambles; that was only to cover up my lie about having cramps, to help me without embarrassing me. I've got to do better than that, if everything *he* has said and done has been a lie, oh, dear God . . . But Marge, what will I say to Marge? No, it doesn't matter, anything to make her stay here with me—to keep him away and give me time to think; to get warm again.

She reached for the shiny blue satin puff at the foot of the bed and pulled it up over her. It felt cold and slithery against her stockinged legs. But why am I lying down? she thought. I'm not sick. Or yes, perhaps I am, and that is where the thought has come from—some foul eruption of the mind, a black bile . . . Connie's room was blue and white and flouncy, nothing like Connie herself: a magazine room. Even the whimsical stuffed animals on the radiator cover looked as though they had been ordered as a set by the decorator. Ann stared at the book lying on the bed table and made out the title on its scuffed spine: *The Mill on the Floss*. Yes, that at least was Connie, Connie's life so like what her own had been—classrooms and uniforms and macaroni lunches, the girls singing out their raucous last-name salutes. "Hey, *Claremont*, wake up, will you?"

There was a knock on the door. She said tensely, "Who is it?"

"Just me," Marge's voice said. "Can you give me a hand with the door? I've brought you some medicine."

Ann reached for the doorknob and turned it. Marge edged into the room, holding two liqueur glasses by their slender stems. "I thought benedictine—that's your favorite, isn't it? Or maybe it's too sweet. I could get you some brandy if you'd rather have that."

"No, that's fine. Thanks." Ann took the tiny glass, propping herself on an elbow.

Marge closed the door and sat down in a small blue armchair at the foot of the bed. "Cheers," she said, raising her glass. "Nothing like a *digestif* for the nerves, to say nothing of the stomach. What's the matter, sweetie?"

Ann set the glass on the table and lay down again. The benedictine left a sticky coating on her tongue; her stomach moved queasily. She said, "Marge, there's something I have to think about that's—terribly important. I can't talk about it. But if you could stay here with me now for a few minutes—"

Marge glanced involuntarily at the door, a quick gleam of comprehension in her eyes. "Of course, darling. You take all the time you want. I thought you were awfully quiet this evening." When Ann said nothing, she added, looking around, "I forgot my cigarettes. I wonder if Connie has some stashed away somewhere. I bet she does." Ann half saw her go to the closet and feel through the pockets of a raincoat and then rummage among the purses on the shelf above. "Here they are, the little devil! Matches, too. I am in luck. Whew! Stale as last year's toast. She must have had them for months." She sat down again with a pin tray for an ashtray and picked up a magazine, after a swift anxious glance at her stepdaughter, who lay on her back now, staring up at the shadowy ceiling, her face pale and still.

Quiet tonight . . . was I? Did he notice it? God. Oh, God. His face on the ferry that night when he asked me to marry him; and that only after he had tried, and failed, to—but she could not think the words. His need of me . . . of course he needed me, he still does, for his own safety. He must have known all along that it might come to that, or at least from the moment I told him what I thought about Bobbie's death. Yes: the law. A wife cannot testify against her husband; or is it only that she doesn't have to? But once bound to him, sharing his life—

And in the meantime, his possession of me: his love-making that shaped my body to his will, the deliberate cultivation of my appetite so that in time my desire for him might become obsessive, unreasoning, slavish. As it has. Yes, even now.

No. Think of Bobbie. His hands on the knife. Impossible—true. I see how his strong fingers curved around the cheap wooden hilt, how his shoulder tensed at the moment of contact. But of course he wore gloves, as the police said; they all do, even the crazy ones, the homicidal maniacs. Thanks to the movies and the comics and television, it must be almost instinctive by now for them to put on gloves, almost as natural and necessary as the taking of aim, the contraction of muscles before the final thrust. Those worn pigskin gloves with the stitching that has begun to pull apart at the seams, the ones I was going to repair for him—

There was a knock on the door. Nick's voice said, "Anything I can do, Ann?"

Ann saw the doorknob turning and flung out a hand reflexively to stop it. Marge said quickly, "She's feeling better, Nick. We were just having a quiet chat."

"Just thought I'd see if she needed any medical attention," he said, waiting.

"Not right now, thanks," Ann managed to say. "You go back to the party. I'll be out in a few minutes."

"Okay," he said mildly. "Just thought I'd check."

Gone. Ann lay back with a pounding heart. Marge had half risen from her chair. Now she sank down, staring at Ann. "What is all this about, anyway?" she asked in a low voice. "You look absolutely petrified. Has he done something . . . ?"

"Done something?" Ann repeated, stifling a wild laugh.

"Yes. For heaven's sake, Ann, this isn't like you at all, to collapse this way. If you've had some kind of fight with Nick—"

"A fight. No, not exactly." She saw that she would have to tell Marge something. She said rapidly, "Nick wanted to announce our engagement tonight, after dinner. He was going to speak to Dad first, of course. I just couldn't go through with it." She turned her head to look at Marge, willing her to believe what she was saying. "I didn't want Nick to know what I felt. That's why I made up this excuse. Or—I don't know, I'm really not feeling very well; maybe that's partly why I got so upset. But I need some time to think about it. To know what to say to him."

"He wouldn't be the easiest person in the world to live with," Marge said carefully. "But then, neither are you, you know, sweetie. All right," she added, flattening the magazine in her lap, "I'll mind my own business. But some uncertainty and doubt is perfectly normal, you know, up to a point. In any case it's better to find out what you feel now, before it's too late."

Too late! Oh, God, the problem is now, ten minutes from now, Ann thought in panic. How to find a face to take back into the room where he is—where right now he may be wondering, pondering, aware that something is wrong. Thinking of a way to test me—

Wait. Oh, God, no. This isn't really happening. It can't be. I've made the whole thing up, hysterically, like a child frightening itself in the dark. Yes, myself as a child, summoning up fresh horrors one by one in order to prove my own courage to myself. Because what do I know now that I didn't know before? Carlo's remark at dinner was only the silly sort of thing he's been saying all his life; in itself it meant nothing. Wait: go over it all again, from the first meeting, step by step.

But this time her mind would not obey; it danced willfully ahead in the new glare of truth, which illuminated scenes at random, without regard for chronology or logic, without mercy.

Ann sat up and pushed the quilt aside in one swift agitated movement. Marge looked up.

"Marge, do you think Aunt Sophie would understand if I just

said goodnight and went on home? I'm—I don't think I'd be much of an addition to the evening at this rate."

"Sophie will understand, certainly, if that's what you want to do." Marge gave her a long puzzled look and sighed, tossing the magazine aside. "If this is what love does to you, maybe you *should* have married that nice BBD and O boy and settled down peacefully in the suburbs. You aren't pregnant, are you, darling?"

"No," Ann said, feeling for her shoes.

"I hope you don't mind my asking. Oh, Ann dear," Marge said, standing up and putting her hands on Ann's shoulders. "I want so much to be able to help you. Can't you talk to me?"

Ann looked up into Marge's face, seeing how square and lined and weary it was without the habitual wry gaiety of the eyes and mouth. She said softly, "It isn't you, Marge. There's no one I can talk to. But if there were anyone, it would be you."

Marge's eyes glistened with sudden tears; she looked away. After a moment she said, "Well, I just want you to know I'm still ready to give you the best damn wedding anybody ever had, and I don't care if you marry the hairy ape himself. Of course, we'd prefer Nick."

"Thank you," Ann said with a bleak smile.

In the black and white music room Moira and Uncle Louis were playing Haydn duets on the piano, while Carlo puttered in a corner with the tape recorder. Moving slowly and stiffly, Ann went on into the living room, where the others sat talking around the big marble coffee table. Nick lounged in an armchair, his gray suit almost black against the soft amber stuff of the upholstery; he turned his head at once as Ann entered and got to his feet, approaching her swiftly.

"Better now?"

"Not much, I'm afraid. I think I'd better go on home and go to bed." She paused. Walk, don't run, she told herself. If he once suspects flight— She said, "If you could come down and find me a cab—"

"I'll go on down to the Village with you."

"No. Really—I'm not fit company for anyone. I'm just going to dose myself and go to sleep. You stay here; Aunt Sophie would appreciate it."

"Ah well, anything Aunt Sophie would appreciate is more or

less obligatory, isn't it?" But he smiled down at her. "You do look
a little green around the gills. Okay, I'll go get your coat."

It had begun to snow again lightly. The pavement shone slick
in the blaze of the cab's headlights. Leaning through the window as Ann sank back against the seat, Nick said, "I'll call you
in the morning to see how you feel. Maybe we can finally get to
the movies tomorrow night. There's something good at the theater
near my place, for once—that French cops-and-robbers thing, the
one about the jewel thieves, whatever it's called."

"*Rififi.*"

"Yes, that's it. Well, goodnight, darling. Sleep well."

The cab moved off at last. Ann saw how he stood watching it
out of sight, as if exerting his power over her until the last possible moment. Their next meeting already arranged . . . Ah, no,
it's too fantastic, it can't be happening to me! she thought as the
cab sped southward along Central Park West, its windshield wip-
ers squeaking. But the sense of her own danger encased her now
like a sheathing of ice, smooth and seamless. She sat motionless
while the cab weaved crazily through the theater-district traffic,
feeling herself for once immune to the random violence of the
streets.

In the city that night, in the cold hours of the early morning, all
familiar noises ceased, as though the million sleepers sucked the
sound of the city into their dreams with each huge collective
breath, leaving a vacuum which nothing could inhabit for long.
Once a dog barked; there was a brief explosion of shattered
glass. The sleepers dreamed of moon-journeys over fields of pitted
rock, of empty halls and fortresses, desert places where the
travelers' garments flapped soundlessly in a dry wind. Within
the vacuum, the wakeful lay wide-eyed and rigid, listening for
the dreadful approach of the day.

THIRTEEN

At ten o'clock the telephone rang. It rang twelve times and stopped. Ann looked at it. A slug or a snail, she thought, black and slimy, like some deep-sea creature that emits its poison rays in a blind, instinctive rhythm, indiscriminately seeking a moving target. The thing to do is just go on sitting absolutely still . . . It rang again. She moved toward it slowly, like a swimmer parting sluggish waves. But it will sting my hand! she thought crazily, watching her fingers close around the receiver and lift it to her ear.

"Ann. I hope I didn't wake you."

"No."

"I tried you a minute ago, but there was no answer. I must have dialed the wrong number."

Her lips moved, but no sound came. Outside the window the Sunday sun was shining on sidewalks greasy with slush. A small boy packed a gray snowball and tossed it at the fender of a parked car, where it smashed wetly, leaving a scummy froth.

He said, "Well, how are you feeling?"

"Oh—not too well, I'm afraid." It's terribly funny, she wanted to tell him, I did get the curse after all; my body at least knows how to defend itself, obeying some ancient system of reflex and withdrawal. It's only my mind that—

"That's too bad. Anything I can do?"

"No, thank you," she said carefully.

"Ann . . . ? Are you sure you're not upset about something? If it's still that business about the hospital yesterday, I—"

"Oh, no," she said, and saw too late that she had made a mistake: this was something she could have used, to give herself time. "I mean, I'm not upset, really, it's just the way I'm feeling."

"Well, look," he said, "let's forget about the movie tonight. I'll come on down around six, see how you are. We can go out for a bite to eat somewhere."

"I—I don't know whether I'll be hungry."

"Then I'll fix you some tea and toast. Maybe you're coming down with something." But his voice had altered; she could see his frown, the droop of his eyelids, the sudden tension of his body; perhaps his hand had even clenched, like hers, around the curly black wire of the telephone. "If you'd rather I didn't come at all—"

"Oh, no, it's just . . . why don't I call you? This afternoon, I mean. I'll probably be feeling fine by then."

A plan! she thought cloudily. Oh, God! How could I have let all these hours go by without making a plan? She looked around the room: to wall herself up within it, or to strip it and flee? The curtains, the pictures, the Hicks animals above the fireplace, all returned her agitated gaze calmly, offering nothing.

"The thing is," Nick said, "I'm not sure just where I'll be. I'd better call you."

"Well, but in that case . . . If I'm not here, I'll probably be at Marge's. Or I'll leave a message there."

"Oh? Plans I don't know about?"

"No, but I might want to take a walk or something. I don't have to stay here all day waiting for you to call, do I?" she said, seizing automatically on an old source of irritation.

"Not at all. You just sounded terribly—elusive, all of a sudden."

His voice was dry, controlled—not annoyed, she realized, not angry. Why not? He has to know, she thought. Of course: he can't afford not to know, to hang up and walk away; he never could. And it was never love that inhibited him, only fear. "We are bound together . . ." But how am I bound to him? If I knew that—

"I just don't want you feeling too sure of me," she heard herself say brightly, flirtatiously, on a note so false he must surely hear its reverberation magnified into shocking splinters of sound, as though she had suddenly smashed a pane of glass.

But he laughed and said, "You don't have to worry about that. I've never felt sure of you yet. Look, darling, take a slug of brandy and go back to bed, will you? You sound pretty punchy. I'll call you later."

"I'm sorry, I—"

"A couple of babies, that's what you need. No more cramps, or so I've heard."

His children: a murderer's children. They would look like anyone else's, clear-eyed, with straight fair hair; they would go to nursery school, learn to swim, skin their knees . . . Wait. There was something she had thought of last night, something she could say to him. A test, it would be, like something you did in chemistry, adding a single drop of acid to a beaker to see if the liquid inside turned cloudy or changed color. Yes, she had even worked out the words—

"Nick?"

"You still there?"

"I got to thinking about Bobbie last night"—No! The danger, it was too dangerous, oh, God, what was she doing?—"and I've decided you may have been right to begin with. About her being pregnant."

"Oh?"

"It really is the simplest solution, the one that makes the most sense. As you said, if she had wanted to marry the man and he refused, and he was someone who had a—position of some sort to maintain . . . He couldn't force her to have an abortion, after all. And if she'd threatened to go to his superiors and make trouble—well, I can see how desperate he might have felt."

A pause. "But from what you said about the men she knew—"

A moving van thundered by in the street below, its studded metal top almost on a level with the window. She lost the rest of his answer and the tone of his voice in the uproar; and could not remember now just what it was she had expected or wanted from him, only that she must go on. There was a thin ribbon of pain behind her eyes that made her blink and rub her forehead with the heel of her hand.

She said, "Yes, but there may have been men I didn't know anything about, like the one Stephanie mentioned—I told you about him, didn't I? Anyway, there are several people, girl friends of Bobbie's, I could talk to who might know something. People whose apartments she might have borrowed, that sort of thing."

He said, "It sounds worth a try."

"You think so?"

"Why not? As you say, it's the simplest solution. And a good deal easier to pursue than your eyewitness theory, or whatever it was."

"Yes. All those gruesome newspaper stories—I suppose I might as well forget them." She waited. "It was probably just a wild-goose chase, anyway."

"Well," he said easily, "it did seem a bit far-fetched."

"Yes."

"Look, darling, I've got to go. Promise me you'll take it easy, okay? I'll check back with you later. Goodbye for now."

"Goodbye," she whispered as he hung up, and laid the receiver down on the radiator cover, leaving it helpless on its back where it could not harm her again. She went into the kitchen, away from the glassy brilliance of the world outside, and turned on the gas beneath the kettle. A cup of tea—he had said something about tea. Or was it brandy? He wants to make me drunk, she thought wildly, to keep me under sedation, anything will do; just as his hands, stroking and smoothing my body, were really seeking my mind all the time, dulling its edges, shaping it to his use . . . No, it must be that I'm drunk already, drunk and giddy with fear—the air so shallow and chill here at the top of this mountain I seem to have been climbing for so long, following his relentless shadow above me. I never asked where he was leading me, but all the same I knew; surely I have known all along. This cold place . . . Oh, God! Bound together, roped together on the sheer mountainside, so that his fall means my own as well—

The kettle whistled piercingly. She took it from the burner and watched the blue ring of flame sputter and die. Gas, she thought: it's what people use to kill themselves with, a convenient home source of death. She looked at her tiny oven, which was mounted above the burners, its handle level with her forehead. It would be terribly uncomfortable, she thought, and besides, could you die standing up? Also, the oven needs cleaning. She began to laugh, at first silently, then aloud. "No, Miss Claremont," she told herself. "I'm afraid you are not the dramatic type, after all."

She took her mug of tea back into the living room and sat down at the desk. There was the notebook, the folder, the sharpened pencils all neatly ranged in front of her. The sight sobered her; she was gratified to feel herself becoming calmly businesslike, detached, ready at last to think things out to their necessary conclusion, and then to act as the facts dictated. Surely that was what facts always did, wasn't it, once you got them arranged in their proper order?

So then, she thought briskly. I have just learned something: that Nick did not have an affair with Bobbie, that wasn't it; did not get her pregnant; is sure—but why so sure, how can he be?—that none of her friends knew about whatever connection there was between them. More than that, that I may have been on the right track after all with my newspaper stories; he agreed with such alacrity that I ought to give them up. Yes, I'm almost sure now that it was something she saw or overheard, something that involved him; and when she saw him at the hospital and he realized that she could identify him, he made his decision and acted —swiftly, confidently, without looking back.

The only weak point in his plan seems to have been me—the only possibility he seems not to have considered. After all, Bobbie might have come home that night and told me the whole story, whatever it was, though as it happened I was asleep and never even heard her come in. Perhaps it didn't occur to him until later that she might have had a roommate. He must have had a bad moment or two until he realized I knew nothing. More than made up for later, of course, by the entertainment of watching me play girl detective, sending me up one blind alley after another with my trusty flashlight in hand—

And then, when I began to see—no, she told herself, resting her head on her hands, I won't think of that now, of how from the beginning it was his very arrogance that attracted me, his hardness and self-sufficiency equal to my own, and the capacity for cruelty beneath it . . .

And now? He would come to the apartment in the evening,

would loosen his tie and make them both a drink and settle down in the chair by the window. And she would say—what? "I'm terribly sorry, Nick, but I'm afraid I can't marry you after all. It's not so much your being a murderer that I mind, though the idea does take some getting used to. No, it's the way you've deceived me and made me deceive myself; nobody likes being played for a fool, you know, and I do have my pride. After all, a successful marriage is based on mutual trust—isn't that what all the books say?" A friendly smile. "Oh, no, I'm not going to turn you in, heavens, don't worry about that! I have no proof, and knowing you I'm sure there isn't any to be found, only circumstantial evidence at best, if it could be scraped together— which I doubt—and probably not enough of that to convict you. Certainly you're capable of committing the perfect crime if anyone is, I know what high standards you've always set yourself. "I've been thinking I might go abroad for a while. It's been a rather nasty experience for me, you know . . . No, I'm not sure just where I'll go, but in any case you have your work, and no time for traveling, chasing a girl around Europe. But maybe we'll run into each other again sometime, who knows? In the meantime, best of luck in your career, and do keep count of the lives you save, won't you? Though I'm not sure just at what point these things begin to balance out; it's like the parable of the shepherd and the stray, only, of course, the shepherd wasn't actually planning to kill the lamb himself . . . You don't mind if I lock the door after you, do you?"

The locked door, the telephone off the hook, the carton half full of books—Ann saw it for the first time, pushed against the end of the couch where she had left it last night, after her first panic had given way to a dazed lethargy. I have already begun to run, she thought. But where? Toward what? Toward nothing in particular, like the people who hurried on home for supper that evening, leaving Bobbie's lifeless body at the foot of the stairs—a little sickened, perhaps, but with appetites not permanently impaired.

She pushed back her chair and stood up. The receiver on the radiator lay buzzing like a summer insect in the silence. She dialed a number, Carlo's, with a steady forefinger; then, decisively, she grasped the slippery black plastic and pressed it firmly to her ear.

Julius's was almost deserted except for a few late-afternoon beer drinkers lounging at one end of the bar, and a comatose couple sitting entwined in one of the booths. Ann took a table at the back and sat waiting in the semi-darkness, her coat around her shoulders. At last the door swung open on a blue sliver of winter twilight, and Carlo stood stamping his feet on the sawdust, unwinding a scarf from his neck while he greeted one of the bartenders. Ann waved, and he came toward her quickly.

"Two whiskey sours," he said over his shoulder to the bartender. "That okay?"

"Fine," Ann said indifferently.

"So—" Carlo scraped out a chair and sat down, blowing on his hands to warm them. "I'd like a new pair of gloves for Christmas, in case you're interested. Fur-lined but not too bulky. Gray would be a good color, size ten. I'd ask Moira, but I think she's knitting me something—she does knit, by the way. Imagine playing the harp all day and then spending the evening knitting. Ah, well, she's a good kid." He looked at Ann. "What's on your mind, sweetie? You look terrible."

"Thanks," Ann said, forcing a smile.

"I didn't mean it that way. As a matter of fact, you look rather magnificent, but as though you'd fly into a million pieces if anyone touched you." He laid his hand on hers with elaborate caution, and then patted it lightly. "Okay. What's this all about?"

Ann said, "Carlo, I want to ask you some questions that may sound"—she gave a helpless laugh—"that *will* sound strange and melodramatic, to say the least. But first I want you to promise me that you won't ask any questions in return. I mean, I can't—I don't want to involve you any more than I have to."

He looked at her blankly. "Well, I'll do my best."

Ann waited until the bartender had brought their drinks and left.

"Suppose," she said, "you thought that a murder had been committed in order to keep someone quiet about a previous—crime or unpleasant incident of some kind. And suppose you could prove that the suspect had been present on both occasions: I mean, at the scene of the original incident and at the scene of the murder. Would that be a case against him? Enough to take to court?"

"My God, Ann!" She met his appalled glance and waited. "Bobbie . . . ?"

Ann said nothing.

"All right, no questions. Good Lord, Ann, are you serious about this?"

"I want a legal opinion," she said.

"But for God's sake—" Carlo laughed incredulously. "I mean, it's not as if I even knew anything about criminal law." There was a pause. He lit a cigarette and blew a pale stream of smoke upward into the gloom. At last he said, "Would there be any evidence of communication in the interim—some sort of contact between the suspect and the victim?"

"No. There might not have been any communication at all— ever."

Carlo stared. "None?"

"Possibly not. Probably not."

"And as for the murder itself—there's no way of tracing the weapon, no witness to the act as such; only the presumed presence of the suspect at the scene?"

"That's all. And even that might be almost impossible to prove beyond a reasonable doubt. But the motive—"

"I take it that establishing the motive would depend on proving the presence of the suspect at the earlier scene. Would that be difficult too?"

"I don't know. Yes, probably."

"And you'd have to prove that the victim had been there too, as a witness to whatever it was. Did this earlier incident occur in a public place too?"

"I think so. I don't know. Oh, Lord, it's hopeless, isn't it?" Ann stared at her drink and abruptly took a swallow of it; her throat contracted at the sugary, acid taste.

"Well, it's all pretty circumstantial, to say the least. A prosecutor would have to dig up a really strong hypothetical motive, something overwhelming, to want to touch it at all."

"Overwhelming," Ann repeated. "But that would depend on

the character of the murderer. What might have seemed overwhelming to him could seem insignificant to someone else."

"Well, but—" Carlo gave a helpless shrug. "If that's the case, I don't know what to say except forget it. I mean, it all sounds pretty vague, sweetie." He took a deep breath and said gently, "Look, Annie—I know you've been upset about Bobbie's death. But you've got to realize that in a city this size these things just happen, either for no reason at all or for so many reasons you couldn't possibly begin to trace them. I don't know just what's on your mind, or why you think you've found a suspect, but I think you ought to be careful of—well, letting your imagination get the better of you. You admit you have no real evidence, so why not forget about it? Please, Ann, listen to me. You have your own life to live. You can't go on worrying about this thing, living in the past—"

"Oh, Carlo, shut up!" Ann put her fists to her temples as the ribbon of pain drew taut behind her eyelids. "I'm sorry. I know you're trying to help, but you just don't know—"

"Don't know what? Ann, tell me, what is it?" His dark eyes searched her face urgently, fearfully. She felt a desperate impulse to comfort him, to put her arms around him and hold him tightly —or was that only the comfort she wished for herself?

She said, "I can't tell you any more, Carlo. As you say, I have no evidence. I didn't think I had, but—well, in any case, it wouldn't be ethical to say anything more, would it, seeing that my suspicions are so hypothetical?"

Carlo received this in silence. Ann took another sip from the sticky rim of her glass and set it down exactly in the center of the paper coaster. This was no more than she had expected, after all. From here on, her course was clear, if only she had courage enough, and skill . . . But oh, God, why hadn't he called during the afternoon, as they had agreed? Had she managed so badly on the telephone that morning that he suspected something already? And if so, what would he do?

One way, one way only to disarm him.

She said, "Then I have another question, Carlo. Or rather a request. I'd like to give you something for safekeeping—literally, I mean. I want you to put it in a safe." She slid the long envelope from her coat pocket and laid it on the table; the heavy pin inside clanked against the wood. "No one is to open this unless something happens to me," she said.

"For Christ's sake, Ann." Carlo stared at the envelope with an involuntary grin. "This is some kind of joke, I trust?"

"Maybe."

"Look, sweetie—this is me, Carlo, not Perry Mason. Just an innocent corporation lawyer with no talent for the cloak-and-dagger bit."

"You're a lawyer," Ann insisted. "You'll know how to put this away for me so that it will be safe."

"Safe," Carlo repeated. He hefted the envelope in the palm of his hand, staring at it.

"Please," Ann said, seeing one of the faces at the bar turn casually their way. "Carlo, put it down. Put it in your coat pocket—or give it back to me. Please!"

Her tone startled him. He gave her a quick look and slid the envelope into the pocket of his coat, which he had thrown over the back of a chair. A white corner protruded from the pocket; he twitched a sleeve over it to hide it, and sat back in his chair with a thump. "Now *I'm* getting the willies," he said. "What in hell is this all about?"

"It's all in there, written down—what I think, and why. If anything happened to me, that would be a sort of proof, wouldn't it?"

"Happened to you? You mean you think you're actually in some kind of danger? From this mysterious suspect, whoever he is?"

"Not now. But I might be some day." Finish this quickly, she told herself, glancing at her watch. Nick may have been calling the apartment. And at any moment Carlo may begin to understand . . . Get it settled first, make him promise.

"But you sound so damned calm!" Carlo was saying. "How am I supposed to believe any of this? Honest to God, it sounds like something out of a bad movie. I mean, I know life imitates art, but can't you at least manage a good clean Hitchcock thriller while you're at it?"

Ann said with a stiff smile, "I can't help the way it sounds, Carlo. Put it down to my hysterical feminine imagination if you want to, but promise you'll do what I ask."

Carlo was silent for a moment, studying her face. Then he shrugged helplessly. "Okay, I promise. I'll take care of it for you."

Ann said, "There's one more thing I want you to promise."

"Oh, God, now what? No, let me guess. If I get a mysterious phone call in the middle of the night exactly six months from tonight—" He stopped. Ann was buttoning her coat, reaching for her gloves. "All right—what?"

She fixed her eyes on his and said quietly, "I want you to promise me you won't do anything else. That you'll put the envelope away and then just forget about it."

"Well, that's easy enough, seeing I don't know what this is all about, anyway. Or—you mean, supposing I do get it figured out . . . ?" She had risen; he got to his feet quickly and put a hand on her arm, saying in bewilderment, "Ann don't go off like this! Can't you tell me, for Christ's sake?"

"No. I've got to go, Carlo."

"But—if you *are* in some kind of danger, can't you at least stop now? Please, Ann, whatever it is, leave it alone, don't do anything more."

She gripped his hand hard for a moment, and shook her head. "I can't," she whispered. "I can't. And even if I could—"

"If you could?" His voice was panicky.

"Justice," Ann said at last, drawing her hand away from the warmth of his clasp. "This way at least there will be some justice." She turned to go.

Carlo snatched up his coat. "Let me walk you home, for God's sake."

"No. Please, Carlo, I'll see you soon. You and Moira—we'll have to get together for dinner one of these days. Goodbye, and thanks for hearing me out."

He stood looking after her in an attitude of comical dismay, his coat bunched over his arm—please God, the envelope, don't let him lose it, Ann thought, looking back over her shoulder—while the barflies grinned at each other. Ann kept the picture in front of her as she went out into the cold darkness. The slush had frozen on the pavement; she concentrated on her footing, helped by the lights of a car cruising slowly along beside her, searching for a house number. Someone rolled down the rear window

and flipped a cigarette butt almost at Ann's feet. She heard the
tiny hiss as it died, and a man's voice saying irritably, "How the
hell should I know? You're the one that knows the Village like
the palm of your hand, remember?"

She came to the corner of Christopher Street and had crossed
the intersection before she realized that the windows of her own
apartment were lighted behind their drawn curtains. Then he
was there. She half ran through the shadows toward the building, her heart thudding violently. In the dark hallway, easing the
swing of the door behind her, she thought: Of course, the surprise visit. I ought to have expected it. He isn't sure of me; how
could he be?

There is still time to run, she reminded herself, standing still
with her hand on the curving, thickly painted wood of the banister . . . Then, through the thin walls, she heard music coming
from the apartment, a rough crescendo of strings bursting into
discord, beginning again, clawing and tearing at the very fabric
of silence. It was the Beethoven quartet, a record she had bought
a year ago out of a vague feeling that she ought to own at least
one of the late quartets, but listened to only once: music of such
heartbreak, of such raw anguish that she had recoiled from it almost superstitiously, with a bewildered sense of her own inade-
quacy before it. She had understood for the first time how for
some people music at such heights could seem an inimical force,
a threat to the slender shell of self, not restorative but destruc-
tive . . . And she had slid the record—thin polished disk whose
bland surface gave no hint, no warning, of the power contained
therein—back into its cardboard casing and put it away for another day: for the unimaginable day when she, Ann Claremont,
virginal and healthy, could match this music's knowledge with
her own.

And now his quick exploring fingers had sought it out and
claimed it, as they claimed whatever caught his intelligence,
for experiment and classification. The late quartets of Beethoven
were supposed to be some kind of musical pinnacle, weren't they?
If he was going to listen to music, he could not be bothered with
anything but the best. And now, she thought, he would be hearing its ugliness and harshness with surprise and doubtless with a
sort of sardonic pleasure; he would feel at most a detached pity

for the exposed nerve, for the great man's soul laid bare—but would never have to feel the knife of its beauty plunge and twist within his heart.

A flare of pure anger, brilliant and exhilarating as the sudden flare of phosphorescence on a dark winter sea, lit her way up the stairs. All right, then, she thought. I will begin now. Why not? What else is there for me, what other way? She opened the door, calling, "Nick? Nick, is that you?" and went in to meet him.

He has taken one life, she thought, raising her cold smiling lips for his kiss. Now let him take another. Let him feel the weight of it. Let him pay.

III. THE NEW YEAR

The doorman

in his heavy winter cloak slammed the door after them with ceremonial violence, and the cab racketed off along Fifty-ninth Street into the lavish glitter of the morning sun. As if dazed by so much radiance after the marble pallor of the hotel lobby, the blond couple leaned back against the scarred leather seat without speaking for several minutes. Presently the young man took a pair of airline envelopes from his coat pocket and checked their contents rapidly, his face intent and satisfied. The girl kept her gloved hands clasped in her lap. Her profile was clear and steady above the trembling petals of the white orchid pinned to her coat; no tendril escaped the thick flow of her hair into the gleaming French knot at the nape of her neck.

"I hope you can get some sleep on the plane," the young man said, putting the envelopes away and turning his head to smile at her.

"I slept all right."

"You did? When?" He put a hand over hers, feeling with his thumb the bump of her rings beneath the taut calfskin glove.

"Oh—sometime."

"Darling—"

She turned her head away from him to look through the window at the uncluttered Sunday face of the city, a geometry of right angles and parallel planes reflecting one another endlessly in walls of polished glass.

"Of course, you've done a lot of traveling," he said after a pause. "But it's all new to me. I've only been in a plane two—no, three times in my life. And never on a jet."

"I've never ridden on a jet, either," the girl said. "That at least will be something new."

He seemed to find her tone unfamiliar and even baffling; he stared at her averted face and gave a short laugh. "Hey—where are you, anyway?"

"I'm right here," she said clearly, turning her gaze full on his face for a long moment. The cab was rumbling onto a bridge above the blue river, which had a suede matte in the light morning breeze. "Look!" she said, turning away once more.

Behind them the famous towers of the city wheeled up into the sky, extravagantly gilded by the sun. From the jumble of stone and shadow at their base—blocks of orange and red and brown, blue depths—the splendid ladders sprang in serene and airy poise against the winter sky. Only the diminishing arcs of the bridges, receding toward the cloudy haze of the open sea, could be seen to link this radiant city to the earth; and that only to another island.

"Farewell, Byzantium," murmured the girl with soft irony.

The young man frowned. "Still looking for your meadows?" he said, not understanding.

"No," she said. "For a city that never was. And probably just as well."

She continued to sit twisted away from him, gazing through the rear window of the cab, until the view was blocked by the contortions of the highway through the anonymous landscape of Queens. Then she settled herself against the seat and said with conversational briskness, "I saw the strangest thing this morning from the window while you were asleep. A policeman ice-skating in the park."

"Oh, come on," he said with a grin. "You must have been dreaming."

"No, I swear it. I could see the light on his badge. He was all by himself, just skating around and around with his hands behind his back. I suppose he was on duty," she said practically, "and it seemed as good a way as any to keep warm."

"No doubt. You should have gone down in your peignoir and taken him some coffee."

"You don't believe me?" she said, giving him a level look.

"Well, you must admit it sounds unlikely."

"I don't know why. After all, the forces of law and order are everywhere, one way or another, aren't they? Even outside the Plaza at seven in the morning of one's wedding night. They're quite recognizable, even on ice skates. Or wearing shorts and knee socks, the way they do in Jamaica. You'll see."

She observed the sudden hooded gleam of his eyes and the just perceptible stiffening of his body before she went on carelessly, "I meant to ask you—did you have a chance to talk to Aunt Eleanor at the reception yesterday? She came all the way from Nashville just for the wedding. She's a dear, but she's aged terribly; I really think she'd forgotten Dad had remarried, she seemed so surprised to see Marge . . . Aunt Eleanor gave us the Georgian candlesticks, remember? The tarnished ones."

"I'm afraid I don't remember the Georgian candlesticks or Aunt Eleanor," he said. "In fact, I spent most of the day feeling like an amnesia case and wondering how on earth you knew who all those people were."

"Oh," she said, "it's up to the bride to keep her wits about her. After all, as the wife of a society doctor—"

"Society doctor? Oh, come on, Ann!"

"But that's what you said," she insisted. She tapped the fat bundle of the Sunday paper beside her. "This morning's spread on the wedding gives you a good start. And I'm planning to develop an absolutely lethal memory for names and faces . . . I'm so glad we finally found an apartment with a dining room. It should be worth the extra rent, considering all the entertaining we'll be doing. We can't have the great Dr. Beddoes eating off his lap, can we? By the way, is he married?"

"No. And he's not exactly the dinner-party type."

"Now how would you know, for heaven's sake? It takes a woman to discover these things. He probably needs a little humanizing away from the hospital."

The young man said sharply, "He doesn't spend much time away from it. Neither do I, for that matter."

"You will, though," she said, smiling. "I mean, as a married man you'll more or less have to, won't you?"

The cab raced on through the brilliant morning toward the airport. She chatted about the wedding, the gifts, the apartment overlooking the Hudson that was only a little more than they could afford. She was glad he'd agreed to let her use some of her own money. Why on earth had she spent so many years being drab and economical, she wondered, when it really wasn't necessary? She enumerated the family social connections, mostly on her mother's side, which could be renewed now that she was a respectable matron and no longer living *la vie bohème* (she brought out the phrase brightly and unsatirically). She talked about curtain materials and teakwood furniture and the car they would buy when they returned from their honeymoon.

The young man watched her in growing wonder, attempting no response. It seemed to him all at once that everything about her person—her skin, her hair, her soft red mouth, the heavy twists of her gold earrings, the glossy leather of her gloves and bag and high-heeled shoes—had begun to gleam with a new and complicated luster which almost obscured the simple clarity of outline that had been the shape of his knowledge of her. The heated air of the cab was fragrant with her perfume—and when before had she used a scent so rich, so recognizably glamorous? He remembered the smell of her skin, the mild aura of a modest cologne. As she talked he opened his window an inch to let in a stream of wintry air; but the scent had done its work already, it clung now to his own skin in a silken caress that was like the sound of her continuing voice, sweet and relentless.

The stewardess pulled the tabs of the Mae West and repeated the safety instructions in rapid, metallic Spanish, her smile decorous and unperturbed above the grotesque expanse of her inflated yellow bosom.

"Don't you want to take off your coat?" the young man asked his bride.

"I always get cold in planes," she replied absently. "I have to have the air thing blowing on my face the whole time or I start feeling claustrophobic."

"You? I didn't think you had any phobias." His voice had a slight edge now.

"Only a few." She smiled at him, a perfect smile that curved her face prettily and widened her gray eyes under their darkened lashes.

He said roughly, "Ann! What in hell is the matter with you?"

"The matter? Nothing that I know of. Don't I look all right?" She raised a hand to her hair.

"Like a magazine cover."

"I only want to do you justice," she said.

He looked away from her meaningless smile. They were silent while the plane taxied bumpily to the end of the runway, past the aluminum glitter of great waiting planes and the tiny darting carts whose drivers squinted red-faced into the bright wind whipping in from the bay. Rousing himself, the young man examined the contents of the pocket sewn to the seat in front of him and sat studying the map of their route to the Caribbean with expressionless concentration. Around him the other passengers joked about their mutual apprehension (a plane like this one had crashed inexplicably on take-off a few days earlier), and secretly braced their bodies against the anticipated shock of departure— seeing the holiday plane for an agonizing moment as a catapult aimed across the abyss that must always plunge between themselves and their pleasure. Only the young man seemed not to have noticed their danger, or not to care. The stewardess, checking seat belts, glanced at him with interest, and sent a belated smile at the blond girl beside him, who was staring straight ahead of her with blank exhausted eyes in a pale face. I hope that one's had some Dramamine, she thought: newlyweds, and no sleep. Damn, is that hair real?

With a cataclysmic roar and shudder of farewell, the plane fired its engines and slammed upward through walls of wind into the sky. As it banked hugely, turning south, the towers of the city toppled and fell away in the bright dust of the morning. Within the remaining world of the cabin, a padded tube furnished with doll-house curtains and plastic breakfast trays, the passengers began to stir comfortably, lighting cigarettes and yawning.

After breakfast the girl slept, or seemed to, her face against the small white pillow which she had wedged between the back of her seat and the window. The young man read the Sunday *Times*, leaning into the aisle to turn the tall pages without disturbing her. Then, as she still slept, he opened a briefcase and studied several of the thick journals he had brought with him. Several times he rose and paced restlessly up and down the aisle, stooping to look through the windows over the laps of other passengers. But there was nothing to see, only the trackless blue of the ocean far below. He sank back into his seat and let his eyes rest attentively on the sleeping face of the girl beside him, as if certain that sooner or later she must feel the pressure of his gaze and open her eyes to meet it. When she did not, he tilted his head to stare at the ceiling, his expression thoughtful and somber. The plane flew on through the cloudless morning with a steady hum that was like the sound of a distant lawn mower heard through an open window, bringing a smell of grass and damp earth to the passengers in their dreams.

She made herself wait until the moment when she felt the level balance of the plane shift a degree for the long descent over the sea, opening her eyes at the first subtle forward pressure but not moving until he turned and saw that she was looking at him.

He smiled quickly. "Hello. Have a good sleep?"

"I wasn't asleep."

"Oh?" He rested a hand against the seat in front of him, as though the plane had given a slight lurch. "Thinking about something?"

"No. I've already done all the thinking I can," she said, as if to herself. "I was just resting. And remembering." She touched the petals of the orchid at her shoulder, and let her hand fall back into her lap in an odd gesture of relinquishment. In a different voice, her old voice, clear and without overtones, like a boy's, she said, "Now it begins."

He stared. "What begins?"

"I know that you killed Bobbie." Calmly, watching his face, she said, "I've known for some time, though I'm still not sure about the whys and wherefores—the exact circumstances that led up to it, I mean. But I imagine I'll find out in time. You may even tell me yourself some day without realizing it."

"For Christ's sake, Ann!"

"The pin," she went on. "You shouldn't have recognized the pin. She was only allowed to wear the company jewelry during office hours. I'm surprised it never occurred to you. When I realized you'd lied about that, about seeing her only the one time, I saw—or rather, I finally let myself see—how everything else fell into place. Including your need to keep track of me, even to the extent of marrying me, if necessary."

"Ann!" He managed the laugh now, shaking his head. The knuckles of the hand grasping the seat still showed white. He followed her glance and let the hand drop, raising his shoulders at the same time in an incredulous shrug. "What kind of wild fantasy is this, for the love of God?"

She said nothing.

"Ann," he said, almost gently. "I thought you'd gotten over all that morbid business about your roommate."

"No, you didn't!" she said sharply. Her mouth looked pale in her set face; she wore no gloss now. "You've seen for some time that I suspected something. I've *let* you see. Don't lie to me. I'm being honest with you, telling you what I know. I can't prove anything—you might as well know that too. If I could, I wouldn't be here. Neither would you."

"I suppose not!" he agreed, with another incredulous laugh. "Ann, please! I don't know what's got into you all of a sudden, but—"

"Stop it, Nick!"

He said coldly, "You're the one who'd better stop it, before you get hysterical."

"Yes, you told me that at the beginning. Hysteria . . . I suppose it really does seem hysterical to you to bother about someone else's death, even when it's a matter of murder. After all, we are all dying at every moment, aren't we? Of course, the time span varies, and some of us have less control than others over the circumstances of our actual, final death. But then some of us deserve to live longer than others, because we're more valuable, we have a greater contribution to make to society—wasn't it something like that?"

K

"I've read *Crime and Punishment* too."

"Well—wasn't it?"

"I never even met the girl," he said harshly. "How in the world could you have dreamt up such an idea? And if you actually do believe it—" He broke off with a gesture of frustration and bewilderment. "Then what is this all about? Why are you here with me, as my wife?"

She looked at him expressionlessly.

"All right. I'm supposed to be some kind of Raskolnikov, I gather. What does that make you—his girl, what's-her-name, the saintly prostitute?" He grinned sharply.

"Raskolnikov was caught and convicted," she said. "Though I never found the Siberian business very convincing, or very—fair."

"You mean things might have been a good deal more drastic for him if the old woman had had a vengeful roommate?" He laughed. "I'd have to agree with you there."

The stewardess had begun breathily intoning the data of their arrival over the intercom. "We shall be landing in Montego Bay in exactly ten minutes. The temperature at Montego Airport is seventy-eight degrees, and the weather is clear. Please remain in your seats until the immigration authorities have completed their check of the aircraft. We hope that you have enjoyed your flight and that you will be traveling with us again soon. Thank you." A string orchestra began to play "Some Enchanted Evening" in swelling tones; the plane shivered lightly in a warm current of air.

The young man looked through the window at a flying rag of cloud and asked tonelessly, "All right, Ann. Why *are* you here? It seems to me you ought to be anywhere but here. Fleeing my presence, as they say. Instead—"

"Instead, I've martyred myself, haven't I?"

He gave her a swift glance full of astonishment and disbelief. "Martyred yourself? My God, Ann!"

"What else could I do?" she asked in a sudden violent whisper, looking down at her clenched hands. "Suppose I never found the proof? What other way was there to punish you?"

"My God," he said again. He began to laugh helplessly. "Of course. It's just the sort of thing you would do; I ought to have seen it. Marriage as the supreme punishment—is that the idea?"

She nodded.

After a moment he said, "And what about you?"

"Me?" She looked at him. "I punish myself too, it seems."

"But why?"

"I'm not such a martyr, after all," she said finally, with a bleak smile. "They were always innocent, or believed they were. Whereas I . . . I was in on it too. With you."

"What do you mean? Don't be an idiot!"

"Yes. I don't know when I first began to know. Almost from the beginning, I think. Only of course I couldn't afford to know . . . That makes me a kind of accomplice, doesn't it? An accessory after the fact, I think that's the term." Their eyes met. She said softly, "But then you were counting on that, too, weren't you?"

Around them the other passengers were shifting busily in their seats, clacking the metal ends of their seat belts together and smoothing their clothing.

"It should be an interesting marriage," he said. "More interesting than most. Unless of course we decide to have it annulled."

"Yes," she said. "And then what would you do? You'd have to keep track of me somehow. I might decide to get a job in Europe —Rome, let's say. It's something I was thinking about before I met you. Or I might marry someone else and settle down in the suburbs behind a nice impenetrable wall of children and charities. But you couldn't afford to let me just vanish, no matter how much you might want to. You'd never know how much I might have discovered; you'd never know when the accusation might come." She paused. "It seems to me that under those circumstances you might also have trouble concentrating on your work—your work that means so much to you."

"And I will be able to concentrate on it this way—married to you?"

She looked at him gravely.

He said, "My work is the most important thing in my life."

"I know."

"So that's what you are going to take."

"You killed her because of it. Let it be the price as well."

She caught the slight flicker of his eyelids and thought: Ah, then I was right about that. I know the sort of thing I'm looking for, at least.

She took a compact from her bag and began powdering her face as a sandy island slid by under the shadow of the wing far below, and said in the new voice she had been learning, "I haven't decided yet whether to stop sleeping with you. It would be a logical first step in a way; but unfortunately"—she snapped the compact shut and turned back to face him—"I still enjoy it a great deal myself. As you may have noticed. That's what I have to get rid of," she said, staring at him. "My own pleasure. Mind over matter, little by little. I don't know whether I can do it, but I have to try."

"Ah, God. Ann!" He took her hand; the fingers lay passive in his own. "Don't you know that I love you?"

"No. I don't believe you," she said flatly.

"Listen—" he began in a low desperate voice.

"You'd better fasten your seat belt. The stewardess is coming this way."

He reached for his seat belt mechanically; even in his agitation, she noticed, his movements were deft and decisive. When the stewardess had passed he turned back to her, his gaze suddenly brilliant with pleading; with a tremor she realized that she was seeing his naked face for the first time.

"Ann, listen. Suppose that I am—that I did do this thing. Do you suppose I could have wanted to do it? Do you think I could have acted out of sheer cruelty, for no good reason? Is that why you think I don't love you—because I'm not capable of love?" She said nothing. "I do love you, Ann. I have all along. I still do."

"No," she said. "We don't know anything about love, either of us. You took one life, and now you're taking another—mine. That's what you really want. Even as a doctor, when you give life you are also taking it. It becomes a part of your power."

"Power?" he said. "But love *is* power! It has no meaning otherwise."

She turned her face to the window and would not answer.

"If you knew the reason—" he began.

"Yes?" Her gaze came back to him swiftly. He took a deep breath. She smiled faintly, turning back to the window.

"If you don't believe I love you, you're a fool not to have run away!" he said furiously. "Don't you see the danger you're in if I don't love you? I mean personal, physical danger. A tragic honeymoon drowning, food poisoning, a fall from a cliff—the possibilities are endless, given a little professional thought." He laughed harshly. "Don't you see that? How do you know what I might not do?" he demanded of her expressionless profile.

"That's already taken care of," she said. "A letter explaining all the circumstances. Not that my death could be considered a legal confirmation of my suspicions, or that my suspicions would prove that I had been murdered. But I imagine it would be more than enough to take the whole thing to court."

He sat rigid, the sweat gleaming faintly on the sharp ridges of his cheekbones. The plane was turning toward the island now, flying over turquoise shallows that flickered white against flat arcs of sand. Suddenly they were over the land: green hills bulged under the wing tips and vanished abruptly into the bumpy yellow fog of a rain cloud.

"Then you are safe," he said.

"I suppose I am."

"Oh, Ann!" he said, turning to her in a last violent protest. "Don't you know that you always have been safe, with me?"

But as though someone had thrown a switch, the space between their bodies took substance, became neutral, dense, insoluble. They were still sitting motionless in their separate silences when the plane burst out again into the full sunlight and flung itself down like a huge bird of prey toward the green, impossible island.